Beneath the Veil

Dear Reader,

I trust if this book has landed with you, you are meant to read her. Please pass on to the person you know needs to read Clara's story.

With Love
x Bernadette

BERNADETTE O'CONNOR

Copyright © 2019 Bernadette O'Connor

www.bernadetteoconnor.com

First published in Australia in 2019
by Karen Mc Dermott
www.karenmcdermott.com.au

Edited by: Natasha Gilmour
Proofread: Jennifer Sharp
Cover design: Maja Otic
Interior design: Ida Jansson

All rights reserved. No part of this book may be used or reproduced by any means, graphic, electronic, or mechanical, including photocopying, recording, taping or by any information storage retrieval system without the written permission of the copyright owner except in the case of brief quotations embodied in critical articles and reviews.

This is a work of fiction. Names, characters, businesses, places, events and incidents are either the products of the author's imagination or used in a fictitious manner. Any resemblance to actual persons, living or dead, or actual events is purely coincidental.

National Library of Australia Cataloguing-in-Publication data:
Beneath the Veil /Bernadette O'Connor
Fiction/Women's

ISBN: (sc) 978-0-6484598-3-5
ISBN: (e) 978-0-6484598-2-8

You love me for the girl I was, the woman I became, and the woman I am becoming, as I unravel my layers and discover what lies beneath the veils.

It isn't always easy being the one who walks by my side in this life, but you astound me with the endless love and adoration you hold for me.

The water to my fire.
The yang to my yin.
The calm to my storm.
The man to my woman.

Luke, my love, this one, I dedicate to you.

Goddess of the moon, divine light of the night,
She who holds the mysteries and cycles of the tides.
Ever changing yet ever powerful.
She who guides and lights the path we weave.
Guide me with your wisdom,
Infuse me with your power,
And hold me in your light as I dance with life.

Contents

Chapter One	9
Chapter Two	13
Chapter Three	24
Chapter Four	35
Chapter Five	39
Chapter Six	47
Chapter Seven	56
Chapter Eight	60
Chapter Nine	73
Chapter Ten	83
Chapter Eleven	91
Chapter Twelve	101
Chapter Thirteen	110
Chapter Fourteen	123
Chapter Fifteen	133
Chapter Sixteen	142
Chapter Seventeen	152
Chapter Eighteen	159
Chapter Nineteen	166
Chapter Twenty	176

Chapter Twenty-one	182
Chapter Twenty-two	190
Chapter Twenty-three	196
Chapter Twenty-four	203
Chapter Twenty-five	211
Chapter Twenty-six	223
Chapter Twenty-seven	236
Chapter Twenty-eight	243
Chapter Twenty-nine	252
Chapter Thirty	260
Chapter Thirty-one	267
Chapter Thirty-two	278
Chapter Thirty-three	289
Chapter Thirty-four	298
Chapter Thirty-five	306
Chapter Thirty-six	317
Chapter Thirty-seven	325
Chapter Thirty-eight	336
Chapter Thirty-nine	343
Chapter Forty	352
Chapter Forty-one	360
Epilogue	364
Acknowledgements	369
About the Author	374

Chapter One

Show them the blood.

The soft silk of my First Communion dress is pressed against the rawness of my back that was ripped apart by my da's whip, at the hands of my brother. I feel the burning as the wounds weep, reminding me of his callousness as he dealt me my punishment. I felt the leather straps tear the skin of my tiny frame, reminding me that I am a sinner and that God punishes the wicked.

He is not God. What gives him the right? Who is he to punish me? I want to scream at them, for I do not understand. Instead, I stay silent knowing my cries, my questions, my opposition will only be met with further punishment.

I sit up and pull my shoulders back. My mammy's

nagging ringing in my ears, 'Don't slouch. Hold yourself with pride. You represent our family. Do not bring shame upon us, Clara.' As I straighten my back I press my shredded flesh against the hardness of the wooden pew, the pain both excruciating and exhilarating. Eyes downcast. My hands in prayer. I am careful not to make a noticeable movement or flinch from the pain as I squeeze the muscles in my back, intent on drawing the blood to the surface and staining the purity of the white silk dress encasing my tortured body.

I had been taught that appearance is everything. That the way we present ourselves—individually and as a family—determined how we were seen and what our place was in our remote Irish village. At the church, it was imperative to meet favour with the parish priest and the wealthier members of the village, especially on a Sunday morning when the whole village would come together. It was always overcrowded because you could not be seen not to attend. That would be a sin and the entire village would know. The church housed the diversity of all the village people from the richer landholders to the Gypsies passing through and everything in-between. I was part of the in-between, perhaps the upper part of the in-between, I know this is what my mother desired. Certain areas of the church were considered more desirable than others and there was an unspoken allocation of church pews, which reflected the social hierarchy within the parish and the village.

I knew what was expected of me whilst on display

in this public fishbowl. I had been conditioned to sit motionless beside my mammy in this same pew since I was a toddler. The pew that was just beyond the half way point in the church. My mammy's fingernail would often furtively dig sharply into the fleshiness of my thigh if I dared to wriggle or murmur a sound. I had felt the wrath of my mammy and da when I was but four years old, for giggling with Agatha, my older sister, when old Granny Malone sitting in the pew in front of us farted as she awkwardly lowered herself to the kneeler. The waft of stale pungent gas almost smothered us as we knelt with our heads lowered like *good* little girls. But we were unable to suppress our innocent giggles, we drew seething glares from our mammy, and righteous condemning stares from others seated in the surrounding pews. Their looks silently chastising us, 'How dare you show such disrespect. How dare you show such reckless abandon. How dare you not play by the rules. You naughty little girls.' I remember that day. The cold hard strips of leather from the horse whip callously blistering the softness of my bottom as my da whipped me into remembering refinement. Never again did I dare smile upon walking into church. Certainly not on my First Communion day.

I sat solemn and demure awaiting the time to kneel before the altar to receive my First Holy Communion. Sitting further upright, I pressed my back harder against the pew. I knew it was wrong and would bring shame on my family and thus further punishment for me, but something kept telling me to press harder and harder to ensure the pristine white of my dress was stained with the blood from my tortured back.

I heard the gasps and murmurs as I stood to walk and kneel before the altar to receive my First Communion. I felt the blood oozing. I felt its stickiness interwoven into the fabric of my dress as the silk clung to my skin. My veil sitting just below my shoulders, untainted as its purity is stark in contrast to the butchery of my dress. I sensed the panic of Mammy, powerless to hide her shame. I felt the intensity of my brother's rage boring into my back as the truth of his brutality was exposed.

I would pay for this.

I had broken every unspoken rule, but something in the petrified seven-year-old little girl in me knew she would do it again.

For this is truth and I knew I was here to expose what lies *beneath the veil.*

Chapter Two

My punishment was immediate and severe.

As the parish priest stood before me, poised to offer me my First Communion, the murmurs amongst the congregation intensified. Our parish priest was Father Colin Stanley. He paused before looking to his parishioners, while I knelt at his feet, eyes reverently downcast.

'She is in no fit state to receive the Lord Jesus Christ, Father Stanley. You must know she is stained by blood, tainted by what we do not know,' said the voice of Padraig McDermott. He was the most powerful man in the village calling out from his front seat pew.

'Is this true, child? Are you stained?' demanded Father Stanley.

I could not lie. I could not bring myself to be labelled in this way. I had heard my parents tell stories from the past of women who were stained by the blood of the Devil. I knew what had happened to them once upon a time. I had also heard Father Stanley speak from the pulpit only last week of those in our own parish community who were tainted. He had been referring to the Irish Travellers. This disregard for the Gypsies was so commonplace. Even when they occasionally passed through and attended Mass, the community, including the priest himself, were in disgust at their presence.

I feared what would happen to me should I be seen as tainted. Would I be ostracised like the Gypsies? Worse would I be hung or burnt at the stake just like the tales of long ago? Fear caused me to stammer and I was reluctant to look into the eyes of my judge in case I saw my fate.

'I am not tainted,' I murmured, nervously to the ground.

'Speak up, child. I cannot hear you,' he bellowed at me. 'Are you tainted by blood or are you not? A simple yes or no.'

'No, I am not tainted.' I affirmed with a confidence that undermined my terror.

'She lies. Her back is covered in blood. Show him the blood. As God's eyes here on earth, it is he who can judge if it is the blood of the Devil,' demanded Padraig McDermott.

I turned my back to Father Stanley as directed and faced the congregation. Standing before them, condemnation permeated the space, and I determinedly raised my eyes to look directly in the face of my accusers. I accessed a voice outside of my own that compelled me to speak truth. *There may be blood on my back, but it belongs to no other. My blood is not tainted. My soul is not tainted. It is the soul of he who raised this blood that is tainted.*

Yet the words did not come from me. Fear had strangled my voice.

The unspoken threat radiating from my brother's eyes silenced my truth. The painfully etched *good* girl story eroded my yearning to challenge, to resist, to fight, to scream, to roar; to allow the wild spirit within me to be free. She was called to open their eyes, to mess with their Sunday *best* lives, to divulge the truths, but she knew they did not want to see, hear her, know her or feel any different, for they too were trapped by fear. Fear of looking beyond the world that they knew where the rules just were and everyone and everything had a place. So long as everyone played to the rules then everything would continue to move the way it should. But who was the writer of the rules? The rules that were defining my life. The rules that said I could not ride my horse wildly through the paddocks. The rules that said I could not roam alone along the cliffs or climb trees with a Gypsy boy. The rules that said while my da was away from the farm, my twelve-year-old brother was in charge. The rules that allowed him to tear strips from my back with a horse whip while my mammy powerlessly watched and affirmed that I was a *bad* girl and that I must learn to obey the rules.

'Life will be easier for you if you just follow the rules, Clara.' Mammy had advised me in a rare moment of tenderness as she dressed my wounds.

Just follow the rules, Clara. I beseeched of myself. Gripped by shame, I humbly turned from the congregation to Father Stanley and as I lowered my eyes, I whispered, 'Forgive me, Father, for I have sinned.'

The look he gave me was one I would see again many years later, that look was stamped in my unconscious mind. I felt a confusing blend of compassionate forgiveness, witnessed by his loyal followers, and vengeful victory that was seen by me alone. The malevolence sent a shaft of terror through my soul which instantly shocked it into submission. That moment between what was and what could have been. I don't know what would have happened if I spoke up. One never knows what lay ahead on the path not taken and it is not wise to ponder the possibilities of untravelled roads.

This was the path I chose. I was the submissive good girl who kept her eyes downcast and her mouth shut. I was fulfilling the role that I was born to be, a daughter, a wife, a mother. This was my path. My mammy desperately taught me how to do it with grace, that involved ignoring any misgivings, repressing any ill-thoughts and suppressing any inner stirrings of discontent. I was to silence the voice that haunted me in the middle of the night, the voice which begged me to speak of the *truth*.

My First Communion day was not the joyous special occasion I had eagerly awaited. I had watched my sister and the other girls from our village school make their First Communion two years before. I was envious of their beautiful dresses and veils, and the attention they received as they were gifted money from family, friends and neighbours. It was one of the traditions secretly relished by all the children, and there was an unspoken competition amongst siblings and classmates to see who received the most money. My brother, Vincent, was the oldest and being a male had understandably received much attention and money. He took his eight pounds to the bank and opened an account—proudly telling everyone he was saving his money—to buy a new tractor, for when he took over the family farm from Da.

My sister, Agatha, knew how to do everything right, she combined just the right amount of gracious reverence and subtle sassiness to have everyone adoring her on her First Communion day. It had always been this way. She knew exactly how to play within the boundaries while making sure she got things her own way. She walked the line with a grace and confidence that I could never achieve, ensuring that people loved her. She somehow played within the lines enough to keep people happy yet danced on the edge enough to be secretly admired. Agatha carefully hid her six pounds in her glory box and told anyone who asked that she was saving her money to buy herself a beautiful tiara to wear on her wedding day, so she could be just like a princess. They would laugh admiringly because everyone knew that Agatha loved pretty things. 'Aye, to be sure, that's our Agatha,' they all crooned in delight that she was planning on marrying, and settling down, and not getting any fanciful ideas of going away to study, or travel, like some of the young girls these days. No, Agatha knew exactly what to tell them to keep them comforted that she was a good girl and knew her place in the world. Somehow, they were oblivious to the fact that she was doing life her way. I know she used her First Communion money to go to Dublin for a raucous weekend of drinking and meeting men when she was eighteen. She visited Maree Maloney who had moved away to study nursing. My brother didn't know that Maree's strict boarding house mistress who had been recommended by Father Stanley had been called home to tend to her elderly parents that very weekend. Every girl boarding in the house took advantage of this rare freedom and Agatha had delighted in re-telling the stories of the men she had met and danced with, and even kissed, whilst drinking and smoking cigarettes as they wandered the streets of Dublin into the wee hours of the morning.

'Oh, Agatha! What will Vincent or Father Stanley do if they find out?' I asked, so fearful for the consequences of such behaviour.

She laughed at me, 'They'll never find out. We all made a pact never to tell, and we were in Dublin, who from here would be out at night in Dublin? Why do you worry so much about Vincent?'

That was Agatha, fearless. And then there was me. My every move and word were underpinned by fear of how I would be seen and heard and the consequences of my behaviour. The incident, prior to my First Communion, was the first time Vincent had taken the whip to me. It was not the last and I moved through life with a nervousness, never knowing when he may strike.

As soon as Mass finished, Mammy hustled me from the church, placing Da's jacket around my shoulders to cover the blood. She was not protecting me, though, she was desperately protecting her own reputation and the quicker I could be ushered away, the sooner people would forget, or so she hoped. I was to learn that despite the Christian preaching of compassion, forgiveness, acceptance and inclusion, many in the village were of small mind, closed heart and without a bone of forgiveness in their body. As I was quickly ushered through the lingering crowd I became aware of the other First Communicants being congratulated with pound notes being tucked into their eager hands. I felt the condemning glares and murmurs of disgust as I walked past and knew that no one was going to congratulate me, let alone give me money, for I had not played by the rules.

Padraig McDermott stopped Da in his path. 'Be sure to keep an eye on that one, Ciaran. I'd be getting her home and knocking some sense into her before she got a day older. Her type won't be tolerated here. Ye know that, don't you?'

'Aye indeed, to be sure, it won't be tolerated in my

own house, let alone in God's house. Ye won't be seeing trouble from this one again. I assure you that, Paddy,' Da affirmed motioning in my direction.

'It is a fine lad you have here, of him you should be proud,' nodding his head approvingly in Vincent's direction.

'A good lad he is, stepping up to be the man of the house when I'm away.'

'That's what we need, a good young man learning to keep this women folk in line,' laughed Padraig McDermott.

I was looking at the ground and dared not look at my da nor catch the eye of Padraig McDermott again. His coldness caused me shivers and my mammy and da's attentiveness to his word nauseated me.

As they were distracted I felt a hand secretly grab mine underneath Da's jacket and the crispness of a note was squeezed into my hand. I cautiously raised my head a little and peeked to my side, my eyes met those of a Gypsy woman, her head covered by a shawl. Her glistening ocean green eyes were familiar and were impassioned as they spoke to me. 'You are not alone.' She moved on quickly, her unspoken words stayed with me, imprinted upon my soul. Her pound note was the only acknowledgement of my First Communion day and was quickly tucked under my dress and into the fold of my stockings to be hidden away when I returned home. No one could know that I received a gift from a Gypsy woman and no one would ever know the power of her gift to me that day. I never spent it on sweets or lipstick or jewellery like the other girls, I secretly held onto it as a reminder that I was seen. I was not alone. I needed to know this in the years ahead and I had a strong feeling she knew I would need this reassurance as I navigated what lay before me.

'We must be getting on now, Padraig. I must get cooking the breakfast for this fine young man and his father,' laughed my mammy, as she motioned me forward, with a firm squeeze of my arm.

I knew my mammy's haste to leave had little to do with cooking the breakfast and everything to do with removing me from the eyes and minds of others. The sooner I was hidden from the view of the scornful parishioners, the sooner my indiscretion would be forgotten, and her shame erased, or so she hoped. I could feel my da's rage brewing as we walked the mile home from the church, it erupted as he entered the house. He clipped the side of my head with a force that landed me on the other side of the room. Huddling in the corner with my arms covering my head, I waited for what was to come next. I could feel my mammy's urge to come to me, and cradle me in her arms, and protect me from the brutality of her husband, but she did not come to me. She did not even look in my direction. She removed her hat and tied her apron around her good dress and began to cook the hot breakfast. I was not allowed to eat even though it was meant to be my special day. I was sent to my room, out of sight from Da who said he could not bear the sight of me a minute longer. I was a constant reminder of the shame brought on his name and the name of his family. I was banished to my room for the entire day. My mammy telling me it was for the best to allow him to calm down.

'But, Mammy,' I queried. 'Does he not want to know what happened and why my back was bleeding?'

'Vincent has told him what happened. It is best to leave it at that,' Mammy retorted.

'Did he tell him how he whipped me over and over til my back bleed, and that he kept going, even when you asked him to stop, Mammy?' I asked.

'He told your father that he had caught you playing with that Gypsy boy and that you needed to be taught a lesson. This is true, Clara. You know not to mix with those kinds and I hope you've learnt your lesson now, my girl.'

'But, Mammy, did you tell Da that Vincent wouldn't stop striking me when you asked him?'

'No, I did not,' her eyes avoiding contact with mine.

'But, you are the grown up, you are his mammy, he has to listen to you.' I protested.

She grabbed me by my shoulders and looked dead in my eyes, 'Listen to me, Clara, I know what you are saying but it is just the way it is. Vincent is the man of the house when your father is away, and we must do as he says. I may not agree with it but what your father says is what we must obey. And when he's not here we must obey Vincent. Do not fight it, Clara. It is easier to just go with it. You must learn to just accept things the way that they are and keep your thoughts to yourself and your mouth shut. It is something that we as women must learn to do, otherwise you will end up in even more trouble.'

She pulled me to her chest and gently rubbed her hand down my arm. It was a rare moment of gentleness, one that I would not forget.

Chapter Three

Alone in my room.

I had many hours to reflect on what had happened as I tried to make sense of it all. I was but a small child, trying to determine how to navigate life, by a set of rules that felt so incompatible with the inner compass which I was used to following.

I had run from the house on Friday afternoon, Mammy said I could go. All my chores were done and there were still enough hours left in the day for me to ride Trinity up to the cliffs. It was my favourite thing to do. I'd saddle Trinity up excitedly talking to her about the adventure we were to have. We would just ride as fast as we could through the open fields. There was nothing like it. It was my freedom. I had learnt early on what was required of me in our home, and only in the last few weeks, Da had agreed with my mammy that if I did my jobs and obeyed all the rules then I was allowed this freedom.

My mammy's only instruction as I left was that I be home for dinner. I assured her I would be as I had each day in the previous weeks. I told her I watched the sun and knew when it reached a certain point on the horizon that it was time for me to head home. Even when it was raining and overcast, I always knew exactly where she was seated in the sky. I was very diligent with this as I did not want to risk losing this privilege.

Aggie did not share my passion for riding. She would rather play with the neighbours when her work was done. And Vincent only ever rode when we had to. For him a horse was a commodity and it served a purpose and he could not understand my connection to Trinity. He righteously declared he didn't have time for the frivolity of riding horses for fun. He took his role as heir to the family farm with great seriousness and was forever trying to please Da by working hard and playing little with us or the neighbours. He was not well liked at school, for he had a sombre nature and had difficulty connecting with others. Most of the other boys in the village and surrounding farms were often getting into awful trouble for the mischief they would get into. Not Vincent. His fear of disappointing Da ensured he had no time or tolerance for the craic.

Trinity and I flew through the paddocks and the open hills and mountains that surrounded the village. My trust in my beloved Trinity was implicit, we moved as one in a harmonious flow. Trinity took me wherever the wind whispered her to go. Her ears would twitch as she left the stable, sensing the callings of nature, knowing she too, was to have the freedom to gallop and stride away from the restrictions of the stable. I would often close my eyes as we rode, giving way to the natural rhythm of Trinity rising and falling beneath me. It was my favourite place to be, removed from the world around me. It was only me and Trinity, the mountains, and the tantalising raging North Atlantic Ocean that took me beyond the rigidity of the life I knew and was becoming more entrenched in. It was all I had known, the rules and constraint, yet here the ocean called to me, the wind seduced my senses and stirred a deep longing which stimulated a familiar unease within my stomach. I welcomed this feeling, the flittering unease, it teased me and although I did not understand it, I knew that it was part of the reason why I found such joy in coming here. It filled me with a desire for something more and I knew as I gazed to the horizon that there was more. A deep longing permeated from my core and pulsated through my seven-year-old body.

I lay on my back, held safely in the arms of the Mother and allowed this vibration to move through me, lingering long enough to activate a deep remembering within my soul.

Remember there is more.

I could not understand these words that seemed to come from within me, but I held them as I had all the silent messages I had begun to receive in recent months. I may not have comprehended the words, yet I felt them. I lay with this delightfully overwhelming feeling of *more* that engulfed me, allowing a brief insight into what lay yonder, beyond the boundaries of my current existence. Sensing a change in the air, I opened my eyes and was immediately jolted from my euphoric bubble to a boy. Perhaps a little older than I was. He was standing directly above me curiously peering down. I squealed in fright and jumped up as quickly as I could to move away from this stranger who had imposed himself into my sacred space.

'Who are ye, how long have ye been standing there?' I demanded of him, as I distanced myself adequately.

'Sure, I was only here but a minute. Truth be told, I wasn't sure if ye were asleep or dead and then ye started grinning like the cat that got the cream. I didn't know if ye were just mad or something,' he laughed mockingly.

'I'm not mad. I was just having, uh, a … rest and I thought of a joke, that's why I was smiling.' Indignantly I put my hands on my hips to try and stand my ground. 'You know you shouldn't sneak up on people like that. I could have died right here and now with a heart attack from the fright, it would have been your fault sure it would.'

'What are you doing up here anyway?' he asked, ignoring my pitiful rebuttal.

'What are you doing up here? No one ever comes up here.' There was a part of me that felt affronted that my private little world, my treasured secret escape, had been discovered by *him*.

'I'm just after looking at the ocean, that's all. Do you really think you're the only one who ever comes up here?

Sure, you are awful daft, if you think that. I come up here every day when we are passing through these parts.'

As he stared out across the ocean I noticed his clothes and shoes for the first time and realised that he was not from the village or even the surrounding region.

'Are you a Traveller?' I asked guardedly. I momentarily averted my eyes as I remembered the warnings I had heard about never looking a Gypsy in the eye, believing you will be cursed.

'And what if I am, what's it to you?' he retorted defensively, turning to face me.

'Well, I don't think I'm supposed to talk to you if you are a Traveller.' My mammy and da's admonitions were echoing in my ears.

'Sure, then don't talk to me, I don't care,' he turned, walked towards the edge of the cliff and stood there staring out into the raging waters.

He was aware of the sneers and disapproving remarks of others. There was much prejudice that came with this life and he already felt ostracised, yet his people persisted in honouring the lifestyle they had adopted so long before. Perhaps he would grow hardened to the judgement of others, yet here, right now he was still softened to the world and he felt the sting of my rejection fiercely. He only wanted to talk and maybe play. He desperately wanted to be seen beyond his clothes, his family and the life they chose to live. He was a Gypsy at his core, but that was not all he was. He already knew this and already had the desire to define himself differently.

'You're not going to jump, are you?' I whispered nervously, standing behind him.

'No, why would I?'

'Sometimes, I think I would like to jump and fly like the birds around the cliffs, just to see how it felt. Wouldn't you like to know how it felt to be a bird?' I asked passionately.

'Nah, I'd like to be a dragon not a bird,' he said with a cheeky look of excitement and awe.

'Dragons aren't even real.' I laughed at him and his wild imagination.

'Yes, they are,' he argued, an assurance overcoming him. 'I've seen a baby one once when we were in The Burren. Ma Ma took me for a walk one night and we saw one hiding in amongst the rocks.'

'You must have been imaging it. Maybe your Ma Ma was playing tricks on you.'

'Nah, it was real. I saw its little wings and everything,' he replied impassioned.

'It was probably just a bat or a weird bird or something,' I suggested unable to reconcile my limited beliefs.

'Nope. Definitely a dragon,' he stated determinedly. 'There are loads of mystical creatures in The Burren. Ma Ma even talks to them. Like the faeries, especially the faeries.' I looked at him with a renewed curiosity and sensing my interest he continued animatedly. 'It was only really little, but she said it must be time.'

'Time for what?'

'Time for the dragons to come back. Because they used to be around all the time, it's not just in storybooks.

For real they were around and then they disappeared. She said it must be time for them to come back to bring the light, slay the darkness they will, to bring the light.'

'What darkness, you mean like the Devil and the sinners?' I asked tentatively.

'I don't really know? Ma Ma says I will come to know the darkness. But I don't know what she means really. I often don't know what she's talking about. She tells lots of stories, but I don't really understand them. She pats me on the head and says, 'one day you will.' Do you think that the birds might look at you and think how they would like to be a girl instead of a bird?'

'No way, there is no way they would want to be a girl. You just do chores, look after the men, get married, have babies, cook the dinner every night, wash the sheets and all that stuff. I would much prefer to be a bird. So much easier to be a bird than a girl,' I declared decisively.

'You are awful queer,' he laughed.

'Yeah, well, so are you because you believe in dragons!' The sting of being called queer, as I often was by my family, was softened by his laughter.

'You be a bird and I'll be a dragon and see who wins. First to that tree over there,' he said pointing to a tree on the far side of the adjoining paddock.

'Go!' I yelled, already running ahead laughing.

We ran together through the paddock, me squawking like a crazed bird and like a ferocious dragon he roared, freedom carrying us beyond the societal imposed boundaries that said we should not be playing together.

Carefully navigating our way to the highest branches of the tree, we sat in companionable silence—as a bird and a dragon—taking in the breathtaking view of the surrounds as the sun began to lower to the horizon.

And then I saw Vincent. He was galloping up the hill towards Trinity where I had left her happily grazing. I tensed. My heart constricted. I panicked by the imposing threat. Sure, he was just my brother and he was only twelve-years-old, but he was no child. He carried a demeanour of solemnity and a steely determination to prove himself to Da, which obscured the innocence of childhood and cultivated a callousness which I feared. He was obviously searching for me and I could tell by the tension through his back that he was angered. I felt confused as I had completed all my chores. I had sought approval from Mammy before leaving home and I still had an hour before Mammy would expect me home. But since Da had been away on business for the past few days, Vincent had been tasked with the responsibility of running the farm, a role he relished and had stepped into with confidence, asserting his power and authority even over Mammy. Sensing I had done something wrong, yet oblivious to its source, I felt the familiar nameless guilt overcome me.

'I have to g-g-go,' I stammered to the boy sitting beside me.

'What's the rush?' he asked, seemingly disappointed that I was abandoning him.

I didn't have time to answer, panic compelling me to get down the tree and back to Trinity as quickly as possible.

I knew I needed to appease Vincent to thwart any further rise in his anger. I had seen him ruthlessly beat my most beloved dog in one of his rages and I feared riling him further. I did not allow myself to ponder what I had done wrong. There would be no point arguing my story anyway. He would see the situation the way he chose, and it was not my place to convince him otherwise.

'You are to come home now,' Vincent ordered, fixing me with a steely stare as I neared him.

Breathlessly, I nodded my head, eyes downcast. I was not sure if I was to be punished here or when I returned home. I was unsure what my punishment would entail but I could sense Vincent's desire to exert his authority.

'Why do you have to go and leave so quick?' the boy asked as he raced up behind me.

I turned quickly from Trinity realising he had followed me, and Vincent glowered at him.

'Who are you?' he spat, disdain dripping from him at the sight of the Gypsy boy.

'My name is Ceallach, it's a pleasure,' he said, offering his hand, choosing to ignore the abhorrent manners of Vincent who stood before him.

Vincent was only a year or two older than Ceallach yet regarded himself with importance and superiority.

Rudely ignoring the proffered hand Vincent demanded, 'What were you doing with my sister?'

'We were just after playing and talking, weren't we?' Ceallach motioned to me as I tentatively watched their exchange.

'Uh, yes. Just p-p-playing,' I stammered, lowering my eyes in shame, knowing in admitting I had been playing with a Gypsy that I was destined for severe punishment.

'Be quiet you,' Vincent ordered without releasing Ceallach from his steely stare.

'You Travellers bring nothing but trouble. Don't you go trying to drag her into your ways. She is queer enough as it is without you filling her mind with your gypsy nonsense. Be off with you,' he motioned as he would a wayward dog. 'And don't ye come back or you'll have me Pa to deal with as well, you hear?'

Ceallach stood rooted to the spot with a rage burning inside. He would not be spoken to in this way. Disregarded like a piece of horse shite. He was better than that. He knew that for sure and would not allow them to think otherwise. He was proud of who he was and his people. He knew they were good people despite the criticism cast on them as a collective. He felt the urge to fight, to put this upstart of a farm boy on the ground, to teach him respect. Yet the wisdom of his father echoed in his ears, *Fighting will achieve nothing, you will just give them what they want, which is to be lowered to their level. Stay true to who you are and your people. Turn and walk away, Ceallach*. He closed his eyes and took a deep breath, allowing the wave of fury to pass through him. Upon opening his eyes, he looked squarely into Vincent's, leaving him in no doubt that he was not intimidated by him.

'Have a good evening,' he nodded, raising his hat. Turning to look to me, so small and scared, my body rigid with the uncertainty of what was to happen next. He said, 'Mind yourself,' as he nodded in my direction.

I did *not* acknowledge him. My eyes downcast. Shamed.

Chapter Four

I mounted Trinity and let her guide me on the path back home. I was too afraid to race ahead, or even look up. I completely trusted in Trinity to bring me home safely. I could hear Vincent on his horse behind me. I could feel the rage burning within him and I felt my body begin to boil as he directed it towards me. He did not need to say anything, I felt it and it scared me. I had never been this afraid of him before now. Sure, I knew that he was awful mean to the animals and to Aggie and me, but that was more in a brother to sister rivalry way, this felt different and I didn't understand where it was coming from.

I don't think he understood it either, but it had taken a hold of him and he couldn't control it. He came up beside me, moving his horse intimidatingly close to Trinity. It was provocative and premeditated. He wanted to rile me, but I knew better, so I kept my eyes downcast and held the reins tight as Trinity began to tense with the threat of the other horse so close. As she fidgeted and began to buckle I grasped tighter attempting to maintain control and turned to see Vincent smirking with amusement at the distress he was creating. He then took his whip and lashed Trinity's rump with ferocity causing her to startle and throw me from her. I landed flat on my back, gasping for breath, winded. I was not sure if I had broken my back or any bones, for the pain was excruciating. I closed my eyes and prayed—not to the God from church—to my God, the one I saw when I stood on the edge of the cliffs. The God that I could only access in my dreams who could take me away like the birds dancing and flying around freely.

I prayed. 'Please, God, take me away from it all. Let this be it.'

I wanted to scream at my brother for his cruelty and run home to my mammy and da and tell on him, but I knew I would not be heard. It was his place, I should learn mine. I lay—still, muted, numb—waiting for something, anything to carry me away from this moment. It did not come. And suddenly, a firm loving voice guided me from within, it said: *Stand up and walk, you are stronger than you know. Every time they knock you down, I will be here to help you rise again.*

I pulled myself up, dusted down my dress, put my shoulders back and my chin up. The well of tears pooled in my eyes, but I would not let him see them. I strode across the paddock with all the strength and resilience I could muster. I would not be a victim of his cruelty, that is what he wanted, he wanted to see me broken. I would not break for him, he despised me for this.

Maybe if I had laid on the ground sobbing or called to him to help me things would have been different. Maybe if I had affirmed his desire for power by breaking he wouldn't have whipped me when I got home. Maybe if I had allowed him to dominate me he wouldn't have needed to dominate me in all the years ahead. Maybe I should have broken then and saved myself the pain that lay before me. But the spirit within called me to rise like those birds at the cliffs and fly again. I craved that freedom, so I rose to meet his cruelty.

I felt his sullen rage each time the whip struck my back. Mammy had agreed that I needed to be punished for playing with the Gypsy boy. My behaviour was shameful and dangerous, and anyone could have seen me and thought ill of my breeding and that I was nothing more than a Gypsy myself. In my mammy's eyes, I should be punished for the potential shame I brought to her name, the family, but I know that this was no longer what drove Vincent's violent hand. I know my mammy thought the first three lashes around my backside would suffice, this was fairly standard punishment from my da for all three of us and in some way was acceptable. Then the whip struck my back repeatedly and began to draw blood. Mammy asked him to stop, demanded he stop, but he would not listen. Vincent was oblivious to my cries and Mammy's fervent screams, he would not lay down the whip. After thirteen lashes, he stopped. Why thirteen? I did not know, but I counted, giving me something to focus on in an attempt to distract me from the pain and shock.

He wiped my blood from the whip with the kitchen cloth, hung it on the back of the door, where Da kept it, turned to Mammy, and said, 'I'll have the dinner now.'

A fair clip around the ear is what he needed to pull him back into line as I had seen my mammy do to him many a time before. Yet she hesitated sensing something had changed in him. Something she feared. And instead of tending to me, she began to serve him his dinner, like the man of the house. A role he had so easily and willingly stepped into.

Possibly, had Mammy clipped him round the ear right then and there, things may have been different. Maybe if she had tended to my bleeding back first and told him to wait for his dinner he would have been put in his place. Perhaps if she had dragged him to Father Stanley that very night to abolish the cruel evilness that had taken over him, the monster he became would never have been given a chance.

A moment in time. A choice.

Mammy served Vincent spuds and stew and cleaned up after him. Her inability to stand in her power, inadvertently handed it over to him.

Our life was never the same.

Chapter Five

I never much liked going to the little village school. There was around forty of us—all different ages—in the one room. The littlest up the front and the oldest at the back. Some of the boys left when they got older and went away to schools in Galway or Dublin. Vincent didn't go away. He didn't want to leave the farm and Da couldn't afford to send him, not that Mammy ever let that be known. She took great pride in telling everyone that Vincent was committed to helping his father run the farm, knowing one day it would be his. She would righteously declare, 'my boy doesn't need a fancy education to teach him how to run the farm, he learns all he needs to know from getting his hands dirty.'

Many of the girls left by the time they were fifteen.

The general consensus being there was not a great need for an education if you were to be married, keep house and bear children. Occasionally, a girl would go away to continue her studies, like Aggie's friend, Maree Maloney, studying nursing in Dublin. This was not looked upon well in the parish. Father Stanley let it be known he didn't agree, as it afforded them too much freedom and exposed them to temptations. He feared that they would forget their place, which, as women was tending to the men and children. I envied those girls who seemed to slip through the noose.

When I was little I longed to learn more and dreamt of one day moving away to study literature. I learnt to read at a young age, guided by my Aunt Maeve, Mammy's sister. She would come around for a cup of tea with Mammy in the early afternoon before the dinner was prepared. Aunt Maeve was not married, she lived with Granny. I once asked her why she was not married, and she told me she preferred a life on her own. Mammy would tell me to mind my own business. Da said that the reason she never married was she was as queer as the Devil.

I adored my Aunt Maeve, she would sit with me before I even started school and read to me. She taught me the letters and sounds of the words. Mammy chastised her for bothering herself with such nonsense. She'd say, 'Sure she'll learn all she needs once she gets to school.' But Aunt Maeve would tell me that if I could read I could handle any hardship because I could always escape into a story and use my imagination to plant myself in the story.

Mammy said to Maeve, 'More feet on the ground and less head in the clouds would have served you well, Maeve. You always had your nose in a book and look where that got you. Serving dinner to Mammy and lying in a cold bed alone.'

'I like my own bed and I like my own space.' Maeve countered passionately.

I remember asking Aunt Maeve what she did with all that time to herself and Mammy claimed she'd go mad with all that time to herself and get awful lonely.

Aunt Maeve's eyes sparkled, 'I read, and I write, I sew, and I go walking around the cliffs, smelling the fresh air, looking at the moon and the stars.'

'You'll catch your death walking around in the middle of the night in this cold,' Mammy chastised. 'And stop putting foolhardy ideas into this Clara's head. She's got a bit too much of the fey about her as it is. She doesn't need any encouragement.'

They both laughed. I liked seeing Mammy laugh, she didn't do it often. When Aunt Maeve was around she seemed more relaxed. It was obvious she didn't need to impress her sister, and when Da was not around she dropped the façade a little. I wished Mammy was like this more often.

'What's the fey?' I asked with the curious innocence of a four-year-old.

'Never you mind, Miss. Get those potatoes and start scrubbing them, you'll be better served learning how to cook a decent mash than filling your head with nonsense,'

Mammy answered lightly.

She never stopped Aunt Maeve from reading to me, or teaching me to read, and opening me to the world of story. A world that would prove to be my only escape in the years ahead.

Following my First Communion, a book always accompanied me to the playground, becoming my comfort from the taunts and isolation from the other children. I'd hear their whispers. I knew what they were saying about me and what their parents were saying about me. I'd see the glare of my brother, humiliated by my presence in his world, his little patch where he'd see himself as someone, someone important, in this small Irish village school.

I don't want to be important in your eyes, in your village. I just want to survive, until I can escape you all. I'd never say it. I just felt something pulsating through me as it held me on that seat, in that playground, impervious to their words, their looks, their judgements. I was so confused because I knew what was expected of me. I knew how I was to behave. I knew what kept my da, my brother, my mammy, my teachers and the priest happy. I knew what to do, but I didn't know if all that was what kept God happy, because when I was being who they wanted me to be, I was not happy. I pondered how I was to navigate this terrain. One which was to become increasingly dangerous. One where I needed to watch myself more carefully now that Vincent had executed his power. One where I had no one to protect me from him.

Not even my mammy.

I knew I should have just gone and played with them. Fit in with their games, their rules. I could see it in Aggie's eyes, impelling me to come play. It would have been so much easier for Aggie to have a sister who was not so odd.

What would it look like if I chose to just fit in? I thought. *What would it look like to not be the girl who longs to ride her horse along the cliffs, who doesn't climb trees with a Gypsy boy, who doesn't destroy her First Communion dress with her own blood in silent defiance of her brother, in defiance of them all who continue to turn a blind eye?* I had to make a choice. I rose to take a step towards them with the knowing that *I* am *me* and they can never take *her* from me—especially if I do not show them *her*—they cannot touch nor destroy her. She will remain mine, sacred and pure. I take another step forward, aware of all that I am sacrificing in an endeavour to save myself and knowing I must silence my voice and keep hidden my truth, as I traverse the rough and unpredictable waters ahead and trust I will find her again. I walk away from my seat and I join the game.

I play by the rules, laughing along with the other girls, remaining aware of the curious piercing stare of Vincent. I feel his hatred towards me and I do not understand it because it never used to be like this. Until last year, we had fun together, like normal brothers and sisters do. Sure, we worked hard to keep Mam and Da pleased, doing our assigned jobs around the farm and in the house, but outside of this we would play for hours into the summer evenings, roaming through the fields, from the beaches to the rock formations and caves. Of course, we bickered and squabbled amongst ourselves, but we knew when and how to behave for our mam and da inside the home and it felt like we were all in it together. There was comfort in that.

I am not sure what changed in the year preceding. Vincent had become increasingly serious and harsh and was spending more time with Da and working the farm. Da had begun spending more time in Galway growing a horse breeding business with his brother, my Uncle Fergus. Mammy was always reminding us that our da was a natural with horses and that everyone knew it between here and Galway. She'd say he was the best in the business. And that Fergus had the brains for the business, but he needed our da for the breeding.

Mammy said, 'There's no business if those horses aren't ready for the breeding, to be sure, and your father is only getting a pittance of the money Fergus is making. ''Tis a disgrace if you ask me. Not that anyone does. And don't you be repeating what I say to your father if you don't want a lashing, ye understand?'

I know Mammy was bitter that her husband was away so often leaving the load of running the farm, keeping house and raising three children, all herself, but I never once heard her complain to him. When he would return from a week or two away, she would tend to him like the return of Jesus himself, risen from the dead.

With his increasing absence, Vincent had taken on more of the responsibility running the farm. A role that placed him in good stead in our da's eyes and yet seemed to diminish his youthful candour and erode the connection between us. As Vincent moved away, Aggie seemed content with the dismantling of our trio and forged closer bonds with the neighbouring girls, who were more interested in sitting around talking than exploring. And so, I often found myself alone. Mammy would say that I had a way with the horses like my da. I had established my love for horses, particularly Trinity, from a very young age, and while Vincent and Aggie would ride, it was never with the same affinity with which I would ride. My connection with Trinity became vital to me as I felt the loss of Vincent and Aggie. A separation I could not really understand.

As I jumped rope with the other girls in the small school playground, I once again felt the sting of separation, this time from myself. A weary acceptance of change tempered the sting and I laughed with the other girls as the ropes became entangled and we found ourselves falling to the ground, tied in knots, as we tried to free ourselves. All the while Vincent and the other older boys sat along the wall watching and jeering in jest, except Vincent wasn't jest, there was a maliciousness to his words. His insults seemingly directed at me. What had I done to elicit his hatred?

You should never have tried to shame me so publicly for whipping you. You should never have crossed me. You will regret ever trying to stand against me. I will not forget. Did he really say that or was it just my imagination? Fear was dancing with my mind, he held me in a place where I forfeited my power and allowed him to control me.

Chapter Six

I hate him for what he did to me.

I hate him even more for what he stole from me, my freedom, my joy. He filled me with trauma and fear that held me in this place for so many years. I should have fought back. I should have spoken up. I should have stood in my power.

I should have *risen*.

But the terror silenced my voice. Gutted my inner strength and blinded my ability to see beyond the lies and deception. The core of who I was succumbed to his brutality, my soul starved of its life force, its freedom wilted. I lost my connection to the powerful little girl who stood before that altar in her blood-stained First Communion dress.

He made sure she would not rise again, not while

he controlled me. And every time he violated me, he knew another piece of my soul would splinter under the pressure and I would lose myself just a little more. I do not know if his methodical destruction of my soul was a conscious plot. I saw a steely darkness in his eyes that sent chills through my bones, other times, I saw a boy becoming a man, treating a girl as a woman, in the way he had become accustomed to seeing on the farm. His penetration of me, nothing more than a functional act performed by the male on the female. He had witnessed animals operating in this way from the time he was a small child and he accepted it as normal.

'It is just what happens.' That is what I heard him say to me the first time.

It was two weeks after the First Communion. The wounds on my back were still healing from the whipping, I felt a sharp pain emanating from them when he pushed me over the hay stack and dug his elbows into my back, as he stuck his member into me.

'It is just like the animals. It is just what happens,' he murmured when he finished.

Was he trying to convince himself or me?

He gathered his breath, pulled up his pants, turned me around, grabbed my tear-stained face, and said, 'This is our secret. Do you understand?' His eyes were piercing. I nodded as he threw me to the ground amongst the horse shite.

I found my way to a restless Trinity and cradled myself against her, settling her as I attempted to calm myself. *Do you understand? Do you understand? Do you understand?* The question echoing through my soul. I understood none of it. Not the part of me that was silently screaming with fear. Not that part that was rasping with an indignant rampant rage nor that which accepted that what he said was true, 'it is just what happens.'

None of it made sense and no amount of questioning any of it helped. I suppose I suppressed the rage, tempered the fear with compliance and surrendered to what was. My mammy had told me it was easier to just keep my mouth shut and go along with it, accepting things the way they were meant less trouble. I don't know if she wanted me to keep my mouth shut about this. I like to hope that should she have known she would have put a stop to it. But I cannot help but wonder if she did know and simply turned a blind eye, preferring to remain oblivious. It was much easier for her not to know. The smears of blood on my underwear silently ignored and the frequent bruising of my back overlooked. The persistent night terrors written off as attention seeking by my da, willingly seen in the same light by my mammy. The social withdrawal and clinginess to my mammy was a desperate plea for nurture, safety and security in a world where I was beyond vulnerable. But I was sent to school where once again I was seen as odd because I could not bring myself to partake in the triviality and laughter of the school yard. I was sent out of the house onto the farm to do my chores, even though I resisted, for I knew what often awaited me in the stables, especially when Da was away.

I was called a lazy sloth for which I would be damned to Hell, it being one of the seven deadly sins, often preached about by Father Stanley. I was dragged to confession week after week for my resistance to mucking out the stables. I begged to be allowed to do extra chores in the house to help Mammy, but she would not hear of it.

'You think I can't keep my home myself? What sort of woman do you think I am? You'll be getting out there and helping your brother, who works his fingers to the bone day after day, to muck out that stable.'

'She thinks she's too good to shovel shite, sure she does,' mocked Vincent.

'Why doesn't Aggie have to do it? How come she gets to feed the hens and help you with the dinner Mammy?' I queried in tears.

'Because I don't even ride the silly old horses, Clara. You're the one that loves them, so you should be the one cleaning up their shite,' declared Aggie self-righteously.

I had no problem with mucking out a stable, the truth was I loved to be there. And when Da was around I would willingly do it with him, knowing I was safe from Vincent. How could they not see that it was he I was trying to avoid?

It came upon me after being dragged to Father Stanley for the umpteenth time to confess my sins, that I would explain the truth of my reluctance and resistance; that I wasn't lazy at all, that my brother was hurting me. That I was scared. Even though I feared my brother finding out, as his recurrent reminder that *this is our secret* constantly pounded through my mind. I reconciled with myself that my confession was a conversation, not with Father Stanley, but with God himself. That is what we had been taught at school by Sister Mary and Brother Padraig. That a priest is an intermediary between us and God, anything shared in the confessional is between yourself and God. My seven-year-old innocence trusted that when I explained to Father Stanley why I was continuing to refuse to muck out the stable that he would understand that I was not committing a sin in being lazy and that God would forgive me.

'Forgive me, Father, for I have sinned. It has been one week since my last confession.'

'And what child, do you have to confess this week?' asked the rather uninterested voice behind the wooden screen.

'I have been refusing to muck out the stables again while my da is away,' I tentatively began.

'I see. Have you still not learnt to obey your mother and brother's directives whilst your father is away?' the voice questioned incredulously. 'You do know that your brother has been assigned charge of the farm in your father's absence?'

How could I not know? My brother had left no one in any doubt about that.

'For that reason, you must obey him and do the chores asked of you, child.' Father Stanley sounded exasperated with the tediousness of this business. He continued, 'Women need to know their place, and they must be taught from a young age, so that nonsense like this does not arise.'

'I do understand that. And I do all that my brother asks of me, but if I may explain about the stables and why I don't want to do it when my da is away?' I asked hopefully.

'Very well, young lady, you may try and explain away your sin to God and it will be up to him to reconcile it within you,' he conceded.

'Thank you, Father. Dear God, I am not lazy. I truly am not. I love to muck out the stables with my da and make sure that Trinity and all the other horses have a clean stable and fresh water. But God, when my da is away, and I must do it without him, I am afraid.'

'What could you possibly be afraid of, child? You have been around horses since the day you were born?' chastised Father Stanley.

'I am not afraid of the horses, Father Stanley. It is my brother I am afraid of. He hurts me when he is alone with me in the stables.' I stammered and coughed, the fear of speaking this truth jamming my throat.

'In what way does he hurt you, child?' asked Father Stanley, suddenly seeming more interested.

'He mounts me against the hay bales like the animals do. He sticks his member into me and it hurts.' I explained, as bluntly as I could.

There was a long pause from the other side of the confessional box and moments later, he asked, 'Do you enjoy it? When he sticks his member into you?'

'No, Father Stanley, I do not, it hurts.'

'Are you sure you feel no pleasure, at all?' he asked eagerly.

'No, Father Stanley, I only feel pain and it scares me when he pushes against me. I fear he is going to break my bones with the force of it.'

'One can only imagine,' murmured Father Stanley, pausing to imagine. 'Now should you take pleasure from this act then that would be a sin. But given you say you experience no pleasure when your brother penetrates the soft fleshiness of your woman with his member then no sin has been committed. Now, say three Our Fathers and three Hail Marys for your penance, pray to God for his help in obeying your brother. One day you will marry, you will be expected to obey your husband, this lesson will serve you well as a wife in many ways. Now, go, tell whomever is waiting to give me a few minutes before they enter.' A stifled moan trailed his words.

I left the church that day more confused than before. I was not a sinner, but I still felt I was being punished for something. There was only one way to reconcile. I simply had to do as Vincent asked and my mother was right. If I just stopped fighting it would be over within minutes and life would continue on as before, until the next time. It seemed easier than the constant battles, I was tired of silently screaming for help and no one hearing me. *Stop being silent*, a voice within me would beg, yet even when I voiced the truth to Father Stanley, a man of God, I was not heard. The futility wearied my soul and I succumbed to this being my story.

I accepted what was for the next five years, until I began to bleed. That day it ended. Vincent approached me in the stables the same as he had done so often before.

As he bent me over the hay bales and lifted my skirt, I pulled away and grabbed at my skirt, 'I'm bleeding. You can't!'

It was the first time I had challenged him in all those years. My initial lack of resistance arose from fear, a silent terror prevented me from fighting back and over time this was replaced by a passive surrender as I completely dissociated from the experience. I had learnt that it was over within minutes and my *presence* was not a necessity to him. I had long learnt how to reset myself after he violated me. First, I would fix my underwear and skirt and then brush Trinity methodically. Her gentle aura was a healing to my brokenness. I would finish mucking the stables before returning to the house and boil a pot to wash myself. My mother would sometimes question why I needed to bathe so often, especially in the winter, but she never sought my truth. She never wanted to know why I would scratch my inner thighs until they bled, the boiling water scalding the broken skin, eliciting a strangely excruciating yet pleasurable pain that in some way helped to expunge the trauma inflicted by my brother.

He stared at me, considering whether to proceed.

'I'm bleeding,' I interjected with a sudden defiant strength.

He slapped my face with ferocity and through clenched teeth he spat out, 'You are a filthy whore, never speak to me like that again.'

And with that he was done with me.

Of course, I did not know that now I bled I could be impregnated by him, but his expanding interest in horse breeding ensured he was well aware of this risk and opted not to take his chances.

Not surprisingly, he took up with Carmel McDermott, the only daughter of Padraig McDermott. They married within a few months. He now had a legitimate female. A wife to mount and release his urge whenever he desired. I felt sorry for Carmel marrying this beast, for I had grown to hate him, but she knew what she was doing, and she chose to accept it as her duty. Reminiscent of so many women before her and of so many who have come after her.

.

Chapter Seven

My childhood wasn't dire, not all the time. There were some good times sprinkled amongst the angst and trauma. I recall a period, when my da was often away for weeks at a time. I hated these times, as Vincent would make the most of these opportunities with me in the barn and would also invoke misery in the home bossing Mammy and Aggie around, demanding to be treated as Master.

Mammy would be so excited on his return, knowing that her world would return to normal. She served Da and tended to his every need, but this was the vow she had made to him when she became his wife. I know she was not comfortable serving her own son in this way, yet she stayed silent, knowing it was not her place to speak up. Her husband had appointed Vincent to this role, she was not to challenge him on it.

On one night, after dinner, Mammy poured Da a whiskey and poured herself a small glass, as well. I watched with curiosity as she glanced at Vincent who sat seething at the table. He wanted to speak to our da about the running of the farm, he wanted his attention and yet he was put in his place by being told it could wait until tomorrow. Vincent stormed from the room with his ego shattered at being dismissed by Da in front of Mammy, Aggie and me. I secretly enjoyed seeing him disempowered, kicked from the throne he had chosen to abuse. I sensed Mammy and Aggie did, too. I feared the ramifications that would come once Da went away again, but I tried not to think about that and allowed myself to enjoy the rare feeling of joy within my home. I saw something in Mammy and Da on these nights that surprised and delighted me. A slight cracking of the armour and a subtle breaking of the rules; what the rules were or who made them up I did not know, but I saw something akin to freedom in their eyes and in it I felt garnered permission to do the same. I know Aggie felt it too, I sensed her loosen her reserve. I did not know whether Vincent was using her in the way he had me, I dared not ask. She did not seem as intimidated by him as I was, yet these nights allowed me to see the impact he was having on us all. My da with a whiskey in hand seemed to leave the outside world behind and in so doing gave us permission to do the same, the façade dropped, and we just were. Needless to say, Vincent never joined us on these evenings, preferring to stroke his bruised ego alone in his room.

'Why don't you sing?' Da said to Mammy. 'You have the best voice in the whole county.'

'Really, Mammy has the best voice in the whole county?' I queried with curiosity and pride.

'Indeed, Clara. The first time I heard your mammy sing was at the wedding of Padraig and Maggie McDermott. That was it. I knew she was the girl who I was going to marry, Mary Smullen, she was standing there by the side of the altar singing like an angel.' He looked at Mammy with a fondness that I had never seen before.

'I do love to sing,' mused Mammy reflectively. 'I couldn't believe it when Padraig McDermott asked my father, God rest his soul,' she continued, as she blessed herself with the sign of the cross, 'if I could sing at his wedding to Maggie, or Margaret Connell as she was known then; I was always of the belief that Padraig did not approve of singing and then he's after asking me to sing at his own wedding. I know it was to impress them Connell's from Sligo, the richest family in the whole of the west coast, so it is said.'

I treasured being part of the banter and invited into my parent's stories. I loved to sing with my mammy on these nights, the two of us would sync into perfect harmony in the rich story of Ireland. I enjoyed singing in the school choir and the hymns in church, but I never felt

I was allowed to really sing then, not like this, not the way I did with Mammy. My da's eyes would fill with tears as he sat with Aggie on his lap, whiskey in hand, listening to us and feeling the soul of the song, we evoked.

These are my happiest memories of my childhood, the light amidst the dark. Vincent was never part of them, making them pure and sacred. Aggie and I got to be with our parents in their truth, in love and joy, without anyone else's rules dictating how they were to live their lives. These memories were a gift, as they were to inspire me in the years ahead to rise above the rules and live life my way.

Chapter Eight

Da died in what everyone regarded as a 'tragic accident' in the back fields of our farm. I was thirteen. Vincent was with him when the tractor overturned, crushing him so there was not a chance of survival.

'An awful tragedy so it is,' crooned the ladies with cup of tea in hand, who visited my mammy on the evening of the accident.

'Sure, it's the way of the land. A fine farmer he was. God rest his soul,' the men would state to Vincent, who had already resumed his position in the home, some six months after abdicating his temporary throne.

In the months following Vincent's marriage to Carmel McDermott, they lived in a small cottage on the

McDermott estate, while he worked for his father-in-law, Padraig. This had been part of the marriage arrangement proposed by Padraig to Vincent and Da. Vincent had righteously declared to Mammy that Padraig McDermott chose him for his daughter because he had shown himself to be a strong man and he believed he would know how to clip Carmel's wings, as she had shown herself to be of flighty temperament. Father Stanley supported the notion of Vincent marrying Carmel McDermott even though she was only sixteen. He said it was better than sending her away to a fancy finishing school in England like her mother attended. A waste of money Padraig McDermott claimed. He believed there were easier ways to bring refinement to the young lady. Vincent had agreed and said it would be his honour to show Carmel McDermott how to be a lady.

The proposed marriage arrangement also required Vincent to work in the McDermott business with a view to inheriting it as Carmel was the only child. And whilst this was a most attractive proposition for Vincent, given his eagerness for the prestige of holding such a position in the village, the reality of living in a small cottage away from the main house and working under McDermott and his existing staff had made Vincent feel subservient.

Da had forgone his breeding work in Galway and returned to our farm to allow Vincent the opportunity within the prestigious McDermott family. For Mammy and Da, it was also seen as a chance for them to elevate their standing in the village, now being related to Padraig

McDermott, perhaps even move a pew or two ahead in the church. Mammy was bursting with pride on the wedding day, standing adjacent to Maggie McDermott and the extended Connell family from Sligo, in the church in front of all the other parishioners. There were many others who were envious of her position that day and she revelled in the glory of it.

'It's not every day that you marry into the richest family on the west coast of Ireland,' Mammy reminded me on the morning of the wedding.

There was no part of me that wanted to celebrate the union of my brother to this girl. I felt sorrow for her knowing the truth of my brother's cruelty. But she also seemed accepting of the arrangement and excited at the prospect of having her own home and no longer having to answer to her father. Vincent had done little to prepare her for the reality of what her future held, having done his best to impress her during their brief courtship.

The untimely death of Da proved advantageous to Vincent who had become increasingly resentful of his father-in-law. It hadn't even been a week since his passing and Vincent was moving back to the farm with his pregnant wife. He took complete control of the home and property.

As I carried Carmel's bags into our parent's bedroom, Mammy objected. 'That is my bedroom, my bed that I shared with your father all those years.'

'He is not here now, so it makes no sense for you to sleep in that bed any longer. As the man of the house, it is only apt that I take the room and share the bed with my wife. You may sleep in with Clara and Aggie. My old room will be needed for the baby coming.'

For the first and only time in my life, I witnessed my mammy lose her mind and dare challenge Vincent. 'Your father is not even cold in the ground and you've jumped into his bed. What are you doing here Vincent? You've an arrangement with Padraig, you cannot just leave and take his daughter with you. Are you mad?'

'I can do what I want with his daughter. She is my wife. Padraig understands the farm is now mine and I have a duty to keep it running. It is impossible for me to tend to the needs of my farm and continue working for Padraig. He will respect me for my commitment to the farm and is pleased with my work as a husband to Carmel, particularly given she is with child, that will no doubt ensure she loses any further fanciful ideas of a life outside of Ireland. Padraig's greatest fear is that Carmel will leave him, like his mother, that mad woman who ran off with the Gypsies and was never seen again. He told me one night when we had a few under our belts. He cannot bear for Carmel to leave him, so I have assured him with a brood of kids under her wings, she won't be flying anywhere.'

'Have you no emotion? How did you become so cold and cruel? Your father would be ashamed of you, sure he would. May he haunt you every night you sleep in his bed.'

Mammy's curse was met with a brutal clout across

her jaw which drew blood.

'You will never speak to me like that again and you will show me the respect that I deserve as man of this house. Do you understand?'

Mammy silenced her voice, but her eyes told another story, one of shock, repulsion, a deep heart-wrenching grief for the loss of her beloved and something far greater, the loss of herself as a woman. While suppressed in most aspects of her life, behind the closed door of her bedroom, she had always risen. A somewhat shameful yet divinely pure secret shared between her and her husband, that was now gone forever. Being kicked from her bedroom stole a sacred aspect of her soul and created a monumental change in Mammy. She disengaged from life, not even the glorious sounds of her grandbabies could coax her from her melancholy, and over time her physical health deteriorated. First the loss of sensation in her hands, rendering her powerless to help in the home, next she lost mobility, unable to leave the home, and then blindness.

'There is no more I want to see anyway,' she moaned the day her vision left.

I was fourteen-years-old living in the home, that had been taken over by my brother and it felt like a prison. I was subservient to a brother who had raped me for five years of my life and beaten me whenever the inkling arose. He had instructed his wife to treat me as her servant and it was my responsibility to tend to her every need, the ever-increasing demands of my ailing mother and the babies that had come in quick succession following their marriage. Vincent took enormous pride in fulfilling his agreement to Padraig McDermott in 'clipping her wings' and Carmel had lost her spark and independence.

Aggie was still living at home and managed to form a strong friendship with Carmel. Together they left most of the work to me, constantly demanding something, 'Oh Clara, will you ever stop that baby from crying? Clara, Mammy is after dirtying herself again, go clean her up. Clara, the breakfast is done you can clean up now as Aggie and I are going to go for a walk.' I often heard them sniggering about me. 'She's awful dull Clara, isn't she?' Carmel would whisper, and Aggie would agree. 'Indeed, she's terrible daft, just doing what she's told and never speaking up for herself.'

Aggie's words hurt. She was my sister and before everything went wrong we were the best of friends. She didn't know that I wanted to run to the edge of the cliffs and scream my head off. She didn't know that I wanted to say 'no, I won't stop the baby crying, she's not mine, she's yours Carmel,' or 'you do it,' or 'feck you, Aggie, you clean Mammy up, I've done it three times today already,' or 'clean your own breakfast up, sure you've got two hands like myself!' But instead I said nothing and just did as I was told, because it just seemed easier to keep my mouth shut, as my mammy had told me so many times when I was little and had a voice.

Vincent would beat me often enough, whenever he was in a mood. I didn't want to give him any more reason, so I obeyed him and them. He never hit Carmel or Aggie. He would rage at them enough so that they feared him, but he would never raise a hand to them. He saved it for me. And they knew it, yet they would not stop him. They watched on, both confused by the intensity of his aggression towards me, yet relieved that it was not them. I did not get much sympathy, as it seemed everyone accepted that this was the way things were and I became accustomed to the blood and bruises and my body aching as I lay each night in bed.

And it was here, in bed at night, that I held onto my freedom, because nobody could take those hours from me. I treasured the stillness and silence of the night and the world that I escaped to while everyone else slept. When Vincent first began whipping and violating me I would have nightmares. The story was often different, but the feeling of terror remained the same, I would wake screaming when the faceless predator's hands grabbed me, as I knew what was to come next. My nightmares were ignored. They never asked me why I feared the faceless man, who stalked me at night.

As I got older, I discovered that I could survive on very little sleep and by avoiding sleep I escaped my nightmares. And in my insomnia, I found my freedom. I would allow my mind to wander into a fantasy land where I would gallop with Trinity across the fields, feeling the wind whipping my face, making my nose run and my eyes water and my heart race. I would remember the feeling of being alive with the blood pumping through my veins and I would stand on the edge of the cliff and imagine myself screaming and releasing all the angst and pain that was piling up inside of me. And I would laugh as I would fall into a heap on the soft grassy ledge, feeling broken yet renewed. And then I would rise and stand with my arms outstretched and call to the wind to take me now and I would fly from the edge of the cliff, and then I would soar through the clouds and dance with the birds in a beautiful harmony. When the dance was done, I would rest on top of the clouds and wait for my angels to come and visit me. Sometimes they joined me and sometimes not and, on those nights, when they would not visit, I trusted there was someone else who needed them more than me. And in some way, I was comforted by that because they must have thought I was strong enough to get through the next day. Nevertheless, they would always come to me, on those nights when Vincent had raped me or beaten me. They would meet me on the cliff top, knowing I might not have the strength to fly, and they would take hold of my outstretched arms and lift me ever so gently into the softness of the clouds like the softness of a mother's breast where I would be delivered to my favourite angel. She was divinely beautiful with a golden glow surrounding her white gown and her wings were so huge and powerful, yet they were so gentle and soft against my brokenness when she wrapped them around my body. She never spoke to me. She didn't need to say words because I could feel her words in the love that abounded me. It was the mother's love of which I was starved in my life and I used her loving embrace to heal me, as best I could.

The throbbing of my muscles would ease. The cuts would stop weeping. The spasms of my vagina would release, and the gnawing anger and resentment would absolve and the emptiness within my heart would be replaced by the love of a mother. And everything would be alright again. Until the next time.

My fantasy life became my saviour and I looked forward to climbing into bed each night to escape to my world. A world where I was not scared and lonely, angry and bitter, suffocating and confused. Here, in the world beyond this one, I was free, loved, supported, protected, safe, assured and I was so incredibly powerful. In my world, I knew me, because no one was telling me what to think or believe or what to do or say. I'd re-connected to *her* and for only a few brief hours, I would remember what it was like to be me, in my truth. I would take her back with me, into my day. I would see Vincent look at me, resenting the fact that despite his best efforts he had not destroyed me, for he could see *her* in my eyes and he hated her. She represented everything he hated about women, the freedom, the confidence, the assuredness, the knowing. He hated that innate feminine knowing, that I carried. It was this he was most threatened by and it is this he seemed most intent on abolishing in me through his words and actions. He relentlessly attacked my intellect, telling anyone he could that I was 'as useless as they come … as dumb as a mule … as thick as two planks of wood.'

He would take the books I was reading from me, saying I was only after pretending I could read and later wouldn't allow any books in the house at all, unless Father Stanley had approved them.

He sat around the table one night with a belly full of whiskey with his father-in-law, whom he had ensured had become his great companion, declaring that only the books approved by Father Stanley, as the eye of God here on earth, shall enter the home. He'd say, 'There's a load of shite being written about women, that's after putting all sorts of fanciful ideas into the heads of them.' He motioned to Carmel, Aggie and Mammy, who were sitting around the range sewing and he spat in my direction as I poured the tea, continuing, 'and especially you,' he yelled. 'You all need to be remembering that you're here for nothing more than to be breeding children, cooking the dinner and keeping us men satisfied in bed.' McDermott and Vincent laughed like a pair of dirty little school boys.

He repulsed me that night. And I turned away in disgust to no avail.

'You, you … fecking ugly whore. You look at me now,' he raged in his drunken voice. I knew it was me he was referring to. It was always me, but I just didn't want to look at him. I simply couldn't look at him without conveying my repugnance. 'I said turn around,' he roared, thumping his fist on the table as he threw the glass at the back of my head.

I grabbed my head, feeling the blood oozing onto my hand and turned to him as he rose from the table and came at me. I went within as I always did when he attacked, my eyes fading to nothingness, so he could get nothing more of me. This act of disempowerment enraged him more and he yanked my head back by my chin forcing me to look into the red tinges of his eyes.

'You think you're so fecking smart, smarter than all of us, you … self-righteous bitch, you're as thick as they come, the cows in that paddock have got more brains than you. You might as well be here helping out my Carmel and Mammy in the house than wasting time in that school. Sure, and don't think I don't know what you've been up to in that school with them boys.' Turning to McDermott, he declared, 'After running around with a Gypsy boy no less, Padraig. That's this one for yer.' Seven years had passed, and he still refused to forget, seething he sought further punishment. 'The sooner you're out of that school and back into this house and under my watch the better. Do you understand me?' He spat, with a ruthless vindictiveness as he shoved my head from one side to another, 'do you understand me?'

Cringing, I quickly said, 'I do,' as I felt my neck straining under the force of his hand. I knew that he could kill me in a second with the flick of his wrist and I wouldn't put it past him. He stared into the emptiness of my eyes, which gave nothing, and he contemplated me for a moment. He hated me, and he didn't even know why. He filled the void of my eyes with a mouthful of whiskey laden spit. As I wiped it from my eyes and rubbed the base of my neck I knew he would never leave me alone until he destroyed me.

Mammy suffered a massive heart attack in the darkness of the early morning as she slept beside me. I had just turned seventeen. She gasped, grabbing my hand and with one squeeze she murmured, 'I'm sorry, my Clara.' And with a resigned moan I realised she had passed, and a powerful peace engulfed the room. I prayed for my angel to come and take her soul home while I held her hand, greedily infusing myself with the feeling of peace that lingered in the room, not knowing when in the misery of my life I would find it again.

I heard the singing of an angel, the words a mystery yet the sound a magical golden thread that reached deep into the core of my soul. I turned to Mammy and traced my fingertips across her face, tenderly bestowing her with my love, knowing she could not brush me away like so often she had, keeping me at arms distance, closed to my love.

As a small child I adored my mammy and I desperately needed her love. She had let me down, not allowing herself to let me in, nor opening to her innate call of nurture. Instead she led with her mind which had been filled with *shoulds* and *should* nots. She was not there for me when I needed her. She would not listen when I silently called to her in my pain. I know she heard because a mother always knows their child's silent cries. If they are willing enough to listen. She could not break through the hardened walls of her own heart to love and protect me in the way I needed.

In the stillness of death, I felt her, and all those who came before her, desperately begging for my forgiveness. I felt a deep sorrow for the ancestral conditioning passed without question from mother to daughter, enforcing the ways of the patriarch. I understood that my mammy was no different to me. A product of her upbringing and a victim to the rules that suppressed her voice, stole her freedom and closed her heart so she was unable to live from love and in joy. I vowed in that moment that I would not be a victim like her, that somehow my story would not end as hers had.

I would do it differently. I would rise.

Chapter Nine

On the morning of my mother's funeral, I stared into the small mirror in my bedroom, not recognising the girl who stared back at me. She was a foreigner. A foreigner I had not seen for many years. Looking at yourself in the mirror was deemed both immoral and immodest and vanity itself a dreadful sin. But mostly, I could not bear to look at myself, I was riddled with shame. A shame imbedded in me, through the eyes of my family, Father Stanley, my teacher, the nuns, McDermott and other parishioners. I was forever being reminded that I was a disgrace to my family, an embarrassment to my parents, that I should be ashamed of myself. No matter what I did or said it seemed I could do no right and so I stopped doing anything of my own accord and only did what I was instructed to do. 'A docile puppet' as Vincent labelled me. I'd silenced my voice. Only spoke when spoken to, giving the answer required of me. The good girl response my mother had prescribed.

Who was this broken girl staring blankly back at me? *Where are you?* A stoic cold reserve had emended me, and I was already too weary to fight my way back to the girl, hidden beyond the brokenness who beckoned me to see her again.

I blamed my mother for not protecting me, for not teaching me, for shaming me for being *me*, and for leaving me with no clue as to how I was to steer my life. I had no voice. No confidence. I didn't know who I was and had no one to guide me. I didn't know how to protect myself. I held each and every trauma within me and they weighed heavily, burdening my body and kidnapping my spirit. I was weak and poorly, years of insomnia reflected the sunken dark rings that engulfed my eyes. My skin parched. I scratched at sores, an anxiety driven habit resulting in bloodied scabs on my face and body. My once beautiful dark curls were now a knotted mess, bald patches scattered over my scalp where clumps of hair had fallen out or were pulled out by Vincent in one of his violent attacks.

Before my father's death and mother's own decline, she would chastise me mercilessly telling me to take pride in my appearance or no one would ever want to marry me. My father would tell me to get to work in the paddock to toughen me up because no man would want a sickly woman as a wife. Vincent degraded me ruthlessly, his words like daggers stabbing further into my emancipated frame while Aggie and Carmel would on occasion try and brush my hair and put make up on my face before we went to church, saying it was an embarrassment to be seen with me.

No one ever asked me if I was okay or why I couldn't eat or sleep or why my hair fell out or why I scratched at my skin. They all just pretended that there was nothing wrong and that it was just me and that I was as queer as the Devil.

When my mother died, I was naïve to the world. I had been pulled from school at fourteen and knew nothing outside of the farm, except for attending Mass. I was not allowed to read or listen to the radio, isolated and starved of knowledge to the ways of the world. I knew nothing about what it meant to be a woman, except from what I had seen my mother be, which was subservient and down-trodden by the men in her life. I did not know what my monthly bleeding meant, except that it was to be hidden and the bloodied rags were to be scrubbed in scalding water to remove the filth and dried secretly in my bedroom, where my father and Vincent would not be subjected to such vulgar matters.

I did not know what happened behind the closed door of my mother and father's bedroom nor in the bed that Vincent took with his wife. All I knew was what I learnt on the farm, that animals were impregnated when one mounted the other. I presumed this bestial act was how women became impregnated and for this reason, given I had already been subjected to such an act on hundreds of occasions and not become impregnated, I thought I was unable to bear a child, therefore would be a poor offering as a wife. I did not want babies, having already tended to every need of my niece and nephews. I had no desire to be mounted by a husband to impregnate me.

My thoughts tumbled through my mind searching for an answer as to what was to happen now. I did not know, yet I knew everything would change again now mother had gone. As I stared into the vast pool of darkness within my own eyes, I prayed that God would take me too, even though I knew this was a sin and I would have to confess it to Father Stanley at my next confession, I knew no other way out.

I tapped at the mirror with the comb in my hand, a little tap at first. *If only it would break.* Then I tapped a little harder as a force outside of myself saw it fragment, slivers of glass danced across the table of the dresser. I lurched at the pieces like a starved animal and took one fragment in my hand. I took the sharpest edge and tore it down my hand from the tip of each finger to the wrist, methodical and without emotion. I watched as the blood pool in the palm of my hand. I squeezed my fingers enticing more blood to the surface. There was so much blood and as the glass frolicked across the edge of my wrist I curiously wondered how much more blood there could be. I felt the urge to show them the blood, the stain on their soul, all those who had failed me. I wanted them to be punished in the way I had been punished. I wanted them to feel the pain that I had felt.

'Now, now, my sweet, Clara. That, my dear, is not going to be helping anyone least assured you.' A voice came from behind. She took the glass from me and wrapped a cloth quickly around my bloodied hand. Bewildered, I tried to ascertain where I was and whose voice I could hear. She wrapped her hands around mine.

'Sure, child, it's not surprising that you cannot remember me, for you were but three or four when I left. I am here to lay my sister to rest. May the Divine hold and heal her soul; may she rest now in peace. I am your mammy's sister. Your Aunt Maeve. Let me have a good look at you, Clara, my girl.' She leaned back, stroked away the hair from my face and gently tilted my chin to her. I averted my eyes, ashamed of myself and what I had become. 'Oh, Clara! What have they done to you?' she whispered, as she stroked my cheek.

I looked to her, drawn by her gentleness. I felt a connection to her like no other I had felt in this life. I began to crumble. Her compassion giving an unspoken permission to drop my guard. I shook my head, for I could not find the words to explain what they had done to me. As she drew me to her chest in an embrace, I sobbed. Being held in her arms allowed the years of silent trauma to release. She did not need to know my stories, she just held me as I released my pain. I do not know how long she held me, yet when the tears stopped, and I raised my head to look at her, she cupped my face.

'Now, child ... is that better?' I nodded, managing a weak smile. 'Good, I do believe that you have needed that for a long while now, so you have.' She leant forward and kissed my forehead resting there for a moment before her demeanour became very serious.

'Clara, I am sorry that I was not here for you. I only wish that I could have been here to protect you from the unimaginable pain you have experienced. Your mother was not a strong woman, even though I loved her dearly. I know she would not have fought for you. I had to leave, Clara. Your father forbade me from seeing your mother when you were but a wee girl. Your father was angered that the farm had not been given to him when my mother passed. As the husband of your mother, he was the only male in the family and it had been presumed that it would be left to him once both my mother and father passed. But my parents knew I was well able to look after the farm myself and ensured that I would have a home and living once they passed. My mother and I ran the farm alone for ten years after my father died. It was the most natural thing in the world for me to continue to do so when my mother did sadly pass. I tell you, Clara Rose, it was the talk of the village upon my mother's death. I was accused of manipulating my parents to inherit the farm. Your father argued that she must have changed the will after he died and that I had forced her hand, suggesting she was not of sound mind. None of them knew your Granny Mary very well.

She was a stronger woman than you would find this side of the Atlantic, there would be no one who could manipulate her. She and your grandfather had told me all along that I was to stay on the farm once they were gone. They were protecting me because they knew I was never going to marry, and I was well able to look after myself.'

'Why did you leave then?'

'In the end I was left with no choice. They conspired to punish me and made it increasingly difficult for me to run the farm. No one would sell me supplies and no one would buy my produce. Sure, it was only a small farm, but from the milk, cream, butter, eggs and a handful of vegetables that I grew there was enough money to keep me going. But without enough feed for the animals I couldn't get the produce and even when I did no one would buy it. Word spread. Led by none other than your man, Padraig McDermott, that I was not to be supported in any way. They pushed me out, squeezing me so tight to teach me a lesson. But it was the animals that were suffering. I didn't want to give up. I couldn't watch them starve. McDermott turned up one night, he offered to buy the farm, as the land bordered his and as he explained, 'it was an obvious inclusion in his land holding.' I refused to sell to him, telling him I had a duty to offer it your father first, but McDermott told me if I didn't sell to him, he would make sure the farm would continue its same fate and my animals would be dead and buried before the winter was through. I knew his power in this godforsaken village and knew he would hold true to his word. He offered me a decent enough price for the land and I insisted that the sale didn't include any of my animals. He wasn't after the animals anyway. He was greedy for the land alone. My farming days were done. I moved away from here, buying a wee cottage just outside the village of Quilty. I gave the animals to your mother and father for your farm here, making sure that they promised when you were old enough to ride, my horse Trinity would be yours. I could always see something in your eyes, Clara. You had that fiery free-spiritedness that both my mother and I knew so well. It is both a blessing and a curse, depending on where you find yourself. I fear it has been a curse to date for you, but trust me, it will be your blessing.'

'How can it ever be a blessing?' I countered, resentful of her optimism despite her obvious failings. 'You gave in. They broke you and they won. Just like they broke me. We can never win, so what's the point of even talking such shite?' I spat with bitter resignation.

She held my chin and made me look at her even though I was done with this conversation.

'It's true. For a long time, I hated myself for giving in and letting them win. But over time I have resolved that within myself. You see, they can only win if I see myself as defeated. I don't. They didn't defeat me, Clara. They made me more powerful than ever before. In ways they will never understand.'

I did not understand. To me they had beaten her. Driven her away.

'Let us get you ready to lay your mother to rest in the way that she deserves. I have had a word with your brother this morning. He agreed with me that it was in his best interest to allow me to spend some time with you today and help you to prepare to sing at your mother's funeral,' she smiled, patting my shoulder.

'I can't sing in front of people. Father Stanley won't allow it,' I stammered perplexed.

'Oh, Clara. You do underestimate your Aunt Maeve, sure you do. I have had words with himself and he seems to agree that nothing made your mammy happier than singing. I know you've quite the gift. You will sing, not in the church but by her graveside, as she is lowered into the ground, raising her spirit and freeing her from this life where she was down trodden for so long.'

'I don't know if I can. I've never sung in front of anyone except Mam, Da, Aggie and Vincent.' I faltered nervously.

'Don't I remember when you were a wee girl the voice coming out of you. Never a purer voice did your Granny Mary ever hear, 'the voice of an angel' she would say, every time we sat around the range in the old farmhouse, singing the old Irish tunes. Vincent and Aggie would join in too. Couldn't sing for their supper the pair of them, but they would snuggle in with their Granny, Mammy and me, and we'd sing for hours. They were such happy days before everything changed. Those are the days I reminded your brother of this morning, for he, unlike you, was well old enough to remember the days before he got too big for his boots. He may have bullied your poor mother, but sure as God as my witness he won't be bullying her today,' she said with a ferocity that frightened me.

Chapter Ten

My heart broke when I saw Clara sitting in front of that mirror, for the loss of her innocence and joy. A childhood stolen from her, left alone in her torture, no one to support and love her. Of course, my own shame and guilt rose. It should have been me who had protected her from what I could only imagine. My sister, rest her soul, was too weak to stand up to that godforsaken priest, Colin Stanley, or her husband, Ciaran, and later to her own son, Vincent. She shunned me at the insistence of Ciaran, banning me from their home, destroying our beautiful sisterly bond. He had brainwashed her into believing the lies that he and Colin Stanley spread about me. The lies that saw me ostracised from my family and the community that I had grown up in.

They were threatened by me as a woman before. What they did not realise was in the recluse they forced on me, I would find a strength far greater than before. In many respects in my solitary life over those fourteen years, I was ignorant of what was happening under my sister's roof. On one occasion that I dared return to the village, I hid beneath a shawl in the back pew of the church. That was Clara's First Communion day. What drew me to the church on that day I do not really know. Just a strong instinctual pull. A knowing that I needed to connect with Clara in some way. I was challenged by this calling, having vowed never to set foot in that church again after the funeral of my mother where Colin Stanley spoke ill of her from the pulpit. He made startling claims about her integrity and having supported me to leave the convent many years before. He had never forgiven my mother for allowing me to come home and renounce my vows to be a Bride of Christ. My mother did not need his forgiveness, in life or in death. But in shaming her good name during her own funeral Mass, he had in turn shamed my sister and Ciaran. They were mortified, and once again blaming me for bringing reproach on the family name. Mary had never spoken to me of my choice to leave the convent after only three years of wearing the veil. It was unheard of in our strict Catholic village for a young woman to leave the convent once having committed herself as a Bride of Christ. And yet, Colin Stanley never spoke of it until Mam's funeral, using his power to bring shame on me and our family for showing such disregard for the holy traditions of the church.

Mary distanced herself from me after the funeral at the insistence of Ciaran. He was fuelled by shame and resentment at my sole inheritance of the farm. I had not spoken to her in all these years. I had missed my sister.

I saw the same look of shame on Mary's face as she scurried Clara from the church that Sunday morning in May. Ciaran's jacket was slung around the child's shoulders covering the disgrace of the blood-stained dress. Not only had her own mother and sister caused humiliation, now her own daughter had brought the wrath of both Colin Stanley and Padraig McDermott, the two men Mary most revered and feared.

I watched my niece stand and walk to the altar with the back of her dress marked with blood. I knew then why I had felt called to the church again that day. Despite my vow never to set foot in it again, Clara needed me. I had always known she was different to Vincent and Aggie, in a way that would be challenging for her. I suppose I saw a lot of myself in the spirited eyes of Clara, I knew her path would not be easy, yet I did not realise how hard it was to be for her. As she stood before the parish with a look of determination in her eyes, a look that wished to challenge the way things were, I felt a wave of euphoria sweep over me, for perhaps she had a strength that I did not, at that time. She was determined to right the wrong, to speak of truth amidst the lies and deception that interwove its way through all aspects of the village. I saw the courage in her eyes and I held her, knowing that was why I was called to be there, that morning, to help her hold the space that I had been unable to hold. To lift her while she spoke the truths I had been unable to speak. To support her while she stood in her power in a way I had been unable to stand.

I failed her that morning and I failed her for all the years after.

I did not hold her, lift her, support her in the way I knew she needed. For as she turned to face Colin Stanley and answer his questions, I allowed my fear for her to wipe away my own strength and she crumbled, succumbing to his unspoken threat to *do* the right thing or *pay* the price.

I saw it in his eyes as he looked at her. I know Clara must have felt it as she spoke those words, 'Forgive me, Father, for I have sinned.'

I gasped with shock because he had won *again* because of my fear. He won because he abused his power, and once again I did not have the strength to challenge it. I let Clara down in the way I had let myself down because of my fear of this man and all he represented. My purpose in being there that day was to give her strength to access her power and shine light on the darkness, and I had failed.

Some years before, I had allowed my own fear of Colin Stanley to silence my voice. As a young girl, I had a deep love of God. I felt a connection to God in a way other people did not. I prayed each morning and night, communing with God in a way that was unique to me.

As I roamed the hills and valleys surrounding the village I would speak to God through the flowers and trees, the wind and the sun, the birds and the sea. My connection to God was pure and untainted by the prayers I was taught in church and school. I would say them, but they were only words and I did not connect with my God through these prayers.

At fourteen, I was convinced by my teacher that I should join the convent, in the eyes of God I would be rewarded in choosing a life of sacrifice. I didn't realise that my God was not the God that they spoke of. I was rewarded every day in the beauty I could see in the world and I did not realise that the sacrifice I was to make, would ensure that my life was devoid of the beauty of nature and replaced by darkened walls and corridors, stale prayer, isolation from family, cruel punishment from the Mother Superior and unwelcomed visits from the new deacon to the parish, Colin Stanley. He was young, already ruthless in his pursuit of power. He positioned himself close to Mother Superior, knowing she had a strong influence on the aging Father O'Brien. He convinced Mother Superior that I needed private counsel to guide me deeper in my relation to God and prayer. What they didn't know was I had a deeper connection to my God and prayer than they could imagine, just not the God and prayer they sought me to prescribe. The private counsel was nothing more than lectures, intense indoctrination and brainwashing to a way of thinking. But it was not my way of thinking and while I did not challenge what I was being told, I also did not blindly absorb it as truth, as was the intention. I would recite passages of the Bible to Mother Superior following these sessions yet lacked the conviction they desired. Through no direct action on my part, I began to be regarded as a troublemaker.

Deacon Stanley took it upon himself to bring me back into line, to show me who was in charge. He forfeited his vow of celibacy to teach me this lesson on more than one occasion, a lesson he increasingly took pleasure in teaching me. I was a virgin—a Bride of Christ in every sense of the word—he took that from me. In the private room he used to counsel me, he mercilessly abused me for his own depraved needs.

He was a little boy lost, starved of the love of a mother, he sought first to be touched, forcing my hand to his leg, his face, his chest. His need for connection confused and repulsed me. His force coming from a place of needing to be seen as a man, not the small runt of a child dumped at an orphanage and picked on by the older children. As he forced my hand to rub against his penis, I felt him becoming increasingly empowered, his eyes became ruthless in his need for more. He thrust my mouth upon his raging penis and squeezed my mouth tightly around it as he released. The voracity of his attack left me stunned, and the warm salty liquid dripped from my mouth, staining the darkened purity of my habit.

'We must clean that,' he remarked, unperturbed as he straightened his clothing, taking a handkerchief from his pocket, dipping it into a jug of water and wiping the front of my habit. 'We cannot let Mother Superior see that, can we now? We wouldn't want her knowing our special secret, would we?' He stared deeply into my eyes, a mix of threat and genuine affection. 'It is our secret. Our special time together,' he said, stroking my face and placing his lips on mine, before sticking his tongue into my mouth and poking around, seemingly mopping up the remains of his salty discharge.

 I did not say anything to Mother Superior or anyone else. I was both too naïve and too shocked to find the words to express what happened. And he used both to his advantage in the years ahead, as he took from me whenever he had the chance in the weekly counselling sessions which he insisted remained a necessity. The first time he penetrated me, as he pinned me across the desk, I yelped in shock as the force of his thrust shattered my determined resolve. He relished this sound, representing a crack in my veneer and bringing me into the moment. Prior to this I had managed to remove myself from the experience, allowing him to take from my body but giving him nothing of me. He craved me and desired connection, yet I gave him nothing, until that first time he penetrated me, and he knew he had broken through in some way. From that point on, he took to watching my face as he thrust himself into me. I knew what he wanted, and I tried not to flinch, but if he didn't get the response he desired he would remove himself and continue to force himself within me, with increasing ferocity until I cried out. As soon as I caved, he knew he had defeated me, and he would release straight away, the sense of power fuelling his eruption.

'You felt it too, didn't you?' He would coo, as he would pat my hair and stroke my face, in some way convincing himself that my cry was a sign of pleasure.

I hated him.

Chapter Eleven

I held that story for so long, not daring to tell another for years because of the shame he made me feel. On one hand, he convinced himself that I experienced pleasure every time he raped me and that satisfied a need within him, yet he also made me feel ashamed for the pleasure he perceived I experienced. He told me I was a sinner, enticing him in the way that I did, that I would be damned to Hell for allowing myself to enjoy those experiences. Of course, I never felt anything in those experiences, except pain and terror, yet somehow, he made me wonder whether I, in some way, was responsible for his behaviour and if in fact I was experiencing pleasure in those moments, for I truly did not recall what actually went on most of the time, immediately taking myself from myself whenever he got that look about him.

After many years, seeking to understand this period of my life, I came to understand that he used his power to manipulate my mind, carefully and determinedly disempowering my own sense of self, and my perception of those experiences. He used his power over my vulnerability to brainwash me into seeing his rape, as an act of love, that I was privileged to receive. And to counter his own guilt he would blame me and shame me, threatening to tell Mother Superior that I had provoked him, and lured him into a sinful relationship. He held a power over me in so many ways that I could not understand. There was a part of me that wanted to tell Mother Superior, a part of me that wanted to fight him when he got that look, a part of me that wanted to tell my mother. Yet somehow, he paralysed my voice and my own shame about not being strong enough to stand up to him, almost made me believe I deserved all of this. That I deserved to be punished for allowing him to abuse me, for not challenging him, for not speaking up, for being a woman.

I deserved to be punished for being a woman.

He made me hate myself as a woman, for it was in being a woman I had brought this on myself. And for that reason, I never told my story. The only time I ever mentioned it was in the confessional box, when I would confess my sin to the man who raped me. He relished these moments. I could hear it in his voice as he told me my penance was to spend more time in counsel with him, where I would be required to go down on my knees and pray for my forgiveness. He would gift me my forgiveness in his own way, that made me feel like I was being punished.

Everything changed when my pregnancy was discovered. I didn't know that my missed periods, enlarged breast and thickened waist was an indication that I was with child. I came to this awareness when I was taken into a meeting with Mother Superior and Colin Stanley, told that it had been noted that I was with child and I was to immediately tell them the name of the father. I don't know what shocked me more, that I was having a baby or that the man who impregnated me was sitting opposite me insisting I name the father. Was he insane? How could there be anyone else? I only got to leave the convent once a month for an afternoon, which I spent with my family. I was lost for words, unable to explain the obvious. As Mother Superior left the room to speak with the doctor who had been summoned, he looked across her desk, his steely threatening gaze met my wide-eyed bewildered one. No words were exchanged. There was not an ounce of fear in his eyes, he knew no one would believe me should I mention his name, for he was the new young priest, revered by parishioners and the higher levels of the clergy alike. There were already whispers that he was destined to become bishop of the diocese in the years ahead, he knew how to play the hierarchy within the parish and the diocese to ensure he was viewed in exactly the right light.

I did not speak the name of the father, despite

accusations being made against Ciaran, who had recently married Mary and my own father. As Ciaran was not a local, he was an unknown and therefore much suspicion surrounded him in this most concerning of circumstances. I defended my father and Ciaran, astounded that anyone could think anything so debauch. I was forbidden from seeing family and the pregnancy was kept a secret. I was taken away to another convent in Galway, which housed other pregnant young women, for the remainder of my pregnancy. My veil was removed, and my true identity was kept hidden. I was counselled to never mention that I was a nun nor where I was from.

Secrets, lies and deception permeated the walls of that place.

Girls were ushered in the dark of night, not knowing where they were going or what was to happen to them. None of us knew what would happen to our babies when they were birthed because once a girl had gone into labour we never saw them again. They were taken to another area to deliver their baby and after that, I suppose we all fantasised that they got to return home to their families with their baby to live happily ever after. Of course, there were rumours from those who were staying for a second time, but the nuns kept a very close eye on those girls and as talking was fairly restricted anyway, it was mostly just whispers in the night about what really happened once the baby arrived.

I was terrified about giving birth as I had only ever seen the cattle on the farm birth and that was gruesome. I didn't have much time to prepare myself, as my baby came earlier than they expected and with a speed that left everyone unprepared. I had only felt one excruciating pain that morning, which was ignored by the sister in charge as I was far from my approximate due date. She called me lazy and accused me of trying to get out of my chores. A few hours later, as I folded the laundry, I was gripped by a seizure of my stomach that brought me to my knees. I felt the gush of liquid release and when I looked at the sheets below me I saw them stained with bright red blood. I screamed in pain and was quickly rushed into the delivery area where within minutes my baby was born. I recall none of it. The ferocity and intensity of the birth put my whole being into shock and many parts of me shut down, in some ways, I am grateful for this because I was not aware of what was happening to recall the pain of having my baby taken from me. As they cleaned me of the myriad of bodily fluids that had released during the birth, Mother Superior came to me to tell me that my baby had died during the birth, 'inevitable really, given it was so fast, so early and a bastard child.' But I heard my baby cry. Despite the shock and the confusion, I know I heard my baby cry. A mother will always know her baby's cry.

And that primal instinctive mother energy surged through me and I finally found my voice, 'No you lie. My baby is not dead. I heard her cry.'

'The baby was dead. You need to accept it. You chose to spread your legs for some man and this is your punishment,' she spat devoid of compassion, hardened by the life she had chosen.

'You know nothing. I spread my legs for no one, ever. He forced himself on me, time and time again.' I countered, as her demeanour altered momentarily.

'You think I haven't heard that before. Do not use that card on me, foolish girl.' She mocked me which roused an avalanche of truth which I had suppressed for many years.

'Colin Stanley forced himself on me every week for the last three years. My baby is his bastard child, I know my baby is alive. I demand you bring her to me before I go to the Bishop himself and tell him what evil that man has done.'

The palm of her hand met my cheek with such fierceness that my head jerked to the side.

'How dare you speak such vulgarity and tarnish the good name of a man of God, you naïve little girl! You think you can go around speaking ill of good people to make you feel better for your sins. You will be going nowhere near the Bishop or anyone else for that matter, you little whore.'

I didn't care about what she said. I didn't care that he had raped me. I didn't care what the Bishop thought. I just wanted my baby.

'Please, can I just have my baby?' I begged of her, as the tears began rolling down my cheeks. I knew if I held my baby in my arms, then none of the other stuff would matter, that everything else that I endured would fade away, that I would forget, because my baby would be worth it all. 'Please, I need my baby,' I screamed as she turned from me to walk from the room. 'Give me my baby,' I screeched again from the pit of my stomach, a primal maternal yearning pulsated through me.

I leapt from the bed towards the door determined to find my baby, but they grabbed me, restraining me with such force, and tied my wrists to the rail of the bed. I fought them with all I had, something stronger than I knew existed. And they held me, slapping my face, throwing water on me, sitting on my legs. But still I would not stop, the spittle frothed at my mouth as a flood of rage spewed from me, every suppressed injustice had been triggered by this greatest of injustice: taking a baby from a mother. I demanded to be released. I do not recall the doctor returning to the room, nor feeling the needle pierce my arm, all I recall was feeling a sense of paralysis come over me, blocking my physical body from moving and turning my mind to mush. I could not move, I could not think, my mouth immobilised, my voice silenced, my heart sealed with a wound no woman can forget.

I have no idea how long I remained in the walls of that convent, in that drug-induced state. Each day as the effects of the drug waned and my mind began to clear, I would remember and feel the surge of agony and rage gush through my heart and I would erupt again, only to be tranquilised once more. Until one day, as the effects began to wear off, a young nun whose job had been to wash and feed me, came close and looked me dead in the eye. They were kind eyes that spoke to me with assuredness and demanded that I listen.

'Now, Maeve, you listen, you are never going to get out of this place if you keep acting up. They'll just keep putting more drugs into you until they are convinced that you've forgotten everything. I've seen them do it before. You need to just settle and pretend like you can't remember, you hear? If you stay here, they'll end up turning your brain to mush completely, then you'll never remember. Do you understand, Maeve?' she whispered with a sense of urgency.

I nodded, somehow trusting deeply in this kind soul. Perhaps it was because no one had been kind to me for the longest of times. I finally felt like someone could see me and care for me.

'It's important you remember, even though, I'm sure you want to forget, but if we forget then they will just continue to get away with it. We must remember our stories, Maeve, yet pretend like we don't, so that one day we can tell that story. Because our stories are important. We must believe that one day our story will be told, we will be heard, our stories will change things. Nothing changes from staying angry, Maeve, nothing changes from being a victim. That is how they want us to feel, because our rage keeps us small. They call us insane and irrational and mad in the head and try to make us forget the story so that they can continue pretending like there is nothing wrong. You are not the first girl to end up in here, delivering a priest's bastard child. Nor was I. There were many before me. There will be many after you.'

'How do you know it was him?' I asked, stunned.

'I was here the day you delivered your baby when you told Mother Superior. We are not supposed to listen or take notice of the *delusions* that come after birthing. We are told to ignore the cries and screams and stories. But I heard you, as I have heard others. I believe you, Maeve!' she reassured.

'If you were here when my baby was born, then you know what happened to her?' I knew she held the answer. 'What happened to my baby? Where is my baby?' I whispered, understanding that I needed to now play by some unspoken rules if I was to ever leave this place and see my family again.

'Your baby did not die, Maeve. She was tiny, but she was alive. And she was given to a family. Good people to be sure, believing that they were adopting a baby that had been given up by the mother. They never know what goes on in here, on the other side.' She stated, sincerely with a loving kindness which somehow appeased the shock and agony of realising my baby was alive, but now belonged to another family.

I was confused, furious and weary. But I had listened and understood on some deeper level that this was how it had to be, for now. My story would matter one day. I must remember it, hold it and when it is time, I will need to use it to create change.

My story, *her* story and the story of so many other girls who have suffered the same fate at the hands of evil will one day matter and will one day create change. I had to believe that, or else I would have taken a knife to my own heart a hundred times over to ease the endless pain I felt for the loss of my baby girl.

Chapter Twelve

I allowed Sister Catherine to wash and feed me, as she tended to me, she quietly guided me. She told me to continue to play the game on return to my own convent, to ensure that I was granted leave to see my family. She did not have a family, an orphaned child, who had no choice but to enter the convent at a very young age. She did not have a family to return to after her own baby had been taken from her. Sister Catherine had committed herself to staying and ensuring that the new mothers were given love and care by at least one person, after their babies were stolen from them. She had the purest of hearts, yet a steely determination to right wrongs, when the time was right. She was the keeper of secrets and knew more than anyone could imagine, and one day she would play a pivotal role in creating change and exposing the darkness that prevailed behind those closed doors.

I returned to my convent the following week after being on my best behaviour while pretending that I had forgotten the trauma of losing my baby and how she was conceived. My return to the convent was a silent affair. My absence was not spoken of amongst the other sisters. It was better they did not know, even if they had suspicions. I kept my head down and did my chores. Solemnly attending Mass each morning, I said my prayers. I prayed to *my* God. I prayed to escape this world devoid of love and compassion. Fortunately, I was not called into counselling by Colin Stanley again, perhaps he was done with me, or perhaps he had moved on to someone else, or perhaps I was too much of a threat.

He wouldn't acknowledge me or look in my direction. But I would gaze at him, and in my eyes, there was a strength that I know he could feel. There is nothing stronger than a broken woman who garners the courage to stand before her perpetrator. I hadn't succumbed to be his victim. I stood there every morning, in Mass, as a woman who remembered the truth of her story, thanks to Sister Catherine's guiding light, I had not forgotten. This was the power that I had over him and he knew it. I had not forgotten.

The following month, Colin Stanley and Mother Superior agreed to reinstate my leave privilege for the first time in almost a year. I knew as I walked beyond the cloistered walls of the convent on that Saturday afternoon, that I would never return.

My parents devastated by my forced absence, for which they were provided with no reason, other than it was for my own good, welcomed me home with open arms. When I told them that I was leaving the convent and would not return that evening as required, they did not ask any questions. It was not discussed, I think they knew. My father went first to the convent to advise Mother Superior that I was leaving and would not be taking my final vows. Next, he went to inform Colin Stanley. To this day, I do not know what was said but he did not object to my leaving. He could have made a fuss and forced me to return, but he never did.

I dutifully went to church each week with my parents, for I still had a belief in the goodness of God and of Jesus Christ. I was not going to allow the actions of a few to steal me of my faith and my connection to my God. I did not realise as I do now that I don't need the structure of a religion or a church to maintain my own connection to the Divine. I had been brainwashed into believing that I did, that the God of the Roman Catholic Church was the only God there was, and those ordained as priests were a representation of the Divine here on earth. I know the Divine is in all, yet I fear that many of those who wore the collar carried a darkness that reflected in the evilness of the acts of power inflicted on others.

As Colin Stanley chose not to take it upon himself to publicly condemn me for leaving the convent, his faithful followers also kept silent their judgements.

If only they knew the truth.

I feared for those who remained in the convent, for there were some younger than I who were trapped within those walls. Nobody really knows what goes on behind those walls, there was so much fear imbedded by Mother Superior that we were too afraid to tell our families when we were allowed visitation. Punishment was severe and swift in all instances, no one dared to shed light on the hypocrisy of this revered institution.

My parents did not need to hear my story to see my brokenness. And as I sat by the fire with my mother, a warm cup of tea in hand, on my first night back home, I knew that the peace I felt was stronger than the fear of the ramifications of my leaving. I was able to maintain that peace, living a simple life with my parents. I did not seek an education or a husband. I did not want a child, as the trauma of losing my first remained raw. I helped with the farm and the keeping of home and spent time helping my sister with her small children, whom I adored.

Until Mammy died and then everything changed.

To this day, I do not know why, but once my mother and father were dead, Colin Stanley relished in revisiting the past. For the first time my leaving the convent was publicly condemned at my own mother's funeral, when he dared to blame her for enabling me to forsake my commitment to Christ. Not only was I horrified that he dared speak ill of my mother when she was no longer here to defend herself, he chose this most sacred occasion to open the door for his followers to begin shaming and ostracising me, all those years later.

Once again, I felt him exert his power over me. Perhaps he saw an opportunity to attack whilst I was so vulnerable having lost my mother. A coward's move that worked nonetheless, as the parishioners led by that man McDermott, now had permission to punish me for claiming my right to choose as a woman and failing to play by the rules of the church. My choice to leave the convent deeply angered those who had committed to blindly living their lives by the rules of an institution, because I chose my freedom and they couldn't, or rather wouldn't. Yet none of them knew why I rescinded my vows and none of them, not even my sister, bothered to ask. I'm not sure I would have been able to tell them should they have asked, not then, but now things are different. I am different.

I am not afraid of Colin Stanley nor the institution he represents. I am not afraid of the Padraig McDermott's of this world. They may have broken me, at one time, but I am stronger because of these experiences and I will use my voice, and my story to create change, in my own way, in my own time.

On the day of my sister's funeral, I amassed my courage and spoke my truth to Colin Stanley, for the sake of my beloved sister and Clara. I had heard of my sister's passing from a friend in my village and I knew I had to be here for my nieces, Clara and Aggie, for the loss of a mother is a torturous experience, especially for girls so young. I entered the church early, before the end of the morning Mass and waited beneath my shawl in the back pews. He entered the confessional box after Mass and I waited until the stream of parishioners passed through, wondering what sins they could be committing that they needed daily absolution. I then entered the confessional box, a place so familiar to me from my childhood and years in the convent, yet now I did not feel intimidated.

'It has been many years since my last confession,' I began with confidence.

'Continue,' he insisted, with a curiosity about who was sitting behind the screen.

'I come here today, before you, to lay my sister to rest and to forgive you. I release to the Divine and the most blessed Mother Mary, any pain you caused me and open my heart to be filled with compassion and forgiveness for you.'

'Thank you,' he murmured instinctively, the shock and confusion momentarily taking him from his place of power.

I had not set foot in a church since Clara's First Communion when the look in his eyes frightened me and I hid beneath my shawl, only stopping outside the church to place a pound note in Clara's tiny frightened hand, before I headed home to my little cottage some twenty miles away. I remained in isolation for several years, ostracised from my sister, her family and the village I had always known. I was filled with shame and guilt for reasons I didn't understand. I knew I had been true to myself, but in some way my truth was wrong in the eyes of others, and without my mother to support and protect me, the judgement and criticism of others wormed its way into my head. I began to believe their lies about me, and I hid myself from the world, ashamed and fearful. It took me a long time, to begin to build myself back up, and it was only by a twist of fate, as is so often the case, that I could reclaim myself, my strength and my voice.

I was walking beyond the village one morning before the sun rose, as had become my custom, when I came across a woman sitting alone on one of the old stone formations so common across The Burren. I was reluctant to interrupt her as she appeared to be in prayer but there was something familiar about her and my curiosity strangely got the better of me.

As I approached she turned to look at me and smiled, saying, 'so you finally came.' I was shocked, not just by her words, but more so with the realisation that I knew this shawled Gypsy woman. She was the estranged mother of Padraig McDermott who had infamously run off with the Gypsies when Padraig was a child at the small village school we all attended.

The McDermott's were well looked upon in the village. Cynthia McDermott was by all accounts a normal woman, a wife, a mother. She was a beautiful looking woman with warm brown eyes and an angelic face. She had a radiance about her, that even as a child I was captivated by, as were most who had any connection to her, which made her sudden decision to leave her husband and child behind to travel with the Gypsies most extraordinary and the fodder for much gossip. Of course, there was whispers of her having an affair with one of the men, darker talk of her being cursed and brainwashed into abandoning her perfectly normal life to live the life of a Traveller.

Old man McDermott put a stop to further mutterings and innuendo when he instructed Father O'Brien to read a statement at the conclusion of Sunday Mass. It was most unusual for matters of this nature to be discussed from the altar, but that was the sway the McDermott's had, and still have, over the clergyman of the village.

'Cynthia McDermott, the beloved wife of James, mother of Padraig, has been cursed by the Devil himself. No woman of right mind would abandon her duty to her husband and child, the darkest of evil surely immersing itself in her body, mind and soul. From this day forth, her name will not be mentioned, her darkness can only bring ill on the people of our village. And be sure to note, the evil that the Travellers bring with them when next they choose to frequent our parts. May God bless us and keep us safe.'

'Amen,' the congregation chanted, intoxicated by the drama and fear. Fear of the Devil and evil had long wielded control over followers of the Catholic faith, this was no different, it was as though Cynthia McDermott was dead. I never heard her spoken of in public again.

My mother was a close friend of Mrs McDermott,

as we called her, and she felt the loss of her friend deeply knowing there was more to her leaving than was being purported by her husband and the church.

I overheard my mother whispering to my father, 'It's less to do with the Devil and more to do with the bottle of whiskey and McDermott's fist I'd say.'

One never knows what goes on behind closed doors, even behind the fanciest of doors in a village.

Chapter Thirteen

She told me she was my mother's sister, but I had no recollection of this woman who had come into my room, showing me a gentleness, I had not felt for so long. She held my hand and absorbed my pain and was familiar in a way I could not understand, for she was never spoken of in our home and my memories of my early years had been destroyed by the trauma that followed. Yet, as she told me stories about my grandparents, mammy and father, things began to make sense. She had strength about her, I don't know what she said to Vincent to be allowed in the house, for visitors were few. But she sat with me, bathed me, washed and brushed my hair, rubbed cream into my face and pressed one of Aggie's dresses for me. Aggie came into the room, but she dared not object to me wearing her clothes, seeming wary of this woman, who proclaimed to be our Aunt Maeve.

She told me that she had seen me at my First Communion, that she was the Gypsy woman who secretly placed money in my hand. I recall her and the look in her eyes, but the woman who was before me was nothing like the old woman beneath the shawl.

'I was not old, I was just broken,' she said.

I did not know how she went from broken to the strong woman before me, but I didn't need to know, somehow, I trusted her. She convinced me to sing at the funeral, and even though I knew Father Stanley and Vincent would not approve, she assured me that they would not object, not today. There was a knowingness of this as she spoke and it both scared and intrigued me.

She took me to Trinity in the stables. She told me that our spirits were suited. I told her that our spirits may have been suited but it had been many years since I had ridden Trinity, having been forbidden by Vincent. She was an old horse now and would not be able to stride through the fields as once she did. I felt as wrecked and weary as Trinity, who I had sadly come to neglect, as any time I spent in the stables rekindled past traumatic memories and thus I tended to avoid it. However, when I brushed her coat and main, and rubbed her rump, I could still feel her in there.

'She is there, isn't she?' Aunt Maeve asked, knowingly. 'That is because she never goes away, Clara. We may be crushed and wrecked, but who we are is still within us, she never goes away.'

I nodded, accepting what she was saying to be true, yet at the same time I was so despondent because while I could feel Trinity, my horse I loved from my childhood, I couldn't feel me, the girl I once was. I wept for her.

'Oh, my girl, she is in there. I can feel her in you. I can see her in your eyes, beyond the pain and hurt, beyond the darkness and struggle, beyond all the trauma. And today, as we farewell your mammy, let her shine,' she assured me, this woman who seemed to believe in me more than I believed in myself.

But I didn't know how to shine from beneath the darkness that had embedded itself within my cells. There seemed no way out.

'Just sing for me, Clara. Sing for me a song you loved to sing with your mammy. Close your eyes and feel your mammy with you.'

I followed her guidance. I took a deep breath and closed my eyes. I saw myself sitting by the range with Mammy, just her and I and she was free. Her face was not drawn and haggard in the way that it had become in recent years, a reflection of her pain and resentment. She was free. Free of the need to be some perfect woman in the eyes of others. She was young, vibrant, and so incredibly beautiful. She began to sing. I listened to her angelic voice float through the words. She smiled at me, beckoning me to join her. I remembered how it felt to be deeply connected and loved by her. I knew she had chosen this song for me and I took another deep breath and let go, allowing myself to fall into the words like there was nothing else in the world, except me and my mammy, in a beautiful harmony.

We sang,

> *'Amazing Grace,*
> *How sweet the sound*
> *That saved a wretch like me.*
> *I once was lost, but now am found.*
> *'Twas blind but now I see.*
>
> *'Twas Grace that taught my heart to fear*
> *And Grace, my fears relieved.*
> *How precious did that grace appear*
> *The hour I first believed.*
> *Through many dangers, toils and snares*
> *We have already come.*
>
> *'Twas grace that brought us safe thus far*
> *And grace will lead us home,*
> *And grace will lead us home.*
> *Amazing grace, How Sweet the sound*
> *That saved a wretch like me.*
>
> *I once was lost but now am found.*
> *'Twas blind but now I see.*
> *Was blind, but now I see.'*

I felt a calm exhilaration as I finished the song, like I had been transported to another time and I remained in that space with my mammy, revelling in the love and connection I felt. *'Twas blind but now I see ...* I pondered these words and I knew that she was telling me, from beyond the grave, to open my eyes, to see once again and to trust in Grace to lead me home. But I didn't know Grace, as so much of my life had been experienced without it and I could not trust in a God that had abandoned me. I was hopeless and truly didn't believe that a wretch like me could be saved.

'One step at a time, Clara. I will do all I can to be here with you and help you,' Aunt Maeve assured me.

I wanted to believe her, but I knew what Vincent was like and I feared she did not know his capability nor his deep-seated hatred of me. And I could not tell her, not today, for today was going to be hard enough and I did not need the burden of my memories and my bitterness to drown me in further misery.

'Clara, will you sing for your mammy today?' she asked me, and I immediately agreed despite my terror. I knew my mammy wanted me to do this, it was for her and for me.

'I have a song that your grandmother used to sing to your mammy and me when we were wee girls. Your mammy loved it, Clara. Every time your mammy sang it she became teary and I would laugh at her because she was so moved by it. Your mammy's real name is Róisín, not Mary, but your old great grandfather was after insisting on calling her Mary. But she loved this song about the blossoming rose. It was her song, Clara, and she deserves to hear it one more time.'

I couldn't imagine Mammy as an impassioned young girl, yet the vision I experienced of her gave me more of an insight into the woman that my mother may have been, beneath the façade in which she found herself trapped.

'How will I learn the words?' I asked. I was so nervous for I knew that the Funeral Mass was to begin in under two hours.

'It is a simple ballad that you will remember. Sure, you won't be able to forget it,' she smiled at me with that same knowing smile that somehow silenced my fears.

She taught me the words as we stood in the stable beside Trinity. We sang it together, and we sang it with Mammy and maybe even my grandmother, for there was something powerful stirring in the barn. I felt nervous about singing in public and so much attention being on me, for I was the one who had been hidden from the spotlight since my First Communion day. I was especially worried about the reaction from Father Stanley, Vincent and Padraig McDermott as I knew they would not approve of me holding space during a sacred religious ceremony. There was no place for women in the church, in those roles and I feared the ramifications, even though, Aunt Maeve seemed assured that there would be none. Despite my nervousness, I knew I would be able to stand by the graveside, as they lowered my mother's body into the ground and sing for her and sing for me.

There were murmurs as I entered the church beside my Aunt Maeve. She had every right to be there, yet the shame of her past was never far from the small minds of these people, who thrived on gossip and scandal. But she did not flinch, even though she must have been aware of the looks and whispers that followed her down the aisle. I was proud to stand beside this strong woman.

Vincent had been unusually quiet as we made our way from our home to the church, which made me nervous. I waited for him to explode and take it out on me. Nonetheless with Aunt Maeve by my side I felt a confidence blossom within as we sat in the front pew. Father Stanley nodded to her in acknowledgement before beginning the service. I felt her hands sweaty and her breathing quicken as we sat there, but to anyone else she epitomised elegant composure.

I felt my anxiety rise as we followed the coffin down the old road to the cemetery that overlooked the ocean. Maeve squeezed my hand a little tighter to remind me that she was here for me, to hold me. Father Stanley said the final blessing over Mammy's coffin and they prepared to lower the casket into the ground. I rose. The congregation turned and looked at me in astonishment, for it was not the place of a non-religious person to participate in these ceremonies, furthermore, I was the invisible member of my family. Vincent and Aggie were well-known and liked within the village, not me.

Who was I—the unseen silent one—to rise at such an occasion.

I could feel Aunt Maeve with me, I cleared my throat, raised my chin to look at the faces of those assembled, took a step forward, placed a single red rose onto the casket and said, 'My mammy, Róisín Mary Smullen, loved to sing, and this was her song.' Pausing momentarily, I closed my eyes and I saw that same young, beautiful woman I had seen earlier, looking at me with such deep love and pride and she roused in me the courage to find my voice. The words gifted to me by Aunt Maeve danced across my lips as I was transported to another realm where I was alone with my mother.

I sang,

'The rose I gift to you,
Hold her close to you each day.
Watch her blossom gracefully,
And never shy away.
And even though she folds and hides,
in the darkness of the night.
The moon will gently hold her,
Nourishing her with light.
And as the sun rises,
on another new day,
Know that she will open once again,
For all the world to see.
Rise Rosa Rise
Rise Rosa Rise
Rise Rosa Rise

Bernadette O'Connor
And open once again.'

My eyes closed, I remained immune to the whispers that permeated the space surrounding me and witnessed her soul rising, shrouded in a sheath of golden light. Never more beautiful a vision had I seen. I was reluctant to return to the reality before me, yet I knew I must, and I could feel Aunt Maeve's hand slip into mine again, reminding me that I was not alone.

As I opened my eyes, I was met with looks of awe and wonder by many of the women who dabbed at their eyes with lace handkerchiefs. While many of the men seemed uncomfortable with the heaviness of emotion hanging in the air and took a sudden interest in their shoes. Vincent showed no emotion and simply nodded his head in acknowledgement, but I could feel the rage building in him. I was quite adept at reading his hidden emotions, my sheer survival had depended on it. And I knew that he would not allow me such power without severe ramifications, despite the assurance of Aunt Maeve.

'Right,' Colin Stanley muttered, before resuming his power, as the Father, finalising the proceedings. He invited everyone to Flannery's Bar to 'celebrate the life of a good woman.'

And just like that the crowd dispersed. Any excuse for hitting the whiskey bottle and bellowing out ridiculous songs without apology. I couldn't bring myself to face the people. It was these people who never bothered looking in on my mother as her health declined. They all knew what was going on, but they were too cowardice to ask questions of Vincent, or about her wellbeing. I would not stand and make small talk with these people under the pretence of celebrating my mother's life. I had done that already. In my own way, a way that I knew I would be punished for, but I didn't have the energy in me to worry about that. I allowed Aunt Maeve to direct me from the cemetery back to the house, where we sat alone in silence over a pot of tea. I appreciated the silence and being alone at home or what was once my home. I was the intruder here now, nothing more than a cook, a cleaner, a child minder.

Sure, you'd make someone a great wife one day, Clara. Not that anyone would have you, given the state of you and all, memories of Aggie's voice mocking me came flooding in. *You're lucky my Vincent puts up with you and puts a roof over your head, and food in your stomach each day. You should be awful grateful, Clara, so you should,* Carmel's words echoed. I should be grateful that I had a place to call home, but somehow, I just couldn't see it that way. I felt cheated out of my own home and I resented Carmel for taking over, Aggie for teaming herself with Carmel so she got away with everything, but mostly I hated Vincent for disrespecting our mother and taking her home from her, and from me. He cared for no one but himself and would do whatever it took to ensure he retained that power. I loathed and feared him but how could I possibly explain any of that to Aunt Maeve over a pot of tea, today, on my mother's funeral day?

'Come home with me, Clara,' Aunt Maeve said, breaking our silence. 'There is no life for you here now your mammy is gone. Clearly Aggie knows how to look after herself and Carmel might have to step up and start looking after her own house and children, rather than continuing to fool herself into thinking she is some lady of the manor.'

'Yes, I know,' I said. 'But ... I can't leave.'

'Why, Clara, why can't you leave?'

'W-w-well, well ...' I stumbled.

'Well, what child? There is no reason to stay on here. Come start a new life with me, leave all this mess behind you,' she declared, with certainty that this time failed to convince me.

'Please, Aunt Maeve. Please, just leave it,' I begged.

'No, I won't leave it, Clara. You can pack your bag and come home with me tonight. We'll take Trinity and head off before sun down.'

'You don't understand, it's not that simple. I can't just leave. Vincent would never allow it.'

It wasn't that I didn't want to leave. I desperately loved the idea of a new life and I fantasied about it every night. The truth was I was not allowed to leave without Vincent's permission. I was programmed to believe that my life as a woman, was not mine to decide, it was to be decided by the men. Once that would have been my father, but with him gone it was my brother who controlled my fate. I allowed him to hold this power over me for I was too afraid to reclaim my power and my life.

'I know what you are going through, Clara, I have been there. Trust me. If we don't stand up one day and say enough and reclaim our lives from the men who control it then we will remain trapped in their world, living by their rules and suffering.'

'You don't know what he would do to me if I left. You really don't know him and what he is capable of doing.'

'I know his type well. And we must find the courage to face our fear of them and do what we know is true for ourselves. Clara, that is what you did this afternoon, you reclaimed your power and faced your fear of them. You rose.'

'Yes, but now I am afraid. Afraid of what will happen because I dared to challenge them. Dared to step out of line. Dared to do what I wanted to do. Dared to live my truth.'

I cried helplessly and frustrated for Aunt Maeve didn't understand.

'I do understand your fear. I have walked in your shoes. I know what happens when you reclaim your power. I know the risk, but the joy of freedom outweighs the risk you take, Clara.'

'No, stop … the price I have paid. My whole life changed the day I chose to stand up and show them the truth, the day of my First Communion. You were there, you saw what happened. But you weren't there for me to see what happened after that. He made sure that I was reminded every day from that day forward who had the power and it most certainly is not me. And no matter how much I detest my life here with him, it is safer for me to stay and put up with his brutality than leave. How do I know that you will be there to keep me safe from him if I leave with you now? You weren't there before, no one was, so why would it be any different now?' I was done with the conversation and I was not going to change my mind.

'Clara, I can't promise that it will be an easy road. The hardest part is taking the first step. You cannot stop living in hell if you do not choose to leave hell,' Aunt Maeve begged.

I was too tired to continue. I stood wearily and washed and dried the cups, filled the kettle and placed it on the range, so it would be ready when they returned from the pub.

Aunt Maeve shook me in her arms and pleaded one more time. 'Oh, Clara, please …'

I stiffened knowing that if I allowed myself to soften in her embrace I would lose my composure and crumble. I couldn't afford to be vulnerable. Not here in the life I was choosing to live. Vulnerability was a weakness and I had to be strong, hard and alert, ready for the attack which could come at any time.

Chapter Fourteen

I curled up in bed. Silence filled the house. I could not recall the last time I was alone in the house. In the solitude that surrounded me I allowed myself to surrender to the aching grief within. I held it. At least until Aunt Maeve left. Even though I felt it beating at my chest, threatening to release. I wanted to leave with her and run away from this life, but I just couldn't do it. The fear was too strong, stronger than me. I was weak and pathetic. I disgusted myself. Who did I think I was to garner all that courage to stand and sing in front of all those people, to feel such pride in myself for being so brave, feeling the adoration of my Aunt and my mammy across the realms. But they wouldn't be proud of me now, for I gave into my fears. I dimmed the light I felt rising within me. I chose to hide away in the shadows, again. No better than a pitiful house dog, who knows how worthless it is, and scurries to the corner in the hope of not being seen.

I don't know why I did it. Why I listened to Aunt Maeve and agreed to sing. I knew it would cause trouble and yet I couldn't say no to her. There was something about her that made me feel that it would all be okay. But the reality was, it wouldn't be okay, I knew there would be ramifications for my stupidity, for daring to break the rules. I should have never listened to her, should never have let her into my head. I should have just kept my head down and minded my own business, kept my mouth shut and been the good girl. That is what Mammy always told me, and that is what I had always done, even though it didn't really keep me out of trouble. Aunt Maeve had implored me to do the opposite. In my vision Mammy seemed to have encouraged me to rise and sing and surrender into the words of the song. She was with me in it and she incited me to stand there with a confidence I didn't even know I had. Why would she confuse me in this way? Why would she inspire me to do something so extreme now when she wasn't here to protect me?

My heart heaved aching for the loss of her. I knew that she loved me, of course, she loved me, but I didn't feel her love, not ever. Well not until today in the barn when I saw her in my mind's eye. I felt her love and it felt so good to be loved, and I longed for that feeling. The feeling of being loved. Perhaps I had imagined it, that it was nothing more than the pathetic longings of a desperate child, creating a fantasy. I was pathetic and naïve to think that anyone would ever love me. I had been told often enough that I was nothing more than a waste of space and no man would ever love me. Who was I to presume it could be any different. I deserved the pitiful life that lay before me.

Aunt Maeve had seemingly appeared from nowhere and offered me a lifeline, and I had rejected her and her love. She believed in me so much, that for one afternoon, she actually convinced me to believe in myself. But I was afraid of the girl who stood in that graveyard, she was strong and powerful and rebellious and no good comes to those sorts of girls. I have heard the stories. I have lived that story. I could not risk losing any more of myself. I surely knew he would have destroyed me, should I have chosen to leave without seeking his permission. I knew he would destroy me anyway for daring to stand before him and sing with power and passion. Even though it was to send our mother's soul home to a peace she was starved of in this life.

I gnawed at my fist, in an attempt to stifle the bestial roar that rose within me, the bellow of a wild animal trapped. For no matter which decision I made, to stay or go, I remained trapped. Vincent had the ultimate control of me.

Why God do you punish me so? I do not know what I have done to deserve such cruelty? Jesus died on the cross so that we would be saved, and yet where are you now, for me, where are you to save me?

I wondered to this God. But how could I believe in this God when I knew he was not here for me. This God who was supposed to love me without condition had abandoned me, just like my father and mother and Aggie. Alone in the house, I fell deeply into my loss, surrendering to the inundation of emotion that swept through me. Perhaps it was residual emotion from burying my mother, or maybe Aunt Maeve in her own way had unlocked the door, for wave after wave engulfed me and for once I didn't try and stop it. Huddled on the bed I rocked like a mad woman as my body pulsated with the release.

Through my tears and moans I heard a ruckus in the yard, the dogs barking madly, Vincent bellowing at them to 'shut the feck up.' His speech slurred. He was drunk beyond his limits. I heard the children screeching wildly, clearly no one had been keeping a watch on them all night and they were as raving mad as the others were drunk. As they stumbled into the house, Aggie and Carmel began singing my song. Mammy's song. The two of them couldn't sing to save themselves, '*Rise Rosa Rise. Rise Rosa Rise. Rise Rosa Rise.*' They laughed with drunken hysteria desecrating the beauty of her song.

'Ah, Jesus, Carmel, who did she think she was

to be standing there like she was some priestess rising Mammy's soul to the ethers? 'Twas awful embarrassing now. I'm not sure what was after getting into her like that.' Aggie's words cut through my core.

'Now don't you be thinking, Aggie, that … that Aunt Maeve of yours, don't you think it was her that was after putting the nonsense into her head, sending her queer like. You know, Vincent was only after telling me this afternoon that she was as queer as the Devil that one Maeve. Says he remembers her from when he was little, she'd often be around the place and then she disappeared and had not been heard of since. Not until she goes and shows up here this morning, on the day of your mammy's funeral, and sure and doesn't she have Vincent himself eating out of her hand. Agreeing to all that nonsense with Clara, sure and even borrowing your good dress, Aggie. Ah, it's true, she's trouble that one. I'd so far as to say she's got the fey in her that one. Sure, didn't she have her way with Father Stanley too by the looks of things, because there is no way that he'd ever have let herself sing unless she'd not got some spell or something over him.'

I pulled the blanket over my head and covered my ears for I dared not hear any more of what they were to say about me and Aunt Maeve, all that talk of spells and the fey scared me. Mam and Da had made sure there was no talk of that nonsense in this house. There would be chit chat about it around the village from time to time, especially when the Gypsies were passing through and stories would trickle back home, but our father would put a firm stop to any such talk, 'there will be no talk of the Devil maker ways in this home', he would say echoing the words of Father Stanley. He made it clear that God himself had no tolerance for pagan rituals, faery folk, spells and the like. On the one hand it was regarded as pure nonsense, despite the deep ancestral ties to Irish folklore. I feared being associated with the work of the Devil, for a firm hand was laid down on those who dared to practice in the pagan ways of old.

I had once seen a new family in the village, forced to move on after only a few months, for they were alternate in their ways of doing things. They were not Gypsies like the Travellers, they were just different. They didn't attend Mass, the mother used herbs and other remedies when her children were ill. Her mistake was an offer to help the child next door who was inexplicably sick, and Doctor Malone was at a loss to explain the rapid and fervent decline in the child's health. Mary O'Toole, desperate to save her child, accepted her help and rumour has it that as soon as she looked at the child, she could see darkness in her, insisting she be taken to the beach, to be immersed in the icy ocean to cleanse this darkness from her soul. She told Mary that it was not the child's, and someone had forced themselves on the child and the soul had gone into shock and fractured and was unable to heal because of the darkness enveloping her. The mother went along with her, and the child was secretly brought to the ocean to be cleansed. Mr O'Toole caught wind of what was happening and fearing his wife had lost her mind and come under the spell of this 'queer one next door' he took Father Stanley with him to the beach, only to witness his dying child running along the beach. 'It was a miracle,' were the whispers of the town. But Father Stanley would not celebrate the renewed life of the child and condemned the actions of the woman from the pulpit. I remember the rage in his eyes as he demanded to know who she was to think she could mimic the sacred sacrament of baptism. The use of those ways, he said were the ways of the Devil, through potions and the like and not tolerated in these parts. Within weeks the family had moved on, whether it was because they were immediately ostracised and forced out or because they realised they could not live with such close-minded bigoted people. Father Stanley applauded his parishioners for uniting in a stance against 'a direct attack on the Divine teachings of the Lord Jesus Christ' and affirmed that there was no room for witchcraft of any kind in our village.

My fears crept in of being associated with Aunt Maeve if the murmurs of Carmel and Aggie reflected the beliefs of others in the village. Yet, I too, remained confused why Father Colin Stanley would be so accommodating of Aunt Maeve's wishes and be seen by his parishioners to be supportive of her ways. My thoughts were grossly interrupted as Vincent stormed into the kitchen demanding a fry up.

'Oh, Vincent, you're not really going to start

eating at this time of night are ye?' Carmel dared to ask.

'Indeed, has a man not buried his own mother this day. I think I deserve a decent feed before I head to bed,' he bemoaned.

'Well, Aggie and I have to get the children to bed. You'll have to get Clara to cook for ye,' she spoke more firmly to Vincent than I had heard her before.

I heard a scuffle and a slap. 'You be minding your mouth ye hear me,' he spoke through gritted teeth. 'Go, get them children into bed.'

'Clara, fix me a fry up,' he bellowed, pouring another whiskey.

Oh, the Lord above help me, I thought, as I jumped from the security of bed and quickly dressed. The last thing I wanted to do was cook at this ridiculous time of night, but I was not about to object. As I laced my boots and tied them secure, he came marching into the bedroom. I quivered ever so slightly, as he never so much had dared come into this room, not while Mammy was alive. I didn't know what he was going to do. I never did with him and I always felt that I was under threat. My heart raced as he approached the bed, yet I did not look up, meticulously tending to my boots.

'I said I wanted a fry up. Why are you taking so long?' he demanded, pulling my head up to look at him by a clump of my hair.

'Jesus look at the state of you. You're all red and blotchy. Finnigan will be after changing his mind if he sees ye looking like this,' he laughed drunkenly to himself as he jarred my head back further. 'You better not ruin this you slovenly slut. This will be the best proposition I'll be getting for you, so you better make sure you move yourself faster when you are called and do something with this godforsaken head of yours, cause Finnigan won't be wanting ye if you can't scrub yourself up to look decent.'

'What? What do you mean?' I asked, baffled freeing myself from his grip.

He laughed with drunken vulgarity. 'Old Finnigan himself got some stirrings,' he rubbed his crotch and raised an eyebrow. 'When you put on your little performance in the cemetery this afternoon. All that singing and rising nonsense, apparently got a rising in Finnigan,' he laughed at the filth of his own joke. 'And he's after offering to marry you to get you off my hands, says he's suffering a lot these days from his injuries. A good young woman to keep house and stoke his fire is exactly what he's needing, and he was willing to pay me. Sure, and isn't he after offering me his two back paddocks, two acres altogether to secure the arrangement. Who'd have ever thought you'd be worth two acres? Wouldn't I have given you away for nothing just to get ye out of my sight,' the laughter ceased, and he looked at me with a vengeance, as if he was remembering something, that memory that stirred his deep hatred of me. 'You deserve everything you get living under his roof, I want nought to do with it or you once you walk from this house,' and he spat at my feet as he turned to leave the room.

I tied my laces tighter, secured my apron firmly around my waist, pulled my hair from my face into a bun and went to cook my brother his fry up.

What was to be. Was to be.

Chapter Fifteen

I did not own much, so there was little for me to pack that morning. I was given a suitcase from Carmel, I neatly packed my undergarments and the two house dresses, I wore on rotation. I was wearing my Sunday dress, a hand-me-down of Aggie's, for she was always buying new dresses now that she was courting Thomas McGinty. She was always off to dances and the like, her and Carmel made an awful fuss over getting her dressed, pinning her hair and doing her makeup. I think Carmel would have liked nothing more than dressing up and going to the dance with her, but she was well and truly married with a tribe of children. She had been married since the age of sixteen to Vincent, so she missed the chance of ever socialising in that scene and it certainly was not appropriate for a married woman to attend. I think she lived these experiences vicariously through Aggie. I would hear their whispers and giggles when Aggie would get home. I was never a part of it, the gossiping and giggles, or the dances. Vincent would never allow me to go, should I have ever asked, I knew that. I had never asked anyway, because I would not have known what to do at a dance. I had enough difficulty fitting in at school in the later years, always the one sitting on the sidelines, the silent observer, often the target of cruel jokes. I knew Aggie was ashamed of me, I would have been an embarrassment should I accompany her to the dances.

'You don't even need to go to a dance to find yourself a husband like the rest of us,' she bemoaned the night previously.

'Indeed, Vincent did a fine job in securing the arrangement with Dempsey Finnigan. A fine piece of land it was he acquired for himself. You should consider yourself lucky. He was a fine man in his day, sure he was Finnigan, so my father says. Went to school with him, so he did, before he went off with the army. He was gone a long while in the army, had a big part to play in the Easter Rising down there in Dublin they say. Was one of the leaders, before he got the injury, a fierce bad limp he has, sure he does.'

'Was good of him to come along to Mammy's funeral. Was a surprise for many to see him there, as he doesn't really get out and about much, except for Mass,'

Aggie added.

'You know, I heard Brigid Malone saying when we were back at the pub, that she wasn't surprised to see him there because he had a thing for your mammy when they were at little school together. But then he went off to the army. Oh, it's a funny thing isn't it, that he's now marrying Clara,' Carmel mused.

I'd listen to their gossip often as I would clean up around them or filled their cups with more tea. This time, I was the gossip. I learnt about the man I was to marry through their idle musings, for I had not met him and because I always kept my head down and eyes lowered at Mass, I had never actually seen the man himself.

I was not part of any of the arrangements, I was just told to pack my bag and put on my Sunday dress, as I was to be taken to the church that afternoon. There was not to be a big celebration like there was when Vincent and Carmel married. I was to go to the church and then leave with him. I was scared. Aggie and Carmel seemed excited for me, so I could not confide in them. I was leaving my home, which in truth had not felt like my home for a long time, but it was the only place I knew. I was still coming to terms with Mammy not being in the bed beside Aggie and me. Now I was to be sleeping in a bed in another home of a man whom I had never met. A forty-two-year-old farmer, who had returned from fighting the British, with a broken body and mind. I heard Carmel say that Brigid Malone, an awful gossip she was, had told her that Finnigan was not right in the head. Her father, Doctor Malone was often after visiting him and giving him all sorts of drugs to keep him right in the head. I feared him dreadfully, what I knew of him. And whilst I despised Vincent and my life here was a kind of hell, it was a hell that I knew. I did not know what my life was to be like living as wife to this man.

I was seventeen when Vincent sold me off.

Carmel and Aggie came into the bedroom as I packed my bag. Carmel handed me a package. I was not accustomed to receiving gifts and was surprised. 'Go on then open it, Clara,' Aggie insisted.

'You're going to be a married woman now and there are certain duties you must see to as a wife,' Carmel explained, with a seriousness that both scared and amused me, for she did not take much of life too seriously, mind you, with me gone and her own children and home to tend, her casual approach to life would be fast changing. I was not sure whether she had fathomed that yet.

I opened the package and examined the night garment that was finished with lace around the collar and sleeves. 'It's lovely, Carmel, thank you,' I said in my confusion.

'Clara, when you go to bed you must make yourself presentable to your husband, that is why your nightdress is so important,' she replied.

Aggie interrupted. 'Mammy is not here to tell you these things as normally it would be up to her to prepare you for these things. So, Carmel, being the married woman of the house, has taken it upon herself to prepare you. She has told me all about it too, so I already know these things, but because you are not, well, out and about and mixing with men then you haven't really needed to know. Because I'm often at the dances, Carmel had to tell me about the men and their urges, so I would be prepared when I felt them against me when I dance with them. Sure, it was an awful shock to me the first time it happened, Michael Malone was dancing awful close to me and next thing I feel this hard thing in his pants rubbing against me. I wasn't sure myself what it was, then I remembered what Carmel had told me and I realised he was after getting himself all aroused, dancing so close with me and the like, his thing had gone and had the erection.'

'Yes, Clara,' confirmed Carmel. 'The thing will have an erection, as a married woman, when this happens, this is when you let him put it in you and push it up and down until he's done. Now, most often this will happen in the bed of a night, which is why it is important to wear a nice nightdress, because you want to arouse him, because they like it and they have urges. Mostly it will happen in the bed, but sometimes Vincent gets urges in other places, like the barn. You have to be ready for whenever the urge comes, be ready to take it. It is your duty as a wife, Clara. Sometimes they will kiss you, even rub themselves on you, or you can rub it and that gets it erect awful quick. Vincent does like me to suck it before he puts it in me. It doesn't taste very nice and sometimes it will hurt you, especially if you are not really ready, so try and be ready whenever. And this act of sex is also how the babies are made. Finnigan has told Vincent that he wanted a young girl like you because he really wants to have a child, a son preferably, to leave his farm when he dies.'

'So, it is really important that you let him do it to you whenever he wants, so that you can make the baby. He's after promising Vincent another acre of his land when you give him a child, so you are going to have to be ready for him to be doing it to you,' Aggie said, smiling with excitement.

They spoke to me as though I was an imbecile, forgetting I had grown up on a farm and understood how the babies were made from the mounting of the animals. And Carmel was not to know that I was far too familiar with her husband's erection and his urges. I was brutally aware that it hurt and to be prepared to take it. I had been trained in this since I was seven years old. I knew what it entailed.

'Sometimes, this is the secret bit that we are not supposed to talk about, but now you are becoming a real woman, I can tell you,' whispered Carmel. 'Clara, when it goes in you and is pushing around, sometimes it can feel really good in there, like a tingling and rumbling, it gets tight and all the pressure builds up and you feel like you are losing your mind with the giddiness of it. But don't let your husband see you feeling this, because it's not meant to be like that for us women. It's meant to be just for him.'

'But …' Aggie chimed in, giving Carmel a sideways glance, lowered her voice, and said, 'Carmel showed me how you can do it to yourself, to get the pressure to build and so long as no one else is around, you can let yourself lose your mind.' She looked at Carmel and smirked, 'Clara, it is just delicious, because I've not had a man put his thing in me, but I'm after doing it to myself all the time now, putting my fingers in myself and rubbing it around. But you cannot let anyone know you are doing it, because it is a great mortal sin to take such pleasure and indulge in the urges that come. I get these urges every day now, don't you too, Carmel?' she asked excitedly.

'Indeed, I do … I do try and resist the urges because I know it is a great sin. But it is such a great pleasure that I make sure I say a decade of the rosary every time after I do it and wash my hands. Make sure that you always wash your hands afterwards. Don't ever confess it to Father Stanley, because the men, they can't know, especially not himself, because he would no doubt put a stop to it and tell us all from the pulpit that we are sinners for taking pleasure from our urges, sinners for having the blessed urges to begin.' She began to giggle, looking at Aggie with cheek, 'Imagine if we all turned up at church and start taking pleasure when we got the urge. What would the men folk do?' and the pair of them descended into fits of laughter.

I didn't see how it was so funny, for I know what

the men folk would do, they would make sure we were punished. That is what happens every time you dare not follow the rules. I knew that more than most, more than Aggie or Carmel. I had taken the wrath of my brother for both of them for so long. I wondered how their lives were going to change with me gone. Who would tend to the house and the children? Who would make them their cups of tea while they sat around gossiping? Who would suffer at the hand of Vincent's rage? My mind was spinning, a million thoughts pounding through my head and their laughter etched on my nerves. I was still baffled as to why they would ever touch themselves in that way, for I could never imagine being touched there as pleasurable, for me, it had been painful and terrifying. The thought that I would now have to be doing it with a crippled old man whenever he wanted repulsed me. What if he hurt me like Vincent had? What if he took me whenever he wanted like Vincent had? What if I didn't give him a child because I never made one when Vincent did it to me? Maybe I can't make babies like some of the cows, those ones who don't calf are deemed useless and traded for one who can breed. Vincent was all about increasing his stock count, he was always after more, more stock, more land, even pimping me to a crippled old man for two acres.

'Enough of the closed door nonsense and giggling,' Vincent thumped on the door. I sometimes forgot that my brother was only twenty-two years old, for he had been acting like a man, a bully of a man at that for so long. 'We need to be getting to the church now, you don't want to be keeping Father Stanley and old Finnigan waiting.'

Chapter Sixteen

Alone at the altar, waiting for him, my anxieties threatened to destroy my unyielding resolve. *Clara, put your head up, eyes down and shoulders back and never let them see what is going on within. Never show them what you are feeling, for it is a sure sign of weakness. Just toughen yourself up, keep your mouth shut and hold your head high. Never bring shame on yourself by getting carried away with your feelings.* Mother's words running through my mind, my heart was breaking, the sadness of leaving my home brought the loss of her closer, the loss of Aggie to Carmel, the loss of the freedom I once had as a child. I had lost it all. When I walked out the door with a small suitcase in hand, I realised the emptiness of the life that I had lived. Aggie had held me and told me she would come and visit me in my new home across the fields, but I doubted she would. I doubted she'd think about me once I was gone. We would see one another at Sunday Mass but that would be it, there would not be sisterly gatherings over cups of warm tea in the kitchen. I did not even know what the home was like I was to live in. It would never be my home, it was his, I was but a lodger, to cook his meals and warm his bed.

    I was scared, as scared as I was the day I stood at this altar to make my First Communion, yet now, like then, I wouldn't show it. Carmel and Vincent, as witnesses, sat in the front pew, a place that Vincent aspired to sitting every Sunday morning. I could sense Carmel's boredom and Vincent's impatience as we waited for him to arrive. I wanted to run away from that church, run away to Aunt Maeve and hide away from the world. This arrangement was not going to work well. I could feel it and I did not know what that would mean for me, but I had no choice, this had been decided for me and I had to just keep my mouth shut and put up with it.

    He arrived. I heard the shuffle of his boots coming closer. I did not turn around to greet him, for I was gripped by fear. I should never have drawn attention to myself by singing at Mammy's funeral, then this man would never have known I existed, and I would not be standing here awaiting my fate. He stood in silence beside me, apparently not knowing what to say or do. I felt his nervousness coupled with an awkwardness that amplified mine. I prayed that this would be over quickly as I felt the waves of anxiety grip me tighter and smother my breath, the panic rose. I quickened my breath to try and appease it, yet this only seemed to make it worse. My palms began to sweat, my hands shook, my head became lighter and then I felt the light changing as my legs collapsed from under me.

He grabbed me by the arm and pulled me upright, 'Slow the breathing, it will calm you,' he directed.

I dared not look at him, but I did listen to him and took slow deeper breaths which did seem to abate the surge of panic. I turned to look for guidance or support from Carmel, but both her and Vincent seemed completely unaware of what had transpired and looked as eager for this ceremony of sorts, to be over.

Finally, Father Stanley appeared from the sacristy, seemingly bemused by the unease of those of us awaiting him. I am of the assumption that in some way he had approved the arrangement of this marriage, yet I was not to know how it had played out. I was just told what to do and expected to do it without asking questions. I was nothing more than a pawn to them.

I dutifully repeated what Father Stanley told me to say, committing myself as wife to a man whose eyes I had never met. There seemed no point in me making a fuss, telling them that I did not want to marry this crippled old man, for I knew they would not listen. I knew this altar and the last time I had stood here and made a fuss only caused me years of trouble. I did not wish to start a marriage with trouble and I was not to know if his fist was harder than Vincent's, his whip thicker or his

Beneath the Veil

vengeance more vicious. I would not tempt fate. I would be the *good* girl my mother had desired me to be and try and be the best wife I could to this man.

There was no celebration, not even a whiskey in the pub after the ceremony.

He, my husband, just nodded his head to Father Stanley and Vincent and said, 'Right we best be getting home.' He hoppled down the aisle towards the door of the church.

I stood rooted to the spot at the foot of the altar and looked to Carmel to guide me, 'Go on with you, Clara. You'll need to be getting him his dinner sure you will,' she shook her head incredulously at me, as if I was daft for not knowing that this was what I was to do.

Of course, I didn't know what I was supposed to do, no one had bothered to tell me. As he hesitated beside my suitcase by the door, unsure as to whether to pick it up and carry it or leave it to me, I realised that he was equally as blind to the ins and outs of this arrangement as me.

As we entered his farm cottage, the smell of cabbage and bacon filled the air. I was surprised by the warmth and cleanliness of the small but modest space. There was little clutter, everything seemed to have its place.

'Would you like a tea? I can put the kettle on the boil, if you would like,' he asked with a polite nervousness.

I looked to him somewhat confused, as no man

I'd come across had ever offered to make a tea. I was surprised by the vulnerability I saw in his stature. I realised that this was in some way as horrifying for him as it was for me.

'I can do it if you would like to sit down,' I said, trying to think of what would be expected of me in this situation, for he may have been testing me, I simply did not know.

'Ah no, it's fine. I'm well able to make a cup of tea,' and he proceeded to busy himself while I stood clutching Carmel's half-filled suitcase looking about the room. It was a typical farm cottage, not dissimilar from my own home, my old home, with a central room that served as kitchen, dining and sitting area, as well as two bedrooms and a washroom. It was quaint yet appeared to serve his needs.

'Would you like to put your bag in the room?' he asked.

Though he walked with the limp, he had an imposing stature when he stood upright, tall and broad of shoulder, but the injury to his right leg caused him to stoop when he walked, emasculating him and stripping him of his confidence. I stammered and faltered, fearing I would say or do the wrong thing, and stood frozen unable to move or think clearly. He moved towards me and I flinched expecting the belt of his hand across my head for being so daft, for it had been many a time when Vincent had pounced on me suddenly for my apparent insolence in not answering a question. I had developed a most unhelpful habit of jamming up when I felt scared. My silence seemed to infuriate Vincent, I was expecting the same from him, yet he did not strike me, he simply took the bag from my hand and moved towards one of the rooms.

'It is best if you sleep in this room, away from me, as I don't sleep well. I will no doubt disturb you. The children will sleep in with you when they come,' he stated, showing he had put much forethought into the decision.

I felt a thrill of excitement about having my own room and my own bed, at least until the babies started to come, for this was something I had always dreamed of, all this space to myself. Yet my excitement was tempered by the confusion about when the babies would be made, for Carmel and Aggie had said it mostly happened in the bed of a night. Perhaps he didn't want to do it in the bed, perhaps he was more like Vincent and preferred to do it in the barn like the animals. The memory sent my heart racing in trepidation, for I knew I would not be able to do it, not if he took me to the barn.

'Are you alright?' he asked cautiously. 'Maybe you should have your tea.'

He promptly placed the suitcase by the small single bed and exited the room hastily. I dejectedly sat on the bed and forced myself to take long deep breaths, the way I had taught myself whenever those memories came to mind.

'The tea is ready. Come it will help,' he suggested,

with a strange awareness of my anxiety. He sat at the small table laid out with two cups, a teapot, milk jug, sugar bowl and a plate of biscuits, with hands in lap waiting for me to join him. I sat in the seat opposite him, momentarily forgetting I was his wife, not a guest. On remembering my duty I jumped with a start and reached for the teapot at the same time he did only to have that frightful moment of touching one another for the first time.

'Let me,' he insisted, and proceeded to pour the tea while I sat and arranged the crisp white napkin on my lap avoiding watching him. As he settled back into his seat and took a sip of tea he began rather apprehensively. 'So, Clara, I can see you are awful nervous. I do hope that with time you will be able to relax and make this your home.'

I nodded and felt a wave of emotion coming over me.

'Should you wish to tend to the home duties, the cooking and the like, you may, your brother said you were well accustomed. I am used to looking after myself, so if you're not inclined, particularly when the babies come, then I am happy to tend to the duties myself.'

I nodded, again.

'Well, like I said if you are so inclined,' he shifted in his seat uncomfortably. 'Now about the children, I'm not sure what your brother told you, but my only reason in taking a wife is to have children, preferably a son to carry on the name and make sure I can hand this land onto someone. My family fought hard for this land and I cannot let their legacy die.' He spoke determinedly and with a heightened passion. I knew he had fought the British to reclaim Irish land, and it seemed of grave importance that his family hold onto their piece of land.

'Why, if your land is so important to you would you have signed part of it over to Vincent in exchange for me?' I queried before I had time to check my thoughts or watch my tongue.

He looked surprised by my question but committed to answering. 'I did not want to do this in this way, but your brother was insistent. He approached me at your mother's funeral and asked if I was wanting a family. I laughed to begin with, because any dream of that seemed lost to me, given I'm nothing but an old cripple stuck in a small village tucked away on the coast. But when your brother suggested you, after you sang there at the cemetery, he said you can cook and clean and being young could give me children, rightly or wrongly the idea did compel me. I asked him if I could meet you. It was then he laughed at me and told me to take what I can get and be done with it. He offered you for the back paddocks. The possibility of having my own family awakened in me and even though I knew I was compromising my families land, I weighed it up and figured it would be a worthy investment. The future return would yield far greater reward than having those extra few acres.'

I was flabbergasted, not by Vincent's actions, for

I knew him to be selfish and ruthless to the core, more by the seeming ease in which my life was traded, like a commodity. I was an investment to him and I felt the expectation to deliver.

'The sooner we begin the impregnating the better. When did you last bleed?' he asked with that same matter of fact demeanour.

Shocked, I stammered overcome by shame, because these matters were never to be spoken of in front of men. As far as I was concerned they were not even aware of the bleeding as it was kept hidden, and yet here he was asking me so directly.

'Uh-h-h, it was, I think, t-t-the week before last,' I faltered as the colour rose in my cheeks.

Unperturbed by my discomfort discussing such matters, he continued, 'Do you bleed regularly, every month? Vincent assured me you were regular.'

The mortification at my privacy being spoken about so openly by these men silenced me, and my reticence seemed to agitate him.

'I asked you a simple question, I expect a simple answer. Are you regular with your bleeding? Yes or no?' he demanded with rising irritation.

'Yes,' I muttered, as I stared at my hands, gripping anxiously to the cloth of my dress.

'Right. Good. You will need to wash and prepare yourself, we will begin this evening. You will remain in your bed afterwards and I will prepare the dinner. I have read that moving about, particularly in an upright position, after the ejaculation, can result in leaking, which will diminish the chance of impregnation. We will not be taking such chances. For the middle week of the cycle, I will penetrate you in the morning before I milk the cows and in the evening before the dinner. You will not be required to do any house chores during this week. You may stay in bed and read. You do read, don't you?'

'I can read, but I've not for many a year now, as my brother forbade me from reading anything but the Bible,' I murmured, shaken by his alarming bluntness and the panic that I felt pulsating through me.

'You may select a book of your choosing from my room. Go now and prepare yourself, I will see to some chores and then, well then, I will come to you. Please be ready.'

He took my cup of cold tea and turned to the sink and began rinsing it. I didn't know what I had to do to be ready. *Do I wear the nightdress for such things? Do I stay in it for the morning when he comes to me again? Do I get out of the bed to go to the toilet or clean myself before he comes back?* I feared asking my questions, in case he reprimanded me for being insolent. I reasoned it would be safest to mind my mouth and just do as I was told. I had witnessed many an animal being broken in and I knew that it would not take long for me to be trained as his wife.

Chapter Seventeen

'Take your hair out,' he instructed.

I stood awkwardly beside the bed, dressed in my white gown with lace trim, as he inspected me and then loosened my long dark hair from the tie, I lowered my eyes, in an attempt to hide behind the mop of dark curls that fell around my face. My legs began to shake as he loosened his belt, was he to beat me with it? The room began to feel hot and small, closing in on me and I feared I might faint.

'Lie down on the bed,' he said as he struggled to remove his pants from his injured leg.

I lay flat on the bed and closed my eyes and began a prayer to my God. *Dear God, help me to make a baby so I might never have to do this again.* And then I disappeared into my mind, roaming the hills on Trinity, feeling the brisk autumn wind streaming through my hair, the kiss of the sun on my cheeks. I felt the bed lower under his pressure, the draft of cold air streamed across my thighs and into my woman parts as he lifted my night gown and spread open my legs. I placed my head against Trinity and felt her heart pounding, I patted her gently, soothing her, calming her, telling her it was all right, that everything was alright. I couldn't breathe, as he lay atop of me, his body crushing me. I did not cry out as I felt his fingers prodding me, opening me for his thing. I did not cry out as he shoved his thing straight into me in one motion. I did not cry out as I felt myself tear. I stroked Trinity assuring her that it was all okay, willing her to settle, to stay calm, her crazed heart beat reverberated through me and I begged her to slow down, to stay with me as it would be over soon. And it was. The thrusts stopped with a primal groan that brought me back to the present. I felt the wetness between my legs as he pulled himself out of me. I felt a wave of nausea suddenly wash over me and the urge to vomit compelled me to jump up, but I remembered I was to lie there, so I swallowed it and placed my hand across my mouth. He did not see, he was already standing beside the bed with his back to me, securing his belt.

'I'll fix the dinner, you're not to move now, you hear,' he instructed decidedly.

I had forgotten to choose a book, so I lay there not moving, my legs still spread with my gown crumpled on my chest.

Please, dear God, make the baby now. Bring the baby into me this first time.

Somehow, I welcomed the chance to lie in bed and not fix a meal. I felt I had been forced to sacrifice myself for this apparent privilege. In his eyes, I knew he was not bestowing on me a privilege, it was part of the arrangement, a necessary step in his endeavour to produce an heir.

As the wetness between my legs dried I was determined that his liquid would not leak from me, so I lowered my gown over my legs and moved myself into a seated position. From here I could see from the window, the beauty of his land that bordered the edge of the cliff to the sea in all its natural wonder. How had I not noticed this when first I came into the room. My mind had been gripped by fear, and only now within the stillness of the room was I able to see. I allowed myself to escape into the dusk, the beginnings of the setting sun flickered on the water enticing me away from the reality in which I was trapped. There was freedom beyond that window and across that ocean and it called to me, as she whispered to me I prayed, not to the God I was so accustomed.

I prayed to her, the Mother,

'Hail Holy Queen, Mother of Mercy.
Hail my life, my sweetness and my hope.
To thee do I cry poor banished child of Eve;
To thee do I sigh, mourning and weeping in this vale of tears.
Turn then, most gracious Advocate,
thine eyes of mercy towards me
and, after this my exile, show
unto me the blessed fruit of thy womb, Jesus.
O clement, O loving, O sweet Virgin Mary.
Pray for me O Holy Mother that I may be worthy to share your Divine Grace. Amen.'

As I took another breath, I felt the tension release and for a few moments I believed I could do this, this life as a woman, as a wife and a mother. As I heard the door open, I reached for the covers and drew them over me, covering myself from him, my modesty a tentative tether to what remained of my dignity. He placed a bowl of soup and a weak cup of tea on the table beside me, before leaving the room, only to return moments later with a stained chamber pot.

'You'll be right to use this then?' he queried awkwardly. 'Save needing to be walking about and the like.'

I simply nodded, hiding my abhorrence, and willing him to leave the room.

'You did not take a book?' he asked, looking about the room.

I shook my head, 'I forgot.'

'I'll choose something for you to read. It is important to read, to keep expanding the mind. I expect you to be well read, so that you can teach the children about more than they will learn in that little village school. I knew nothing of the world from what I was taught by the nuns in that place. My children shall not be limited by their geography. An expansive mind ensures they can travel anywhere in their own mind, even if they find themselves tied to one place,' he stopped himself abruptly, seemingly embarrassed that he had exposed to much of himself.

I was curious about him and did not know whether the stories I had heard from Carmel and Aggie were true or merely the gossip of the small minded who had never left the village. He both repulsed and intrigued me, this complexity seemed to exhaust me even more. I did not feel called to read, despite him placing a decrepit copy of *Moby Dick* on the bed beside me before he left the room and quietly closed the door behind him.

It was to be a fitful sleep, my insomnia and anxieties waking me in the darkness of the night. I had no clue as to the time and I was not familiar with the noises surrounding the cottage to guide me. I felt the darkness surrounding me and compressing my chest, the feeling reminding me of the pressure as he lay on top of me only hours previously. The terror began to rise, and yet I was well used to this feeling, as for many years I had suffered the same attacks during the darkness of the night, when through lack of distraction, my body recounted its terror which demanded release, the silent screams insistent on being heard. I had mastered holding them in, breathing deeply and willing myself to silence, for fear of the consequences of being heard. I could not awaken him, who slept in the next room, for I did not know what he would make of my hysteria and I knew I would not tempt this fate.

    I tried my regular escape to the hills with Trinity, but my mind was too busy, the fear of the unknown was so demanding of my attention. I recklessly poured over every detail of the last few weeks, condemning myself for my actions that had brought me into this situation. I deserved to suffer at the hands of this man in his desire to sire a child, for he made no attempt to hide his motivations, and in failing to have the courage to stand up to Vincent and leave when Aunt Maeve invited me, I knew I was responsible for this situation. As Mammy would often mutter to herself, 'You made your bed, you lie in it.' I never understood those words until now, as I lay in this bed, in a stranger's home, a stranger who in a few short hours would penetrate me again with his thing. The thought brought on a fresh surge of trepidation that I felt within my female parts which still felt raw and bruised from the first encounter. He was not rough in the way that Vincent was. It was different with him, he did not intend to be violent, but he seemed so disconnected from what he was doing that he was completely unaware of the force he was inflicting.

This was the pattern I was to become accustomed. His determined focus on the outcome ensured he remained emotionally detached from the process. I realised his time in service to the Irish Republic had conditioned him to disconnect himself emotionally from his experiences. In some ways our pairing may have been for the best, for I had no emotional demand of him as a husband, nor he of me as a wife. It was an arrangement devoid of emotional connection, that was designed to serve a single purpose. A purpose I seemed unable to fulfil.

After three months without becoming pregnant, Vincent was summoned to the home and I was banished to my room. I spent much time in my room reading, devouring the books offered to me. For one week of each month, during the peak impregnating period I was confined to my bed and whilst I felt imprisoned, I made the most of this time, in expanding my mind, my imagination billowing with the possibility of a world beyond the one in which I found myself. Another world to flee to during the night when sleep evaded me. We were not accustomed to having guests, no one had visited the cottage since I had arrived. I had not seen Aggie or Carmel save from passing them outside of the church after Mass. Our greetings were cordial yet lacking the warmth I craved, my soul becoming increasingly starved of human connection. Even my niece and nephews were reticent around me, his presence beside me a threat to their innate carefree nature.

I cradled Jane Eyre closer to me as I heard Vincent arrive. I wished to escape into Jane's world, where I related to her misery yet found inspiration in her strength to claim her freedom, *"I am no bird; and no net ensnares me: I am a free human being with an independent will."* And I, I am a pathetic girl, weak of will, hiding away in a room while two men meet to determine my life.

I heard the raised voices and became fearful for my own safety, for no doubt Vincent was to blame me for his promise, to deliver a fertile young woman, not coming to fruition. I felt the shame rising through me as they spoke of me as they would a filly failing to impregnate despite rigorous attempts. They discussed my cycle, my smell, the look and feel of my woman parts, how he did it and how often. The rage at being spoken of in such an inhumane manner pulsated through me and beseeched me to storm into the kitchen and demand to be respected, but the pure mortification crippled me. I found myself rooted to the spot; powerless and filled with shame, guilt and disgust. Disgust at myself for my weakness as a woman.

Chapter Eighteen

The descent into darkness began in earnest after his first meeting with Vincent. He became even more intense and obsessed with having a child and rearranged his life to accommodate their new strategy. He brought on a farm hand, a local boy to keep the farm in order, as he was to remain in the house to tend to the domestic duties and to me. It was determined that there must be something wrong with my bleeding cycle, so he was to try all month to find the right time, it was what they did in the horse breeding world when a filly wouldn't impregnate, and by my brother's account, it worked to good effect. As a result, I was not allowed to leave my room, nor my bed for that matter. I had heard whispered stories when I was younger of women being bedbound whilst pregnant to hold the baby in, it appeared I was doing the same to hold the possibility of a baby.

    I craved the warmth of the summer sun on my skin, the fresh green grass under my feet. I was trapped. I could see through the window to the world beyond, but it was fast becoming an alternate reality. I had been excused from attending Mass by Father Stanley due to unspoken medical complications, so I was not even afforded this one outing each week. Whilst I read book after book, my mind spent much time in turmoil. I did not know what would happen to me should I never deliver him a child. I did not know if I would ever get out of this room. I could not leave, for he ensured he remained in the cottage all day, cooking and cleaning, reading and praying. I heard him moving about and his persistent shuffling unnerved me. I would flinch each time I heard the door handle creak, not knowing if he was clearing away the chamber pot, bringing me food, or himself.

    I was oblivious when he came to me, as it was the same each time, sometimes three times a day. I closed my eyes and disappeared into some other world, where I do not really know because it was not some fantasy land, it just took me away from here, from him. I would block the stabbing pain, the incessant creaking of the bed, the smell of stale tobacco on his breath, the grunt at the end. In my oblivion I discovered it did not traumatise me as much, I became immune to it.

    I began to sleep during the day, through both boredom and exhaustion. He called me slovenly and insisted I read and study encyclopedias to build my intellect, in preparation for his children. I did not tell him that it was not my mind that needed expansion it was my spirit, for my spirit descended into dark spaces during those months of recluse. I kept my mouth shut, for fear of what he would do if I spoke out, yet I could not think of what else he could do to me. He robbed me of my freedom, my dignity, my body, my spirit. It was when I began talking to the spirits that haunted me during the dark of night, that he began to medicate me. A solution to my insanity that ironically created it, for he stole my mind. He told me they were sleeping tablets that he used to help him sleep, for he too had trouble sleeping. I did not question why, for I was in no doubt that the trauma of the battles he had fought and kept hidden within tormented him. I could see it in his eyes, when he shuffled into my room, his soul was troubled deeply. The pills did force me to sleep but the residual effects destroyed me, the essence of who I was. My brain became foggy, my awareness of days and weeks and time in general was lost. I was a scattered mess. I could barely put the pieces together to remember who I was, yet it seemed the memories of my past became amplified and began to infiltrate my thoughts. Crazy, wild thoughts, that tortured me, flashes of those moments in time that I was convinced I had forgotten all came crashing back in. The whippings, the blistering of the skin across my bottom and back, the slaps across the face, the kicks in the back, the smell of hay bales as my face was pushed into them, the excruciating sting with urination, the bruising and swelling of my tender woman parts, the sound of him closing the door to the barn, the tree and the Gypsy boy, laughing and playing, the blood stain on that pure white dress, the taunting at school, the wetness dripping down my legs, patting Trinity, calming Trinity, rejecting Trinity. My mind was constantly abuzz. I was in a relentless state of confusion that made my head throb and I began hitting it to make it stop, first with my hand, then against the wall and door. He gave me more pills to calm me down, to stop me pacing the room, banging my head, muttering to the voices that taunted me.

It worked.

Everything stopped.

I existed in the room in a manufactured state of calm and no longer fought it. He no longer called me slovenly or tried to get me to read, so long as I was not disturbing him, he could pretend I was not there, until he did his thing on me, yet even then I am sure he pretended I was not there, just as I did. I remained in a comatose slumber for what must have been a number of months, before he entered one morning and said, 'You are late by seven days, you should have bled last week.' He kept meticulous records of my cycles, which was fortunate in some regards for I had no recollection of what day it was, let alone counting days.

'You are with child. You will no longer take the medication for it may damage the child. You will learn to sleep without the need and you will still your own mind and recommence your studies in preparation for the child. You will be allowed from the room to sit with me by the range. We will talk and read. I will continue the home duties while you carry the child,' he spoke with assuredness as if he had prepared for this moment, and there was a confusing gentle edge to his words.

I had so many feelings arise, but none had enough power to touch me and I barely reacted to his news, which riled him. He wanted me to be joyous, but I did not know how to be. He wanted me to be excited, but I did not know how to be. He wanted me to at least be something, a real wife, a real mother, but I did not know how to be. After so many months trapped in the bedroom, in forced isolation, I had lost my ability to function in the world and he could not understand that. He could not understand how I couldn't just step back into life, as if nothing had happened, and suddenly pretend this was normal, that I was normal.

The sudden withdrawal from all the medications caused my body to go into shock. I vomited and fevered for three days, and on the third day I began to bleed. As I awoke to find the blood-stained sheet under me, I screamed, my terror was not so much about losing a baby, a baby I was not convinced I was carrying, rather my fear of what he would do to me for not being able to hold his child. I had no doubt he would blame me and punish me further.

He came to the room and saw the stained sheets.

'Clean yourself and your mess,' he said, before walking away and leaving the cottage. This was the first time he had left me alone in the cottage for months, he too having been excused from attending Mass. Father Stanley made a point of bringing him the Communion on a Sunday afternoon, where he would stay for a whiskey and they would discuss 'the progress of the project'. It seemed he had as much interest in the project as Vincent did, who would check in at the end of each month. Never did they bother checking in on my progress, I was but a cog in the wheel, an unimportant commodity, that was easily replaced should I not prove able to finish the project. On one hand, I wished he would replace me, on the other, I did not in fear of what would happen to me should he throw me out. Vincent had made it clear when I left to be married, that I was not welcome back at my childhood home. Aggie and Carmel had never looked in on me, in all these months, despite the rumours which must have abounded, I knew they would not want me back. The only other family I had was Aunt Maeve, but I felt so much shame at refusing her offer and ending up in this circumstance, that my pride would never allow me to ask her for help. I reconciled that this was all I had, this was my home now and I must do my best to mend my wrong doings that had resulted in me losing his child. I would seek his forgiveness on his return and pray with him to be blessed with a child.

Chapter Nineteen

'Our Father, who art in heaven
Hallowed be Thy Name;
Thy kingdom come,
Thy will be done,
on earth as it is in heaven.
Give us this day our daily bread,
and forgive us our trespasses,
as we forgive those who trespass against
us; and lead us not into temptation,
but deliver us from evil.

Amen.'

I knelt by the bed and prayed, incessantly awaiting his return, desperate to be forgiven for my sins. I was weak with fever and the cloth stuck between my legs felt heavy with blood and my unborn child. It was a reminder of my sins and I knew that God was punishing me for all my sins. Even though I had tried to do the right thing and not cause him any trouble, I had proven as useless as Vincent always claimed. I needed to prove myself worthy of being in this house, of being his wife for I had failed him, and he had given me every opportunity to succeed and my poisonous rotten soul had sabotaged his dream. I would pray more for I had become lax with my prayer. Perhaps I was being punished for not attending Mass, for I knew it to be a mortal sin of the highest regard, that is what Father Stanley had always said, but I thought because he had pardoned me that I would be forgiven for committing this most grave sin.

I remained on my knees, with my head lowered and my hands clasped as they entered the room. He had brought Doctor Malone and Father Stanley, one to tend to my physical defect, the other to heal my spiritual disease.

> *'Amazing Grace how sweet the sound,*
> *That saves a wreck like me.*
> *I once was lost but now I'm found,*
> *Was blind but now I see.'*

The words played over in the emptiness of my mind. I was lost, my soul a wreck and I saw these men as my saviours, delivered to me by my husband. I cried silent tears of gratitude as they hovered by the end of the bed discussing the awfulness, both mine and of the situation that had become with him.

'Stand, woman,' Doctor Malone ordered.

As I awkwardly brought myself to my feet with the weakness and pain taxing me, I felt the blood gush onto the cloth, the stench brought bile to my mouth.

'Have you no pride in yourself?' Doctor Malone asked, repulsed by the sight. 'Ah, she has proven herself to be dreadfully slovenly. A disgrace to her family, and embarrassment as a wife,' he spoke with fierce disdain.

'Indeed, it is a good thing that Ciaran and Mary, God rest their souls, are not here to bear witness to this, this abhorrence. For they were good, fine standing people and this ... this here should bear no reflection on them. It is her and her alone who has brought this on,' Father Stanley preached, whilst staring at me with repulsion.

'Shall I begin, Father Stanley?' Doctor Malone asked, respectfully.

'Yes, do, the sooner we get this over with the better for all,' he muttered.

'Take off your clothes, that cloth.'

I was mortified as the three of them stood staring at me. This was the most sacred of a woman's business and I was to expose my shame to them. And they expected me to do it there, in front of them, without replacing it with a clean one, the blood was dripping down my thigh and onto the ground at my feet. I obeyed. He placed a handkerchief over his mouth, to stifle the stench, as he examined the remnants of my bloodied excretion.

'Yes, Dempsey. Yes, indeed you were right. She was with child, the large clots here, would be the remains of your unborn child, God rest its soul, and take pardon on those who failed to bring it to life,' his eyes determinedly boring into me.

I did not know how I had contributed to the death of my unborn child, but the burden of guilt, shame and remorse brought me to my knees. 'Forgive me for my sins,' I cried out, begging their mercy for my failings.

'How long had she been stealing your medications, Dempsey?' he asked earnestly.

'Ah, now I can't be sure, a few months, perhaps more. You know I did wonder why I was running out so quickly, after having to call for you so often for more. Yet I never realised, until a few days ago, that she would have dared to take from her own husband and let me suffer my pains. An insult it is to all those I stood alongside and fought for the freedom of the Republic, her freedom.'

'A pure selfish act indeed, and a mortal sin to steal and disrespect the husband,' proclaimed Father Stanley.

'And you are after having done the right thing, Dempsey. By taking all those drugs away from her as quickly as you did, for the good of your unborn child. I would say though, by the look of the remains that the damage was done, whatever she had been taking for all those months, was in her system already and would have killed the poor wee infant before it had the chance to thrive at all. ''Tis true, and don't we all know it, one cannot grow within toxicity,' Doctor Malone concluded with authority.

'Indeed, 'tis true, 'tis true. And a fine mind you have, Doctor Malone, to be able to examine those bloody masses to determine the cause and all so quickly,' acknowledged Father Stanley.

'What shall be done to fix this mess? Is she worth keeping, to try and breed again or is the damage done?' he queried of them.

'Please forgive me, I will try harder to be the wife you need me to be,' I begged of him.

'Silence,' he roared in a manner I had not heard before. 'You shall not speak unless spoken to, do you understand me?'

I nodded fearfully.

'The stink and sight of ye is enough to make me turn you out. You've proven you are not able to care for yourself, let alone me, so I indeed have my doubts as to whether you will be able to care for a child, for you've shown yourself inept at even carrying a child, killing my first with your own indulgences.'

Clara, rise up! I heard the faintest whisper calling to me.

I had not stolen the drugs. I knew he had not even allowed me to tend to my own basic needs, nor my duties as a wife, for he had locked me away in this room and drugged me for the last few months. This truth lay within me, and it begged me to speak—to speak of these truths—but there were so many layers of shame, guilt, regret and unadulterated humiliation that I could not believe the whisper of my soul. And what was the use in trying, it would make no difference, they would never believe me. I ignored the whisper and absorbed their story. Their story that condemned me for killing the unborn child, his unborn child, I carried. Was there even a baby? It didn't matter the truth. In their mind, and thus mine, there was a baby and it was my fault that it had died. I had killed it with the toxicity of my being, my poisonous dark soul.

'She will recover. Plenty of strong tea, a shot or two of whiskey before bed. And when the bleeding stops get her out into the yard and doing a bit of descent hard work. A good bit of hard work is good cleanser for the soul, so it is. And dear Lord and God above, get her to wash herself, for I am in many doubts about how you ever went near her yeself, Dempsey, to create that child in the first place.'

'To be sure, Doctor Malone, it was most certainly not a pleasurable experience. I thank ye for your time and wise guidance,' shaking Doctor Malone's hand he escorted him from the room.

While they were gone he stood there staring at me as I hung my head in shame. I could feel the disgust in his eyes and I wished to be dead to save me from this torment. It was true, I had disgraced myself and my parents, no doubt the stories around the village would not be serving my reputation well. Aggie and Carmel would be mortified by their association to me, their lack of contact evidence that they had detached themselves from knowing me. And Vincent would be ropable that I had failed, and he had not been able to collect on his end of the arrangement. It surprised me in some ways that he was not present for this inquisition, though for this I was grateful.

Father Stanley's silent condemnation heavily permeated the small room as we waited for my husband to return. I dared not move from the position beside my bed even though I longed to cover myself, the indignity at standing before him in my dirtied blood-stained gown devoid of undergarments was crippling.

I lowered myself to my knees beside the bed, and began praying aloud, 'Dear Lord God, Father Almighty, I ask you to save me. Save my tainted soul from the pits of Hell. Forgive me for killing my unborn child, the child of my husband. Forgive me for my failings as a wife and woman. Cleanse my soul of the darkness cursed by the hands of the Devil. Forgive me Lord, Father for opening myself to the temptations of the Devil himself and welcoming him into my soul. May you rid my mind and body of this most vile scourge. Cleanse me, dear God. Cleanse me so I may be of value to my husband and bear him child. Amen.'

'For God to touch you, you must first clean yourself. Scrub yourself thoroughly from top to toe, and then burn these bed clothes, they carry the stain of the child killed by the Devil you invited into your bed. Air this room from dawn to dusk. You shall not lay around in bed any longer. You shall tend to your husbands needs in the home, while Dempsey here returns to the farm duties. I will come daily to counsel you, until it is determined that your soul has been cleansed of the darkness of the Devil. Dempsey, you shall not penetrate her again until we are assured she is clean. We do not want the evil within her to pass onto you, nor a child of the Lord.'

'Yes, Father, thank you. You are indeed a good man, a soldier of the Lord God here on earth, protecting us all from the evil of the dark. I shall be guided by your counsel in these grave matters of the soul,' he crooned, taking Father Stanley's hand in his own.

'I shall return tomorrow morning to begin my work,' he stated solemnly taking his role as my saviour with great seriousness.

In my bewilderment I welcomed him as my saviour. I trusted in him to cleanse my soul, so I might be blessed with a child, to fulfil my husband's deepest desires and prove my worth as a woman. As soon as he left, I asked that I might wash myself. I took such pleasure in scrubbing the filth from my skin, the scalding water on the rawness of my flesh was in some way ecstatic, making me feel more alive than I had in the last year. I scoured my hair and then meticulously untangled the knots that had become so entwined that I feared I would have to chop it all off. I sat with an unyielding focus, intent on reclaiming some aspect of myself. Mammy had always said that my long dark curls were my most endearing feature and I longed to recapture an essence of my old self.

'Might I prepare your dinner for tonight?' I asked, tentatively once I had removed and burnt the sheets, cleaned the room and opened the bolted windows to air it. I loved the feel of the breeze on my skin and stood looking out the window at the world beyond, believing I was emerging from a dark cave following a long winter. I longed to breath in the air, feel the sun, move my body with vigour and touch the land once again.

He eyed me with suspicion, unsure of my motive and whether to trust in this path that had been laid out for him that had seen me awaken within hours. It seemed Father Stanley had freed me from his imprisonment and I sought to move with this vitality that was working through me. He nodded his approval.

'Are there any fresh vegetables in the garden that I may use?'

Again, he nodded, wary as he watched me carry the basket out to the garden. It was the first time I had stepped outside in months. I breathed in the freshness of the air, intent on filling every corner of my lungs and turned my face to the sun, allowing myself to bake in the warmth of its kiss. I patted a cat who curled herself around my legs, meowing in greeting. Then soaked in the sight of the abundance of the vegetables in the garden and the beauty of the flower beds surrounding the cottage. I absorbed the vitality in the soil as I dug out the spuds and carrots, and nibbled on the greens of the leaves, the freshness activating my taste buds and making my mouth water with a remembering of life.

I found myself humming and smiling as I pottered in the garden, gently pulling the weeds and picking flowers to place on the table and in a vase in my bedroom. I did not seek permission from him, I did not even think to ask. As I prepared his dinner, I felt useful and hopeful. Perhaps this was the turning point. Perhaps I had to descend into the depths of the darkness to make my way back. Perhaps Father Stanley had already begun his work on cleansing my soul. Perhaps everything would change now.

I was naïve.

Chapter Twenty

I was naïve and stupid. I deserved all that came to me.

He lured me into his filthy evil trap and I allowed him to take me there. He did not counsel me as a man of God as he had promised me, as he had promised my husband, he groomed me. And it only took him two weeks of sitting with me in the sunshine, roaming the hills, walking on the beach, listening to my troubled soul releasing her pain, feigning compassion, to lure me into a space where I trusted in him. He made me feel better. He brought me to life. He awakened my light again, that spark I had been missing for so long.

And then he destroyed me, again.

Methodical and calculating, he chose his moments to subtly assert himself on me. A gentle supportive touch of the arm; an understanding hand on the knee; a compassionate look that held the eyes too long, a brush of the cheek to remove windswept hair. All a premeditated plan to open my trust in him, before he executed his plan. The plan that he purported to be God's plan to cleanse my soul.

'Make some tea, Father Stanley will be here shortly,' I was instructed on Sunday morning after my husband returned from Mass.

Father Stanley still thought it was best that I should not attend Mass with the rest of the congregation, in case the last of the Devil, was to transmute itself onto others. Despite the lightness I had begun to feel within myself, I was often subtly reminded that I was still dirty, infected by the Devil himself, which shamed me and fuelled a desperation for my soul to be repatriated.

After his tea, with my husband standing watch he lay me down on the bed. I did not fight him as he spread my legs to inspect me.

'One must look for all signs of evil,' he explained to my husband, who had vowed to protect me, yet stood motionless, powerless in many ways to the will of this man who called himself a disciple of Jesus.

He donned his white robe with ritualistic care and prepared the thurible before lowering the chains between my thighs, so the burning incense diffused into the darkness of my woman. He prayed to the highest Heavens that the Devil would be released from within me and following more muttered prayers he handed over the thurible, so he could prepare the holy water and cloth. In some perverse way I trusted in him as he knelt between my legs, and massaged the blessed cloth into my woman, beginning gently at first before more forcefully pushing his fingers through the cloth and into the dark corners of my woman. I did not flinch, I allowed myself to be cleansed, welcoming the blessing, opening to the blessed cleansing. He handed the dirtied cloth to him, who impassively stood in wait like a dutiful servant and instructed him to put it aside to be burnt that evening. He then washed his hands in the sacred holy water.

'It is the hands of God, through my own, that shall determine if the curse of Satan remains imprinted on her soul. Dempsey, you shall watch for any sign of pleasure, for as you know, for a woman to experience pleasure is a mortal sin and a sure sign of the presence of darkness hidden within the crevasses of the woman. She who sighs or moans or murmurs under examination, no doubt has been cursed by the Devil himself. Watch for these signs, the flicker of an eye, the hardening of the nipple, the tensing of the hands, all indicators that she is experiencing pleasure,' he spoke with assuredness, indulgent in the importance of his self-appointed authoritarian role.

The rigidity of his finger pressed hard against the inside of my opening. I did not flinch with the pain or the shame. I closed my eyes and allowed him to explore my inner woman. His finger prodded the edges, before he pushed his hand in deeper, just as I've seen the men do many a time when checking on the cow before she births, feeling around to make sure nothing is amiss; no dark spots, no hidden pleasure spots laid down by the Devil. He poked and prodded, seeming intent on finding something, yet I felt nothing but the pain with which he forced himself into me and the shame and indignity of lying with a man's hand inside of me, while my husband stood watching and waiting for the sign of my pleasure.

There was none.

He viciously scrapped his nails along the edge of the wall as he removed his taut cold fingers. He demanded a cloth to wipe his hands, before soaking them once again in the bowl of sacred holy water. I opened my eyes to see him staring intently at his hands, contemplating his next move. I thought he was done, as I had not responded in the ways he was looking. I was sure the Devil had not cursed me. Yet he was intent on proving me wrong, that the presence of evil was still within me, even if he had to put it there himself. Without explanation, he lowered himself to kneel between my legs and again opened me with his fingers. But this time it was gentle and soft, this time he stroked the outer edges with a light touch, slowly circling around my opening. It felt different as he inserted his fingers into me, allowing them to lightly dance up and then down again in a smooth rhythm. I closed my eyes and allowed myself to feel his gentle playful touch, and as he stroked me, my body began to move with the rhythm of his touch. A pressure built in my core and I felt dizzy with the intensity as it rose quickly. I gasped as it moved in a wave through my body. I gripped the bed as I arched my back, allowing the wave to rise even more, and moaned as it passed through my throat.

It stopped abruptly as the bowl of blessed water was thrown in my face, followed by a fierce whack across my mouth, my husband bellowing, 'You, heathen whore of a wanton slut, how dare you bring the curse of the Devil under my roof.'

'Stop now, Dempsey,' coddled Father Stanley, wiping his hands methodically. ''Tis a grave time indeed, but we must not lose our focus. You have just witnessed Satan himself working his evil, as a disciple of the Lord Jesus Christ, I must eradicate this filth from within her, cleanse her once and for all, your baby had no chance of thriving and is best it died. One can only imagine the deformity and inflictions it would have been born with, for one cannot be held in the darkness of the womb with the Devil himself every day without serious consequence.'

'Ah, right you are, Father. May the Lord Bless the child and let its soul rest now in the hand of God, freed from this woman and her curse,' he murmured.

'Amen,' he chorused, as he blessed himself and removed his robe. The bulging mound in his pants explicit. 'The Lord God is calling me to wipe clean the remains of this darkness, to destroy the evil perpetrating within her.'

I wiped the water dripping down my face, now stained red from my bleeding mouth. I stared at the blood on my hand, transfixed.

I felt him pull me down by the shoulders as instructed, 'Hold her there, Dempsey, to be sure the Devil himself will fight.'

I did not fight him as he forced himself within me, inserting himself deeper and deeper with each thrust. I did not fight him as he gripped at the flesh of my thighs, spreading me open even further, angling himself even higher, I did not fight as his eyes burrowed triumphantly into mine, as he drove himself into me intent on crushing my woman. I did not fight because there was no Devil within me. I closed my eyes and melted into the darkness of nothingness that beckoned me to take refuge.

'Open. Her. Eyes.' He panted furiously, determined I should witness his desecration of me. Freeing my shoulders, he prized open my eyes, yet I saw, and I felt nothing but the darkness. Even as he ripped open my bodice and clawed at my breast; even as he roared victoriously with the release of his cleansing waters; even as he blessed my mind, my mouth, my heart with the remains of his most sacred bodily fluids; even as they walked from the room leaving me lying in the bloodied sheets, battered and bruised.

I felt nothing. I was nothing.

Chapter Twenty-one

The nothingness stayed within and around me for weeks.

I moved within it, feeling the nothingness whilst doing life. Allowed from my room, I played the wife, cooking and cleaning with gusto. The purpose of doing something cutting through the intensity of the nothing. He did not speak to me. He could not even acknowledge me and avoided being in the same room. He did not lay a hand on me again. I felt both his repulsion and fear of me. Perhaps it was of himself, as I was the reminder of his own disempowerment as he pathetically stood watching while another man raped his wife. Of course, I was not thinking these thoughts at the time. My thoughts were vague and confused, my mind having been shut down with the shock of what had transpired. I was grateful for the space I had away from him and the world, for both he and the world scared me and in some perverse way, it was here in his farm house, the place where I had suffered such horrific abuse that I felt safest. There was some strange comfort in being held by the walls that carried my story, the walls which knew I was a victim. They would speak to me: *'We know what they did to you, we saw it all, we will not let you forget. Clara, you are the victim here. If you forget they will forget, and they will all get away with it, again.'* The walls held this for me as I moved within the nothingness.

The days and weeks passed by in somewhat of a blur. It was different to the months before where I was trapped in the room with my mind altered by drugs, then I couldn't recall days from nights, weeks from months. Now I moved through the days and nights methodically with an eerie stillness that the darkness could not penetrate, but in some ways, I preferred the darkness to the nothingness because at least I felt something. Then I felt the darkness and I struggled with it—an unpleasant frightful dance to be sure—but at least it moved. Now I felt nothing and that scared me even more because I knew it was waiting for me—lingering just outside of me, a thin veil lying between here and there—I didn't know when it would hit me or when it would violently erupt from me.

I feared this day and others should have too.

The first month that I did not bleed passed without comment. There was no declaration that I was with child, unlike the previous occasion. His disdain was now teamed with an iciness that sent shivers through me as he passed me in the kitchen on his way outside. As the second and third month passed with no bleeding it became apparent that my body was changing shape, my small breasts blossoming, my tummy and hips rounding. I hated to see my body changing in this way and tried to hide it by loosening my dress and apron, for it was evidence of a truth that I did not want to acknowledge. I was carrying a child that did not belong to my husband. I was carrying a child that belonged to Colin Stanley. I was carrying the spore of the Devil and it was devouring me from within, a parasite that was taking over my body. I hated what it was doing to my body and I hated it because it came from him, the poisonous seed that he planted within me. I knew he would have noticed, he must have for he was so accustomed to counting my days and watching for signs of my bleeding when he had been intent on impregnating me himself. I did not know what he was going to do to me, or this unborn child. The tension in the cottage grew tighter the more obvious it became that I was carrying a child and it was not his. On one hand he wanted to convince himself that it was his and proceed with life as if this was his plan all along, yet on the other he could not ignore the truth: a child born to his wife from another man would never be his and it would be a constant reminder of his own emasculation.

It became apparent that we were both of the mind that if you ignore something for long enough it will eventually go away. I did not know what I was to do, and I had no one around me to ask for support or guidance. I was still absolved from attending Sunday Mass on the grounds of ill-health, but I know Colin Stanley simply couldn't bear to see me, for he no longer brought me Holy Communion like once he would. He had no contact with me and I'm certain he was hoping if he ignored me for long enough I would eventually disappear.

It was not meant to be. I would not disappear, the walls of the cottage holding me, silently reminding me why I had to stay. Why I had to wait for the right time. Why I had to be ready when the time came.

As the light began to rise on the Sunday morning, I felt the fierceness of the tightening in my belly and the heaviness of the ache below. I recognised this ache—a duller version coming before I would bleed—I breathed deeply, innately, knowing the veil was lifting.

I quickly covered the blood spotted sheet and prepared the cloth to soak the blood that I felt engorging me, ready to release. I prepared his breakfast without fuss, despite the spasming pain that periodically gripped me, hoping he would leave quickly to attend to his chores before heading to Mass.

I stripped the sheet from my bed and placed it on the floor between my legs before I lowered myself to my knees, leaning against the bed, legs spread wide, I allowed the blood to gush from me, as it flowed from me desecrating the sheet I surrendered to the agony that had been held in the walls of this room and allowed it to engulf me. It moved through me in waves and I moved with it, intent on allowing it to infiltrate every cell of my being. As the pains gripped me I recoiled deeply into myself, finding momentary refuge and as they passed, I opened, everything within me expanding, the raw ragged edges stretched wide to the allow the rage to ravage me, to chaotically gush through me, stomping at my throat, demanding to be released, to explode in truth, to be free. I pushed when my body screamed at me to push. What I was releasing I did not know, but I forced it from me with ferocity, dispelling this thing from within me.

This thing.

I felt her rise. The powerful spirited little girl within me. It was time and she screamed and thrashed savagely as she unleashed the fury that had kept her hidden for so long. Mercilessly she obliterated the mass that had discharged onto the sheet. She ripped it apart, her nails clawing it, shredding it into pieces, squashing it viciously in the palm of her hands, determined to destroy it. This thing. This filthy poisonous thing. She tore at her face, the divine little elfin face, that was once so innocent and pure. She dragged her blood-stained nails across it, tearing the skin, savagely destroying it. She pulled her hands through her smoky black hair that hung in waves around her mutilated face, a guttural moan echoing around the room as she rocked herself back and forth, her hands pounding her head, leaving clots of blood knotted through her hair. She hated her, that pathetic little girl. That stupid weak little girl. That dirty vulgar little girl. She had begun all this and now she was to be destroyed. She thumped her core, willing the poison that lay within her to consume her, until she collapsed onto the ground, the evidence of her murderous spree surrounding her, her exhaustion depleting her.

That is where I found myself, lying amidst the remains of the dead baby. For I was sure I had seen a baby, a minuscule conglomerate in the form of a baby lying in my hands. And then I was lying on it and in it, with it streaked across my face and through my hair. My insanity terrified me and I curled into foetal position, in a futile attempt to calm myself and to draw myself out of the mania that continued to send waves violently through my body, each one carrying a stronger charge, compelling me to rise, demanding I find them and show them the truth. The truth of what they had done to me. What they had all done to me. They were responsible for this, this abhorrence. As the fervid rage flew through me, I rose and stormed from the cottage. A calmness meeting my derangement, a deep knowing of exactly what I was doing—being guided from something stronger than I that came from both within me and from a calling in the winds that seemed to bellow—urging me to go, to go to them.

Despite my fragility, I walked methodically to that church. My wrath fuelling my power and as I opened the doors that encased them in their spiritual righteousness

I saw him standing behind the pulpit preaching of goodness and love, things he knew nothing about. He was bad, and he was evil and as his eyes struggled to adjust to the influx of light into the darkness of his den, and comprehend the sight of me, daring to darken his holy grail. His sudden silence forced others to turn to look, their frightful gasps a testament to the horrendous sight that met their eyes. I strode forward aggressively, wanting them to feel uncomfortable, needing them to be terrified, mortified, repulsed. I needed them to feel me and all that I had carried for all those years.

I was a mad woman who strode confidently into the church that day with bright red blood strewn across every inch of the precious night gown that Carmel had gifted me to please my husband. My face streaked by the blood that hardened and amassed in the ridges left from scratches. My hair a matted mess, clots of blood, the remnants of his demonic baby, clumping it together in a mass that encased the lunacy of my eyes. I determinedly did not deviate my eyes from his as I strode towards the altar, even as I heard them murmur 'stop her'. I stopped purposefully and grabbed at my crotch and squeezed hard, soaking my hands in the freshness of the clotted blood that continued to release unobstructed from within me. And raising my blood-soaked hands, I spoke with authority as I looked directly at him, standing self-righteously behind his pulpit.

'You will not touch me. You will not silence me. This is the blood of the purest of evil and I will not hesitate to inflict its curse upon you, upon you all. I will be heard.'

I heard the gasps, the whispers, the children cry. I cared for none of it.

I had no fear of what would happen to me after this, I did not care for anything but this moment. This moment, which I had waited patiently to arrive. This moment, I was to re-claim my freedom, the freedom that could only come from owning my story and speaking my truth.

It was time.

Chapter Twenty-two

I stood on the altar, taking his stage and I looked to the congregation. The shock, horror, repulsion evident on their faces. The face of my sister showed confusion, humiliation, sadness. I'm sure I saw sadness there, but I did not want her pity, not now. I wanted her to know the truth, the truth that none of them wanted to acknowledge. The truth of what has been going on *beneath the veil*, the one that they refuse to look beyond for fear of what they will see, what they will see in their own lives.

Carmel tended to her children while their father, Vincent, sat stony faced, his eyes scathing, his mind racing in an attempt to determine what to do. For sure they could have brought me down, but they were so fearful of evil and the prospect of being cursed that they stood down, waiting for himself behind the pulpit to issue them instructions. They failed to see the curse that had already been inflicted upon them. In their righteousness they could not see their own failings, the evil that they perpetrated on others. The Devil was alive and well in many in this small village, but it was not in me.

'The Devil lies within, but it does not lie within me.' Raising my hands and motioning to the blood covering my body, I continued, 'This is the blood of evil, the remains of the foetus that he implanted in me, when he raped me, first with his hands and then with his penis under the disguise of cleansing me. He cleansed me, while my husband stood watch and did nothing. He raped me using the name of God. He did not cleanse me, he poisoned me and today this poison released. And it is time for the poisonous infliction of my soul to be released.'

I paused. I calmed. I steadied.

I looked to Vincent pointing my bloodied finger at him, 'When I was seven years old, he whipped me and when that wasn't enough he began to violate me. For years he violated me in the barn of our farm house, in a way no brother should do to a sister. In a way no man should do to a woman. I hope Carmel he has not raped you as he raped me, causing me to tear and bleed. I hope he has not laid hands on your daughter. Watch him, for he is a beast and cannot be trusted.' I ignored the commotion as Vincent raised from his seat and propelled himself at me. I stood my ground and held my hands at him, like a sorceress of old, holding a curse within my bloodied hands and I was not afraid to use it. Sensing my insanity, they dared not challenge me for they really did not know what they were dealing with. Indeed, it appeared as though something had possessed me. I was possessed, so beautifully possessed by the power of my soul who held me and compelled me to speak my truth, to tell my story, to free myself from the hold they had on me.

I continued. 'I told him in the confessional box when I was but seven years old. I told him what my brother was doing to me, confessing my sin, for indeed I was convinced it was my sin. And he did nothing to stop it. Nothing, but ask me if it gave me pleasure.' I turned from Colin Stanley to Vincent, then to the wider congregation holding them in this truth. 'How can a little girl get pleasure from being raped by her brother?' I asked. 'And that was all he wanted to know. He did nothing. It was my sin, not his for raping me, not his for not stopping it. It was mine and I have carried the shame for all these years. And today I release that shame, this blood, this is my shame and now I return it to you Vincent and to you Colin Stanley. You stood dressed in your holy gowns proclaiming to do the work of God, as you systematically raped me. You did not cleanse me, you did not release me of my darkness, you used your power to inflict your own evil onto me. And you …' I pointed to Dempsey Finnigan, '… you were meant to protect me as my husband, instead you stood and watched while he desecrated me. You coward and weak man. You bought me to be your wife, yet you allowed him to do this to me. It was bad enough that you inflicted yourself on me relentlessly, so you could have a child of your own, locking me away in a room for months at a time, coming to me whenever the urge came, drugging me so I would forget where I was and what you were doing. You blamed me for killing the baby you put in me. You all blamed me. I was not to blame, it is not my shame. It is yours for filling me with toxins and starving me of life and mercilessly forcing yourself on me, treating me like nothing more than an animal. You did this. Let this sit on your soul all the days of your miserable life.' I turned away from him as he sat humiliated in his own self-repulsion. I turned to my family, the family who had so readily abandoned me, who now cowered with shame to be associated with me, this mad woman. I moved ferociously towards Vincent, fearlessly, knowing he had no power over me in that moment. 'You are responsible for this. How could this body carry a baby? How could it possibly ever carry a baby after the terror and trauma you inflicted on me? It stays with me, every day I feel it. Every day I feel it here,' I spat, grabbing at my groin, 'every day and every night, the memory of you bending me over those hay bales haunts me. How could a baby ever thrive in that darkness? You all wonder what went wrong with me, how did Agatha turn out the way she did and me so queer, I know you do? I have seen it in your cruel condemning eyes, from the time I was a child. The looks, the shakes of the head, one so right and one so wrong. How did it happen, did any of you ever dare to ask me what went wrong? Aggie did you ever think to ask me if I was okay, did you ever wonder why I woke screaming with nightmares? Did you ever wonder why I was petrified to do the chores in the barn? Did you ever wonder why he beat me with such venom? No, you never asked me, you didn't care. And Mammy and Da never asked me, they didn't care either. Did you know, Aggie, did you know and just not care? Did he do it to you, Aggie, or was it just me? Why did you pick me? I never did anything to you, to deserve that. I never did anything to anyone to deserve any of this. I wanted to be a little girl and explore the magic in the world and you wouldn't let me. You destroyed me. I wanted to be a good wife, and cook and clean for you, but you wouldn't let me, you just wanted someone to give you a child.'

I returned my gaze to the altar, as he stood still shocked by the outburst, more so by the fact that none of his loyal followers had silenced me.

'And you, Colin Stanley! All I wanted was to be a good girl, you could not let me believe that, in some way you had to see me as the bad girl, the sinner, the one who needed redemption, so you could redeem me, so you could feel almighty and powerful. You knew what he was doing to me as a child and you did nothing. You came to that farmhouse every week to bring me Communion. You knew what he was doing to me, locking me away and drugging me, and you did nothing. You waited for them to destroy me, so you could claim your glory and save me. Cleanse my soul you proclaimed, yet all you were doing was waiting until I was broken enough, until he was desperate enough, weak enough, to allow you to bring your wicked heathen ways into his home and desecrate me. But you did not cleanse my soul, for my soul didn't need cleansing, because none of you … none of you were ever able to reach my soul. My soul is sacred, and she is Divine, and you may have broken my body and you may have broken my mind, but, you did not break me. I am not my body. I am not my mind. I am *her*. None of you touched *her* and none of you broke *her*. She remains within me and it is *her* who has given me the courage to speak my truth, it is *her* who is holding me. She is a reflection of God, the pure Divine Light. Not the God that you speak of. The God who does not love. The God who controls through fear. The God who takes advantage of the weak and misuses its power.

That is not my God. My God loves me and holds me. My God is light and is truth. It is not the Devil in me today, it is my God. Divine. Grace. Light.'

Exhausted, I collapsed on the altar.

Free. Finally, free.

Chapter Twenty-three

I don't know how I got there.

My welcome on arrival to the Magdalene Laundry, in Galway, defined exactly what was to come for my stay. My bloodied clothes were striped from me. I stood naked in a freezing shower block as they inspected me. There were two of them, old with hardened faces. One the superior, the other her dutiful servant. They looked with disdain, up and down my body, pulling at clumps of my tangled mass of hair.

The exhaustion of what transpired earlier that day in the church silenced me. My mind awash with the nothingness that I had become so familiar with.

'This one is trouble to be sure. And I have seen

plenty of bad ones in my time here, don't you know it, Sister Therese,' Mother Superior crooned, as she circled me like a black crow planning her attack.

'Indeed, you have, Mother. Many a very bad girl has crossed this here threshold, stood where this one stands, sinful and a disgrace to her family, a threat to the community. Best locked away here with us, under the watchful eye of you Mother, and God himself,' the dutiful one chimed, desperately seeking approval.

'Father Colin Stanley, a grand man he is, says she's well and truly possessed by the Devil himself. Clearly insane to all who witnessed her demonic attack on himself, her own husband, and brother. I've a right to cut that venomous tongue from your mouth right here and now, so ye never will be able to speak ill of those fine men again. But no … cutting away your tongue will not serve. I see, too clearly, that those heinous stories, are well embedded in your mind. The lies, the heathen tales of those good men, come from here,' Mother Superior said, as she thumped the side of my head with the base of her hand which sent jarring waves through my whole body. 'Not from here,' she concluded, slapping the side of my mouth fiercely.

I did not react. She did not realise that I was held by the nothingness, where nothing more could touch me after the trauma I had already experienced. I know she wanted to break me, and she would prove herself relentless in this pursuit, but right then, her venom and violence could not infiltrate the steely layer that engulfed me. Not even the bitter icy water from the hose she pelted over me, like nails piercing my skin, could rouse me. She ensured every inch of my body was scrubbed, eradicating any sign of the trauma that brought me here. They took scissors to my tangled mass of hair, clumps falling at my feet, before scouring it with soap and boiling water and scrubbing until my scalp bled. They were cruel and merciless. A part of me thinks they enjoyed it, playing their part in the cleansing of society, asserting their power over fragile young girls and vulnerable women. They claimed to be saving souls from the perils of evil, yet they inflicted further evil under the guise of goodness and destroyed many a young girl.

I would not let them break me. I would not allow myself to go through a never-ending revolving door of Hell, from one soul destroying experience to another. I had to do this differently, I still felt the power within me, the power that took me into the church and gave me a voice to speak, to release the rage that had crippled me and kept me powerless for so long. I would not allow myself to be disempowered again. Not by these women who were intent on punishing me. They had been well-informed of my actions in the church that day and were under instructions to ensure that mad woman never opened her mouth again. I knew I needed to be wise and cunning, listening and watching, hovering in the wings, so I was not seen and didn't draw attention to myself. Whilst keeping my head low, I needed to learn who was *who* and what was *what* to decipher whom I could trust, who I could use to help me. I knew my discernment became blurred by fear and it was imperative that I held onto the nothingness so that the fear had no power over me. I didn't know that the nothingness would prove to be my saviour during the months that I was held prisoner within the walls of this hell, called The Magdalene Laundry.

An institution that destroyed the lives of thousands of women, it was a cruel and sad place. I knew I could not connect with any of the girls, for if I opened my heart to them, to be sure it would have broken. The more broken and vulnerable you were, the more you proved to be a target for Mother Superior who seemed repulsed by their weakness. I saw more than one woman dying a sad and lonely death. I saw a number of girls removed from their beds at night never to return. I didn't know what happened to them. I couldn't let myself think about them. I needed to keep my wits about me to ensure I was not one of those women or girls, nor one of those picked out by Mother Superior to spend the afternoon with the visiting priests. I heard the whispers amongst the girls, I was not naïve to what was going on. I took no part in it. I did not speak to the others. I was polite when asked questions of the nuns and I did my work. I had spent a lifetime blending into the background, intent on not being seen or drawing attention to myself, it was a skill that stood me in good stead to safely navigate the minefield that was that godforsaken place. Perhaps, Vincent's years of abuse was a gift in disguise because my innate survival instinct served me well.

Mother Superior spent the first few weeks bitterly punishing me or directing others to. I would not take her wicked bait as she lured me into rage, relentlessly questioning me about what my brother, husband, and her beloved Colin Stanley had done to me. I knew what she was doing provoking me in this way and I would not walk into her trap and allow the rage. The rage could not blow my mind, not then, for it had lost its power over me when I finally allowed myself to release it. She wanted to push me over the edge, to prove my insanity, but I would not budge. I gave her nothing and she soon became bored with me. I was neither weak to repulse her, nor strong enough to threaten her; therefore, I was not of interest in her quest to exert her power. Gratefully she moved her attention from me within a matter of weeks and I became just another of the dull grey souls who existed within the walls of this depraved institution.

I prayed every day, not to their God. I prayed to my God, the one I knew loved me and was holding me safe in the nothingness. I didn't know what a life outside of here would look like now, for I was certain I would not be welcomed back by my husband or my brother. I knew that village would never be home to me again and I never wanted it to be. I fantasised about a life across the great Atlantic in the Americas. I had read about the Americas in all those books. How I was to get there I truly did not know, but it gave me great peace to put my mind to something so expansive as the possibility of one day living a life in a whole new world.

Prayers are often delivered in the most unexpected of ways. As I stood folding sheets at my station devoid of conversation and connection, Mother Superior came striding across the room towards me. I was stunned that her attention was focussed on me, for I could not figure out what I had done which might draw her attention.

'You! Come with me immediately.'

I could tell she was irritated and that something was unsettling her. I was offered no explanation as I followed her nervously to a part of the building I had never been. It was beyond the closed doors, which we were never allowed to go past, a completely different world, one that was almost resplendent in its luxury compared to the cramped cold conditions in which we were kept. As I walked into a room, I was surprised to see Aggie, she was sitting on a chair waiting patiently, confidently, looking more assured and beautiful than ever before.

'Thank you, Mother Superior. I will deal with her now. I will be sure and tell Father Stanley that you were most accommodating in his request for information,' asserted Aggie, as she stood, moving towards me.

'Right you are then,' she replied somewhat cautiously. 'And yes, make sure you get all you need for Father Stanley, a grand man, sure he is, and so good of him to remain concerned for the state of this one after all she did to blacken his name. I don't know why he'd bother myself, a lost cause no doubt. I'll leave you to decipher that for yourself.'

    Mother Superior turned, walked from the room holding her head high, proud of her accomplishments, righteous in her way forward, intent on saving more heathen souls.

Chapter Twenty-four

I looked at my sister warily, I was reluctant to be here with her. I felt a well of emotion rising from anger and resentment, to grief and shame. I needed the nothingness to hold me, but something in Aggie's presence made me feel more vulnerable than I had in all the months I had been here. As Mother Superior exited the room, Aggie turned to me and her eyes conveyed a sadness, yet she spoke with coldness and disdain.

'Right you, I have come here to check in on you. Father Stanley has asked me to see to the state of your head, to check to see if the madness has left you. Let me look closely at you.' She approached me slowly and as she stood in front of me, she looked deeply into my eyes, whispering, 'Clara, I am so sorry,' a tear rolled down her cheek, then she sternly raised her voice, 'you certainly don't seem to have much to say, Father Stanley will be pleased to hear that,' she winked, and pointed to the door and her ear. 'I will rightly inform Father Stanley that Mother Superior has done wonders with you. He did say she was a remarkable woman, tough but fair, he will be pleased to hear that she has not disappointed his expectations.' Aggie paused as we heard Mother Superior marching away from the door, her sense of self-importance overflowing.

Aggie grabbed me, wrapping her arms tightly around me. I did not respond, for I did not understand. I was unaccustomed to acts of affection and could not recall the last time someone had hugged me. That made me sad, ever so sad. As she released her hold on me, she looked at me and ran her fingers through my short ugly fuzzy hair.

'Oh, Clara, what have they done to you?' she cried, overcome with what I could only describe as deep remorse. 'I must be quick, Clara, she is no fool that Mother Superior. I'm after telling her that himself sent me to check in on you, but he never did, no one knows I am here. I couldn't sleep another night not knowing if you were alive or dead. Vincent went away to Dublin and Father Stanley is off visiting his family somewhere in Cork, so I told Carmel I was going away myself for the day. I didn't tell her I was coming for ye, Clara. I couldn't, for I know she would have told Vincent and then there'd be awful trouble. What sort of sister, am I? I am sorry I didn't know. I should have known. Maybe I did, maybe I just didn't want to know, but I am riddled with guilt, for either way I let you down,' she paused, looking so sincerely at me, desperate for me to respond. The words would not come from me and as I was so accustomed to remaining silent, I allowed her to speak without interruption. I listened intently to her words, soaking up the connection I felt to her, for I did not know when, or if, I would ever feel such a connection again.

'You see, I believe you, Clara, I think a lot of people believe you but are too frightened to admit it to themselves, or anyone else. It is easier not believing you and calling you mad. When I thought about it, after you said all you did in the church that day, I knew what you were saying was true. I could see it in your eyes. Everyone was after saying your eyes looked like a mad woman's, but I saw you in there. I saw my fiery spirited little sister, the one I hadn't made enough time to even realise was missing. I just thought you went all strange when we were kids, I was too caught up in my own nonsense to really take much notice. When I thought about it, it all made sense. You did go awful odd, but it was at the same time, that Vincent started picking on you fiercely, especially during the times our father was away. And you would have the dreams and then not sleep. I was only ever after thinking of myself and being annoyed that you'd be waking me up with your screams. I never asked you why you were screaming. I never asked you why you would cower whenever you were in the same room as him. I just thought you were queer. And you always were a little different even before all that, always after running around and talking to the animals, especially Trinity, and talking to the flowers and the trees. A right queer little one you were, but there was so much joy in you then, and I realise that was what disappeared. There was no joy left in you, no spirit, Clara. I don't know why I didn't seem to care, or Mammy, I don't know why she didn't do something to figure out what was going on. I think she was afraid of him. I think we were all afraid of him, the way we are now. He beats the kids awful fierce these days. After the church thing, he was so angry, scarily silent in his anger, and he took it out on little Mary. Oh, Clara it was a terror to watch and we couldn't stop him, no matter what we said, Carmel and I, he wouldn't stop until she was beaten and bruised, the wee little one, only four years old herself. They missed you awfully, Clara, when you left to live with himself. I should have come and visited you, checked in on how you were going and the like, you know, all that married people stuff. But Vincent forbade it and I'll admit I was too caught up with my own romance nonsense to give you much thought. I am riddled with guilt, Clara. I have failed you. I have to make good of these failings, in the hope that one day you will find it in your heart to forgive me,' she looked to the floor in shame.

    I had never seen Aggie so vulnerable, nor had I ever heard her speak such truths, especially daring to speak ill of Vincent.

'Aggie, I forgive you. It takes too much of me, to keep resenting ye all for letting me down. I let that all go, the day in the church. And you are right, never was there a day where I was more myself than that very one. It saved me from me. And sure, I ended up in here and it's a dreadful place, Aggie. The Devil's work goes on beyond these walls at the hands of that woman, so you be careful, you hear me? She is dangerous and won't take kindly to trickery.'

I realised Aggie was not as strong as I had always thought. I had held her on a pedestal for so long, for she appeared so assured of herself, and even though she knew how to manipulate Mother Superior to get herself through the door and access to me, I could now see her powerlessness and I feared for her if she didn't escape from Vincent, Colin Stanley and the whole malicious village.

I continued, 'Aggie, you have to get out, away from them. Why don't you take yourself to Dublin, England or even the Americas? I've read about it. You could be free then, Aggie. You're not meant to be stuck in a farm house in a small village, you are meant for more in this world. You always were.'

'Clara, please don't worry about me. I will get myself sorted somehow. I know I will get myself out of there. You showed me the truth of it all, the truth I and others were reluctant to see. And while many prefer to stick with what they know, and the way things were,

I cannot. It's impossible for me not to see what you revealed, the darkness that dictates our lives. I will get out, but first I must free you from here. I will never be able to live with myself in England or in the Americas knowing you are stuck in this dreadful place.'

Aggie squeezed my hands tightly and gave me a look of determination that reminded me of the Aggie of my childhood. If she put her mind to something she would no doubt get her way. I felt a flicker of hope, yet I dared not allow it to ignite, not now. Hope was dangerous in a place like this, it could only lead to more desperation and heartache.

'Get Aunt Maeve! You must find Aunt Maeve, tell her to come. She will know what to do, she will know how to get me out of here. She begged me to leave with her the night of Mother's funeral, but I said no. I was too scared of what he would do. I should have gone with her then. You have to find her, she lives in the village of Quilty, it's about twenty-miles along the coast line there from home. Perhaps now she will come for me,' I said, quickly knowing that we would not be left for much longer.

'I will go to her, Clara, I promise you. I will figure out a way to get there myself and I'll beg her to help me get you out of here. And then, you can start all over again.'

Aggie grabbed me, this time I softened into her embrace, allowing myself to feel her sorrow and her love. There were many experiences in the years that were to come that helped me to heal, but none so profound or transformative as this one. For love and compassion are the most powerful of healers and Aggie and I shared that gift in that moment.

As we heard the brisk footsteps marching towards the door we quickly separated, and Aggie gently pushed me to my knees before her. She began circling me. I lowered my head so as not to smirk at her trickery as Mother Superior entered the room and stomped towards us.

'I trust you have completed your investigation for Father Stanley?' she inquired directly.

'Indeed, I have Mother Superior. I look forward to passing on the good news to Father Stanley, for it is clear that the good work that you do here in exiling the lunacy from the fallen ones, most effective, I say. This one has no recollection of any of the events she once spoke of in God's holy house. It appears she is completely mute, I am confident that there is no chance of further malicious outcry against Father Stanley nor the other fine standing men of our village. Indeed, you have done your finest of work in saving this one's soul, for as one who witnessed the debauch performance that day, I had my doubts whether anything could save this one, so depraved was she!' Aggie exclaimed, indulging in her own performance.

'Well that is what we are here for, be sure to tell Father Stanley should he be needing further assistance with any other ones of her kind, to be sending them my way. I will do my very best to serve him and the good Lord in ridding them of their heathen ways.'

Mother Superior walked Aggie from the room, leaving me to pray secret silent prayers to my God, that one day, Aunt Maeve might come and take me home with her.

> *'Mother Mary, brightest light, watch over me and guide me home.*
> *Keep me safe within these walls sparing me from the suffering and abuse, maintaining my strength through my silence and my courage through your deepest love.*
> *I remember that I am worthy of your unconditional love and nurture and I welcome it now to shelter and protect me, until their return.'*

Chapter Twenty-five

Aunt Maeve arrived some five weeks later.

Those five weeks were by far the hardest of my time in the Magdalene Laundry. I clung desperately to the nothingness, yet the possibility of a life beyond here certainly challenged it, and the ugly realities of life inside began to touch me. I knew it was crucial that I did not allow myself to feel, because in feeling I would become vulnerable. My mind would begin to reconnect to old pains and the voice I had wisely kept silent for so many months would demand to be heard once again. I knew should that happen there was no way I would ever be allowed to leave; the label of insanity would stick permanently. I had instinctively held myself so well and I felt the risk of all that crumbling, each day a little more.

I had trusted in Aggie and I had begun to wonder whether I was a fool to do so. She proved herself to be a master manipulator, fooling Mother Superior, yet I wondered if she was playing me the whole time. I questioned if she was ever intending on finding Aunt Maeve, if she just needed to come here to see me and clear her own conscious. These thoughts wreaked havoc on my resolve particularly of a night when, despite the physical exhaustion, I found it impossible to sleep. That space, in the darkness of the night, was dangerous and I found myself increasingly turning to prayer to get me through.

I prayed in desperation to Mother Mary. I begged her to help me to hold onto the nothingness which had been my saviour yet became more and more tenuous. And one night, as the darkness tickled at my throat, I grabbed the sanctioned rosary beads which I had previously refused to touch, subtly rejecting all they projected onto me. It was a sliver of independence in a world strictly controlled by the programs of others, but I had spent a lifetime controlled by the church and I refused to allow myself to willingly partake in any form of prayer that was prescribed when I was not forced to. I was forced to attend Mass daily and mutter the rote prayers, but I was not the one saying them, it was my voice, but I was not that voice. They forced me to receive Communion, but I was not in Communion with the Jesus Christ that they projected onto me. They forced me to confession, and again I was not the voice who recited the scripted

'Forgive me, Father, for the sins of my past. I seek absolution from the darkness of my soul.' I would not say the rosary prescribed to me for my penance, instead I would kneel and pray deeply to Mother Mary, whom I did not need to seek forgiveness because I could feel her love for me at all times.

Yet on this night, during those challenging five weeks, I instinctively took the rosary beads in hand and connected with Mother Mary. I walked with her through the decades of the rosary. I haltered as I began the Our Father, as I did not want to pray to their Father, but I clearly heard a gentle nurturing voice telling me 'Honour the Father, Clara, for he lives within you, too.' I did not understand those words, not then, but I trusted her wisdom. All my years of isolation and insomnia was proving to be a gift, as I had developed a very strong sense of intuition, which allowed me at times like this, when I needed higher guidance, to listen to the wisdom which was always there, but so often hard to connect with. It was only when he drugged me for all those months, I truly lost this connection and it wasn't until it was gone that I realised how much I had relied on it to support and guide me during all those years of trauma. I suppose this was my greatest fear, that if the nothingness left me, I would lose this connection and I would be truly lost.

As I focussed on each bead and connected to each word of each prayer, the structured repetitive nature of the rosary proved powerful in holding me in the nothingness. As I connected with the rosary it took me beyond the walls that threatened to close in on me, it took me into a great expanse of nothingness which was where I felt safe, held, protected. My rosary went with me everywhere, tucked safely away around my neck during the day, secured in the palm of my hand of a night. It was the rosary that saved me from imploding while I waited for Aunt Maeve to come for me.

Word came through in whispers that there was a visitor, for they were few and far between, and a sense of anticipation filled the work room. Every girl and woman in that place dreamt that one day someone would come for them, that they would be released. And it was true, some were, one every now and then, but for many it proved a life sentence, dying as old women having not lived in the outside world for decades. A tragedy of monumental proportion, that threatened to break my heart whenever I thought about it, and the possibility that it could have been my story.

Aunt Maeve came for me.

Aggie having secretly sent word via a Gypsy she met in the village. She took a huge risk in speaking to him, for had she been seen, she would have been in awful trouble. He told her he knew Maeve and had heard what had happened to Clara.

I was marched from the work room to the waiting room where weeks before I had met with Aggie. I did not collect anything from my bed, for there was nothing of mine to collect. I did not say goodbye to the other women, for I had never connected with any of them. I did not turn around as I walked through the front door with Aunt Maeve gently guiding me, her hand on the small of my back, for I was determined to leave this behind me. I already had enough burden to carry without letting everything within and about the Magdalene Laundry infiltrate me.

I ached with curiosity to know how Aunt Maeve had managed to secure my release, but I dared not ask and the look I got from Aunt Maeve was one that suggested it was better I did not know. I didn't care. I was finally free. Completely free for the first time since that fateful day with Trinity and the boy in the tree, the day that seemingly changed everything.

It was too long a journey to return to Aunt Maeve's home that day, so we stayed in Galway the night. My father's people were from Galway, something I had not even considered whilst locked away. There had been no contact with them after my father passed. I later discovered from Aggie that the gossip suggested they did not take kindly to Vincent and the manner in which he took over the farm as soon as father died. They also had not so subtly expressed concern about how father had died, given he was so experienced on the tractor, having driven one from the time he was a child himself, to flip it over. It had been suggested that Vincent may have had something to do with father's death, with the intent of claiming the farm. My spine tingled when I first heard of these rumours from Aggie, for I did not doubt that

Vincent was capable of such a murderous act.

    Aunt Maeve insisted she bathe me once we had settled into the lodgings. As I lay soaking in a warm tub, she gently washed my mop of cropped hair. The nuns kept all the women's hair short to prevent lice and the like from running rampant, not that it worked. I think it was just another way to dehumanise and demoralise the women, taking any form of beauty from the self or life away. Whilst somewhat wary of Aunt Maeve, given our last meeting had seen me blindly trust in her and suffer severe punishment as a consequence, it also felt so good for someone to care for me. The last time anyone had tended to me was on the morning of the funeral when Aunt Maeve loving helped me make myself presentable once again. The irony was not lost on me. This was the second time she had come to my rescue, nurturing me. I knew that nothing was going to stop me from going with her, for I had nowhere else to go. Whilst I felt a deep loving connection to her, I was intimidated by her power. It was evident that she was incredibly powerful at getting what she desired. I was to learn that she knew when and how to use this power and it was not something that she needed to activate often. She seemed drained since we left the Magdalene Laundry, she was dreadfully quiet, only murmuring gentle instructions and basic information about our movements for the evening. I do not know what transpired between her and Mother Superior in that room, even though she had triumphed as she walked away with me, her victory looked to come at a cost.

It was only the next morning, after a solid sleep and a decent breakfast, which I greedily devoured, did she seem to regain her spark. It was then that she informed me of how Aggie had got word to her and how she had made her way to me as quickly as she could, hoping desperately that she was not too late. Aggie had told her that I was fine in the head but seemed very vulnerable and she wasn't sure how much longer I would last in that place. Having come out the other side, I was able to reflect on how I had navigated that experience. Surprisingly, I felt a pride for holding myself so well, for being so strong.

'Clara, the spirit is powerful, especially when it is returned to you. I have a rather strong feeling that you reclaimed your spirit when you walked into the church that day and told the truth about those men. Oh, yes!'

I was shocked that she knew about that day.

'Your old Mother Superior there took great pleasure in dictating to me the extent of your 'lunacy' and warned me that you were indeed a 'darkened soul' riddled with the Devil before you came into her care. She was most proud of herself for ridding you, of himself, and silencing the voice of lunacy which preceded you.' Aunt Maeve continued, in a teasing way, mocking Mother Superior, she said, "Be sure I left her in no doubt that I was able to rid you of all that wickedness, you heathen!" she laughed. Although, I was a little confused by her, I giggled partly through the shame, it was such a relief to make light of it all. It always felt heavy and so serious. And here Aunt Maeve was making light of my insanity.

'From what I have learnt through my many years now, my girleen, is our insanity is our freedom. From within the chaos of lunacy comes a sense of calm, as you release the shackles that kept you trapped in a world prescribed by another. It is insane to stay chained to a world dictated by another, when the world itself offers us such freedom. Our world is full of wonder and beauty when we open our eyes and mind, when we allow ourselves to finally see once again what is there, waiting for us each morning as the sun appears, and each evening as the moon rises to bless us with her magic light. Do you remember the magic and beauty of it, Clara?'

I nodded, as a well of regret rose within me. 'A little, I remember how much I once loved being outdoors and roaming about with Trinity, but I can't remember the last time I looked through those eyes that you describe, Aunt Maeve. Those eyes that look with wonder at the world. There's been so much happen and it's been so long since I felt like that about anything. I don't know where she went that little girl with those eyes. I don't know if I can get her back?' I said, as the tears rolled down my cheek. I began grieving a loss of part of me, which until that moment I didn't realise was missing.

'I was witness to the day you lost her, your beautiful free spirit, my Clara. It was on your First Communion day, when you stood in front of himself, at that altar, a wee girl dressed in white, stained with blood. I saw you, the magical spark in your eyes, that had always excited and intrigued me, fade away when you chose to stay silent. When you stopped yourself from naming him, he who had beaten you. Do you remember that, Clara?'

Once again, I nodded. Deep regret and shame surged through my stomach.

'I was so scared of them, Colin Stanley, Vincent and McDermott, all standing there in front of me filled with self-importance, all imposing and judgemental, and I thought keeping my mouth shut was the smartest thing to do.'

'You thought,' Aunt Maeve paused, patting my now cleanly brushed hair, 'that was the problem, my dear. You are not meant to be a thinker, you are a feeler. Do you understand?' she asked with affection.

I understood her words but not her meaning.

'All babies when they are born, innately feel their way through life. If they feel hungry they cry, cold they cry, wet they cry. They use their feelings to guide their behaviours, much like animals do because their brain is not so developed. As babies grow and develop and their minds grow they start to become thinkers more than feelers. They think what they should do, rather than feel into what to do. But you were different, you didn't let the mind detract you from feeling your way through life. You were so connected to the animals and the land from such a young age, you would act from that place, where you just knew things, rather than thought things.

I could always see it in you and I loved that you held it for so long.'

'I do sort of see what you mean. I can remember that, but Vincent use to tell me I was daft and queer, I really did feel like I was not as smart as him and Aggie.'

'Oh, Clara, he would belittle you in that way, because he knew that you were wiser, more knowing than he could ever dream to be, and often this is a threat to the like of him. You are smarter than the two of them combined, you always were. It was desperate to watch you on your First Communion day, not because of the blood on your dress, nor because they shamed and threatened you. I despaired as I saw you start *thinking* what you should do, and as your thinking overtook your sense of knowing, you lost your connection to your beautiful wise spirit, and because of that he was able to get to you. They always do, the like of Colin Stanley and Vincent. If they don't break you that first time, they go at you again and again until they break your spirit and then they take advantage of you. Indeed, it is a tragedy, but it is a story as old as time, one that we as women must learn to break. When we hold our spirit regardless of their attack, nothing can touch us.'

'I know that.' I surprised myself with this knowing. 'Aunt Maeve, I know this. I know the nothing and when the nothing is there then nothing can touch me. I did not know what the nothingness was, but it came to me after … after he …'

'Colin Stanley?' she asked.

'... yes, after he did those things to me. It enveloped me, and nothing got in. The same thing happened when I was there, in that place, it held me sort of in a bubble, this awfully strange but lovely feeling of just nothing.' I smiled reflecting on that feeling, and then realised that it was no longer with me. 'Why can't I feel it now, the nothingness? Does that mean my spirit has gone again? Will I have to go through it all again? Oh, I couldn't possibly!'

'Settle down, it's grand. The nothingness as you call it, has lifted, that is all. It doesn't need to protect you in the way it was. Indeed, Clara, you must have been sending some powerful prayers out there to someone or something to have held you in such a cocoon like that. You are blessed. Blessed indeed!' she shook her head with an amused awe on her face.

My life had been anything but blessed, I certainly did not feel blessed, but through Aunt Maeve's teachings, which had just begun, I would learn that my life had indeed been a blessing, should I wish to see the blessing. Often her teachings left me confused, yet I believe that was her purpose because when we are confused, we simply don't know the answers, possibility exists, and when we know all the answers we limit ourselves, to exactly that which we know. Many a time, she left me completely bewildered and I learnt to embrace the mystery of not knowing—letting go of the need to know—allowing myself to *feel* my way through life once again. I connected into my feelings. I gradually

connected back into the flow of life.
>
> This time life was completely different.
> Life was beautiful.

Chapter Twenty-six

Clara was true in sensing my exhaustion as we walked through the darkened doors of the Magdalene Laundry, both silently vowing never to return. Whilst exhilarated that I had managed to secure freedom for my niece, I was burdened by the guilt of leaving so many others behind. Other women who may never have someone come for them. Other women whose stories were no different to mine or Clara's, but whose ending would be different.

That night, as Clara lay sleeping peacefully beside me in bed, I prayed silent prayers of forgiveness, seeking the forgiveness of others and in turn forgiving myself and releasing the guilt which threatened to plague me. Clara needed the best of me as a nurturer and teacher, if she was going to rise above the traumas of her past.

And so, I prayed,

*'I am sorry to all the girls and women
I did not free. Please forgive me.
I am sorry that I let you down. Please forgive me.
I am sorry I did not give you a voice. Please
forgive me.
I am sorry that I was not strong enough to fight
for you. Please forgive me.
I am sorry that I used my power only to placate.
Please forgive me.
I am sorry I did not believe in my strength as a
woman. Please forgive me.
I am sorry I was not ready to step into the
fullness of my power. Please forgive me.
I am sorry to every woman who had a baby
stripped from her. Please forgive me.
To every woman who was disrespected and
disempowered by a man. Please forgive me.
To every woman who suffered at the hands of
the patriarch. Please forgive me.
To every woman who was shamed into believing
she was worthless. Please forgive me.
To every woman who was told she was insane.
Please forgive me.
To every woman who was made to believe she
was powerless. Please forgive me.
To every woman who forgot her strength as a
woman. Please forgive me.*

*I am sorry I didn't know how to make it different. Please forgive me.
I am sorry I wasn't ready to make it different. Please forgive me.
I vow I will make it different now, through my words and my teachings, I will make it different.'*

I felt enormous relief wash over me as I made this vow and I also chose to forgive all those I held grievance towards, so I was not attached to the stories connecting me to them. In forgiving them I freed myself from being a victim to their actions and I moved beyond the story and empowered myself to truly be present with Clara. It would be through the work I did with her that I would fulfil my vow to make a difference.

She was the one who took my baby from me all those years ago, the woman they called Mother Superior, an unworthy title for she was not the superior mother. She tarnished the name of the Mother by the wickedness she inflicted onto other women, allowing herself to be nothing but a puppet of the patriarch. She condemned those women who entered her door, relishing her role as judge and holding women in their shame and trauma. The Mother I knew was one of love and it was this love that freed women of their trauma. It was her that I connected to when my own mother passed, she was the Mother that guided me to my freedom, she is the Mother that Clara will grow to love and honour, the Mother who taught me how to embrace my power as a woman, the Mother who embodied the essence of both Mother Mary and Mary Magdalene.

> *She, the nurturer and the fighter;*
> *the sun and the moon;*
> *the light and the dark;*
> *the day and the night;*
> *the gentle and the fierce.*
> *She, the Mother and the Teacher.*

I forgave Mother Superior for what she had done to me and to others, allowing me to see her through a compassionate lens and to remember she is no different to me, an essence of the Divine, having a human experience. I accepted her for where she was in her own evolution, in her remembering of her true essence. I prayed that she may find this within herself and share it with those she was entrusted to care for, that she may return to love and live from this place. This was not the first time I had done this work with Mother Superior, for my forgiveness of her had been an instrumental part of my own healing. Yet my encounter with her that afternoon, had triggered some of my old memories, revealed aspects that required further healing and in turn gifted me with remembering the power of forgiveness, compassion, loving kindness. I was grateful for the experience as I knew that I would need to teach Clara these tools so that she may truly regain her freedom.

One of the greatest lessons I learnt, all those years

ago, after leaving the village and the people who treated me so cruelly was that freedom does not come from being outside the walls of a building. I naïvely believed that in moving away from the limiting constraints of the village, church and closed-minded people that I was freeing myself from all of them. But my memories and the stories I had created about my life in the village and other people came with me. I believed that I was a victim of their cruel actions, but the truth was I chose to be a victim to their actions by creating a story that kept me trapped in that space. My freedom did not come from being outside the boundaries of that village, my freedom came from being outside the walls that I had constructed within myself. No one kept me imprisoned except my belief that I was a victim, and the stories I created to keep me in that space. It was these stories I relentlessly told myself about what occurred that proved to be the only thing that was trapping me and keeping me separate from the freedom that was always there, and available to me, should I wished to remember it and choose to claim it.

Every experience I had and continue to have is an opportunity for me to evolve—it is never the actions of another that limits me—it is the choice I make, in response to each experience I have that determines whether I am free or whether I imprison myself. To get to this point, I had to look to my past and own my stories, which was extremely distressing, because I, like most people, had chosen to try and forget. Yet when I looked at all the stories I had created around my life experience to that point and took responsibility for the part I played in each story, I learnt that every experience offered me the opportunity to be empowered or disempowered, to rise from the victim or remain stuck in the victim.

I learnt that it was never the actions of another that limited me, it was what I did with the experience. My experiences were gifts to enable me to grow into my greatness, when I allowed myself to receive them like this. When I released myself from the stories I had told myself about who did things to me, and let go of all the blame and accusations, all the I'm right and they are wrong, and offered forgiveness and compassion, it was then that I began to break down the walls of my own limited thinking. It was then that I began to blossom and truly live again, in peace and contentment.

Clara had much to heal and much to learn. I recognised that it would not be an easy path. In many ways, I knew the trauma she had experienced was deeply embedded in her soul. Her eyes told me she was a victim and that she was powerless to the world, that all these experiences happened to her and she was unable do anything to change it because she had never been in control of her own life, she had allowed other people to control her experience of life.

The more she spoke of the nothingness that enveloped her after Colin Stanley raped her, the more I realised that something profound had awakened in Clara during that experience. Sometimes, it takes the most shocking events to derail life, to destroy all that we were. I believe that this is what happened to Clara. The shock was so great that she stopped functioning as the puppet she had become and this allowed the 'nothingness' as Clara called it, the 'loving protective nurture of great spirit' as I call it, to come and hold her—while she reset and realigned back onto her true path—where none of the outside realities of life could touch her, because she was held. It was in this space that her beautiful soul began to reawaken, and while she had been propelled into further trauma by ending up in the laundry after she revealed her true self that day in the church, I knew she was still there. Fortunately, Mother Superior had not been able to touch her, the real Clara. The great spirit had come and held her in the wonder of her nothingness. I knew the real Clara was still there because I could see a flicker in her eyes of a fiery spirit that was intent on being remembered, waiting to be guided through the unravelling of layers that was keeping her true essence trapped within her.

I was to guide and teach her the ways of reconnecting to the powerful wise woman who lived within her, just as I had been taught by Cynthia, my beloved teacher, and friend.

It was a chance meeting, that morning in The Burren, all those years ago, but Cynthia assured me that it was not a coincidence that she was sitting there that morning, waiting for me. She had known I would leave the village one day, when the time was right, and she would find me and take me under her wing and help me to rise again. She had recognised the 'otherworldliness', as she called it, about me when I was a child and she had kept a close eye on me. She had heard along the gypsy trail, for she herself never returned to the village from which she escaped, that my deep devotion to God had seen me enter the convent and she prayed that it would not steal my soul and destroy my connection to the true beauty of God. I didn't understand to begin with what she meant by the 'true beauty of God', but that is where she began her teachings with me, reconnecting me to the God that lives within the world around us.

Cynthia was a friend, the only friend I had at that time. We would meet in the early mornings, sometimes of a night, to walk amongst nature and talk. She would bring vegetables to my cottage and we would delight in cooking clean fresh meals together, honouring the food that nature had provided. We would sit under the moon and the stars and she would talk to me about the vastness of the Universe, beyond the west coast villages of Ireland, the only world that I knew. I would look in awe and wonder at the magnificence of the Universe that I had sadly forgotten. As the stars twinkled in the darkness of the night sky, she reminded me that even amidst the darkest of nights there is always light, even if we would not let ourselves see it.

Cynthia would reflect and gently remind me, saying, 'Maeve, even in the middle of the darkest nights of my soul, where I struggled between a deep calling to leave the life I was living to reclaim my freedom against my duty to my child and a husband I despised, I would stare for hours out the window at the moon.' She said, 'There is always hope even if it is only a sliver, it is always present, just like the moon. And it is this belief, that the light is always there, even if we cannot see it with our own eyes, that reminds us that we are never alone, and we are always in beautiful union with the Divine Light.'

I did not fully understand then.

I just listened as Cynthia shared the power of her story, 'I was sick of looking at the moon from behind a pane of glass, separated on so many levels from the Divine Light that called to me. I wanted to bask in her glory, to remember my union with her and dance in her light, free.'

I sacrificed my son Padraig to dance in the moonlight and reclaim my connection to the Divine. A selfish act many may say and one that has caused me much grief over the years, especially when I hear of the man he has become. I feel so sad for he represents the masculine that suppresses the beauty of the feminine, yet I know that this was his destiny because this was his father's path and he chose to follow him. I have reconciled within myself, that should I have stayed in that home with him, I would be betraying my calling to my true Self and living that life for Padraig. I would never have been powerful enough to influence him differently anyway, for I was so removed from the true essence of myself as a woman. My calling was to reclaim my own feminine, and in turn be the teacher for other woman just like you, Maeve, as you will be for others.'

Whilst contemplating the power of Cynthia's words and learning of the sacrifice she had made to be with me, as my teacher, I asked, 'Will I teach others?'

Cynthia explained in our conversation a deep knowing, guiding me, 'Yes, and you already know who your first student will be, just as I always knew that one day you would come, when the time was right.'

I replied, 'I think it is Clara. My sweet little Clara, but Cynthia they are already destroying her, your son and Colin Stanley and the like. Just as they did to me. Why can't I save her now, why does she have to be broken like me before I can teach her?'

'Because she is not yours to save, Maeve, just as you were not mine to save. It is the path that she must take to learn how it feels to be so disempowered by the masculine, which in turn will stimulate her rising.'

'But why does it have to be that way. Why must she be broken before she rises again?' I asked.

'She doesn't. We can learn our lessons through joy or struggle. But for now, she chooses struggle, for that is all that she knows. She does not yet know how to allow herself to grow from joy, for she does not have great women showing her a different way. Not yet anyway. My vision is that one day all women will know their power and all little girls will grow knowing no different. They will know their power as women, they will know both the beauty and fierceness of the feminine, they will know her, and they will honour the masculine that resides within themselves and within all men.'

'But why don't we just fix the men? Why don't they just stop disrespecting the feminine and destroying women?' I asked.

'They are part of the story, but they are not the problem, Maeve. When, in our struggle, we first look outside of ourselves to blame another, to claim we are right, and they are wrong, we neglect to look within ourselves to see how we are responsible, to recognise the part we have played in the story that has created the pain.'

I was challenged by her words and wanted to argue, as much as Clara would in the years ahead, when I passed on these teachings, but I was wise enough to open my heart and mind to look from a higher perspective.

Cynthia continued, 'It is understandable to feel anger towards those men and women who disrespected you, and me, and your little Clara, under the dictate of the patriarch. But we cannot hold onto the anger, we must learn to release it, because anger will never be a creator of change. Our anger will be met with anger and further suppression. A vicious cycle that must be broken if we want change, if we want the feminine to rise, if we want harmony between all.

First, we look to ourselves and we make changes to ourselves. We reconnect to the light within our self and remember our oneness with the Divine and seek to understand why we allowed ourselves to become separate in the first place. Because when we forget our true essence and separate ourselves from the Divine Light, we disempower ourselves, and in turn, allow others to do the same.'

She paused to allow me to reflect on my own life. I could see how I had lost myself in the more challenging experiences of my life and become separate.

'The feeling of being one with the Divine, God, Universe, Creator—whichever name you choose to give her—is powerful beyond measure because you remember you are *her*, a perfect reflection of the Divine, your adoration and honouring of her, is reflected in your adoration and honouring of yourself. And when you love yourself in this way, you will never allow another to dishonour and disrespect you.

When those who seek to suppress you come, you are called to rise in this power and they will never be able to access *her*, for she lies within you and nothing can disempower her, unless you allow it. It is time to stop fighting to be seen and heard as women, in fighting we disempower ourselves. It is time to *rise* and *reclaim* our place at the table, to reclaim our voice, to reclaim our power, because this is our birthright. It is a given.'

Again, Cynthia's silence allowed me to contemplate her teachings. I was unsure that I was able to walk this path, let alone guide others.

'You will learn this, Maeve, as you unravel the layers that have kept you separate from this truth. You will witness its power as it gently leads you through life, especially the tough times. Just as I have learnt from Athena, an incredibly wise old woman, who called to me one night to meet her under the moon light and begin my passage home, so too you, will learn from me, and as I pass my knowledge onto you and others, so too will you, as will Clara and all those who come after us. As more women remember their truth, and embrace the beauty of their whole Self, the feminine energy will rise once again, it is inevitable.

But first we must stop disempowering ourselves by being victim to the stories of what the patriarch has done to us individually and as a collective to women. This begins with forgiveness. There will be no greater tool I can teach you than the power of forgiveness in freeing yourself from the stories that says they are wrong, and you are right. These stories keep you separate from your truth, the presence of the Divine within you.'

I simply did not know where to begin and I appreciated the overwhelm Clara was to experience as she began her passage home. I chose to surrender to my teacher and listen to the wisdom she was to share with me, and in so doing, Cynthia guided me *home* and reconnected me to the Divine that lay within me, and all around me. This is exactly where I began with my Clara.

I would teach as I had been taught.

Chapter Twenty-seven

I sat under the moon and the stars, gazing at the vastness of it all, the first night I was at Aunt Maeve's home. She lived out of the village so there was nothing surrounding her small cottage but an expanse of fields and stone fences. She had bought the cottage off an English landholder, who resided in the big house a mile down the road and in exchange for helping about the farm, they gave her milk and eggs and a small payment. It was ample to meet her needs, and she grew her own fruit and vegetables in the plot of land surrounding the cottage. It was a very simple life that she had chosen to live, with her two dogs and a cat. She had lived happily alone in her cottage for many years now.

I feared I would disrupt the life that she had

created, but she assured me that she had always known that one day, when the time was right, I would come. And when the time was right, I would once again leave. I could not see myself ever leaving, for within a few days, I felt more at home than I had ever felt in my life and I vowed to myself that I would hold onto it forever.

'Put on this jacket to keep you warm, we will need to be finding you one of your own soon enough. But this old thing will do you for now, it was your Granny Mary's, you know,' she enthused, as she passed the threadbare jacket to me. I tucked it in tightly around me, feeling secure in the arms of a woman I had long forgotten.

'Where are we going?' I queried nervously, as I couldn't recall ever having been out at night, the darkness scaring me.

'And that my girl, is exactly why you need to be out there amongst the darkness, instead of tucked away telling yourself you are safe inside here, like you have for all these years gone. Sure, and you will feel as safe out there in the darkness, once you get used to it. It's a matter of doing the things you've not done before, Clara. Otherwise you will just stay stuck in all the old stuff. And if you're after wanting to be truly free, not just away from them, then you have to put yourself in these situations that you have always avoided because you were scared,' she was firm in her knowing.

'So long as you promise to be by my side and hold my hand whilst we walk through the fields.'

'Of course, I will, you think I'd be after sending you out there in the dark all by yourself?' she chuckled. 'Mind you, I'll count the days before you're heading off yourself without the need for me. Mark my words, the night is a magical place and does wonders for your soul.'

I found myself sitting on top of an ancient rock. Aunt Maeve on one side and Sandy her collie on the other, surrounded by nothing. And once my nervous chatter stopped, my worries appeased by both Aunt Maeve's reassuring squeeze of my hand, and the nuzzling of Sandy's head under my arm. I took a deep breath and felt the nothingness which I had become so familiar with surround me once more. My curiosity sparked, wanting to know where it had come from, for I associated it with places of distress, not places of calm like this. But I silenced my insistent curious mind and allowed myself to sink into the quiet and stillness of the night and the familiar nothingness embraced me. Everything else slipped into the darkness surrounding me.

It was here, through this ritual of our night walks that I learnt to trust in the darkness, knowing she was a friend not foe. Aunt Maeve was right in her prediction, within days my initial hesitation about leaving the cottage at night had dissipated and I eagerly awaited the darkness to descend over the fields.

On the sixth night, as I put on Granny Mary's jacket in readiness for our nightly walk, Aunt Maeve told me she would not be coming with me as she was meeting with friends. I was taken aback and felt a sense of abandonment, my fears of being alone in the darkness threatened to overwhelm me, but also because I did not know she had friends. She had never spoken of these people whom she was meeting in preference to supporting me. I felt a sudden wave of anger swell within me, fuelled by my own fears, I wanted to scream at her and beg her to not leave me, to come with me, but she cut me off before I had a chance to protest.

'The night sky is filled with light tonight because the moon is at her fullest. She will guide you, Clara. I know you are ready to sit in the darkness without me. She will both challenge you and hold you tonight. It is time to be brave. Sandy will go with you to calm you should you become overwrought. I do not know what time I will be back.'

Aunt Maeve had an intensity about her which I had not seen before and whilst I wanted to ask to go with her, or for her to cancel her plans because I was scared by myself, I knew I had to leave her do her own thing. I had to find the courage within to go alone.

The moon was brighter than I had ever seen her before. I convinced myself that it wasn't really the night at all, just the early afternoon, which somehow felt safer. With Sandy loyally by my side, I made my way to my favourite rock and sat companionably with Sandy waiting for the nothingness to come. Without the darkness I could see more, the moonlit shadows danced around me, teasing me, unsettling my mind. I thought the light was my friend, but it made me feel more uncomfortable than the darkness ever had. My eyes trawled the shadows of the landscape trying desperately to latch onto something to reassure me, and then I saw it, sitting on the stone hedge not more than ten feet away from me. Still, wide-eyed, staring at me. I did not flinch. Sandy raised her head sharply, eyes and ears alert scanning, only to come to rest on the owl, whose stillness seemed to permeate the space. Rather than being startled by the intrusion of this creature in her space, Sandy immediately relaxed and seemed to nod at the owl before returning to her position with her head on my lap.

'Shoo, shoo, be off with ye,' I said, motioning to the owl.

The owl's presence unsettled me more than the shadows that danced around us. It did not fly away. Not even flinch. I wanted desperately to run home to Aunt Maeve, but I knew she would not be there, or perhaps she would be. So many thoughts bounced around in my head, and the owl's stillness seemed to only mock my chaos.

I took a deep breath knowing that the nothingness would come if I settled myself, despite the shadows that threatened my space. I wished the light would disappear, so I could return to the safety of the darkness which I had quickly mastered. I stroked Sandy rhythmically, slowed my breathing, closed my eyes to the world around me that had been illuminated by the moon. I had faced more than this before. I reckoned with myself and the owl watched on. *You don't scare me. I am not running from you. I am staying right here and remembering what Maeve said. Moon, please hold me in this discomfort.* Every time my fears sparked with the sound of a bird squawking or the rustling in the bushes—for it seemed everything was awakened with the fullness of the moon—I would take another deep breath and extinguish the fear desperately wanting to pull me into hysteria. I danced this dance with my fear, with the owl watching, waiting for the nothingness.

It was only when I felt the curl of my rosary beads around my fingers and my devotion to the Blessed Mother, flow from me, that the edge of my resistance fell away, and the nothingness enveloped me once again. I finished my rosary before opening my eyes and looked at the moonlit night with different eyes.

The owl had moved closer, within arms distance.

Now I did not feel threatened. Now I could see her and the wisdom she wished to share with me. I wondered how long she had been watching me. I wondered if she had been there every night in the darkness, but I was just not able to see. I wondered at her beauty and commanding presence. I listened in awe as she spoke to me, the nothingness freeing me to hear the silent vibrations of her wisdom.

'Just as you learnt to become one with the darkness, now you must learn to look into the shadows. It is the magic of the light and dark dancing that creates the shadows, and it is in

honouring the magic of the light and dark within you that you will be freed. One is no more than the other.'

And she flew away into the shadows, leaving me to absorb her words.

I lay my head beside Sandy. We were held by the majesty of the moon in her fullness, surrounded by the nothingness. I sank deeply into sleep where the wisdom of the owl embedded itself deep into my consciousness.

Chapter Twenty-eight

I woke much later than normal, the mid-morning sun already piercing through the curtains. I was not sure what time I had made it to bed, as I had woken on the rock in the early hours, disoriented yet strangely calm. Sandy guided me home and I curled into bed and fell back into another deep sleep.

I was relieved when I came from my room and saw Aunt Maeve still in her nightgown sitting at the small table with a pot of tea in front of her. I feared I might get in trouble for being slovenly having not risen early to help her with the chores.

'I'm sorry to be so late rising,' I began cautiously.

'Never mind at all, Clara. I'm only after rising

myself. Come have a cup of tea with me and tell me about your night,' she invited me reassuringly.

It was only when I sat opposite her that I noticed how drained she was, her skin pale and her eyes circled by shadows.

'Are you not well, Aunt Maeve? You are looking fierce pale and drawn out,' I observed with concern.

'I'm not the best, but it is grand, Clara. This is just my way,' she motioned to the bucket on the floor beside her.

'Oh no, you've been poorly, should you not go back to bed and rest? I can do the chores about the farm and look after the cottage,' I offered.

'Truly, I am fine, Clara. I will rest when I've done what I need to do. Like I said, it is just the way I do it,' she smiled wearily as she heaved once more into the bucket.

'It's just the way you do what?' I asked, wincing with each heave that purged what was only now bile from her.

'It's the way I release when I am shifting things through. The full moon is powerful and has an intense energy, a time to let go. My friends and I meet each full moon and set intentions about what we wish to release for the next cycle, and there was obviously much for me to let go of this cycle. The next week as the moon wanes, is an important time for you and me, as it is the time to release all that doesn't serve you anymore.'

'But why would you do that when it makes you so

sick. That can't be a good thing, especially if it happens each time there is a full moon.'

'It is a wonderous thing, my Clara. She is a powerful energy and is impacting on all of us—whether we realise it or not—and I have learnt to work with her cycles to better myself. When she is full, we are given a wonderful opportunity to cleanse ourselves of what we no longer need, what is holding us back. For me, I don't even know what some of this is anymore, so I just set my intention to release what no longer serves me. And this time, there is obviously much for me to release because I have not been impacted like this for a couple of years.'

'I don't really understand how it works and I'm not keen on getting sick and the like,' I resisted.

'You don't need to understand how she works, just honour her light and open yourself to being held and supported by her guiding light. You are only given that which you can handle, Clara. I know this to be true. In life we will be tested, but it is never more than we can handle. When you look around beyond the world that you know, there is so much support as we move through these challenges. I know that much of what I needed to release is connected to you coming into my life in this way. For me to teach, and guide you, in the way I was guided, I must release a great many beliefs I carry about myself, most significant the one that tells me I am not worthy to be your teacher because I am still learning.'

'But you are so wise, Aunt Maeve. I cannot believe all the things that you know. All the things that other people don't know about life and the moon and releasing stuff. You are teaching me so much already.' I wanted to reassure her that I valued her wisdom because she seemed to be doubting herself.

'I am coming to know that in teaching you, I am teaching myself. I am remembering more about my true self the more I guide you to reconnect to your true Self. I know that this is all perfect, we are both going to be doing much growing over the months and years ahead. But be aware, Miss Clara, it is not always lovely strolls in the moonlight, gazing at the stars. As you can see, sometimes it is not pleasant, but when you just accept what is happening it is much easier to move through it …' she paused, taking a deep breath as yet another wave of nausea swept over her. 'Any challenge that you are going through is only temporary, but you, my dear, are forever. You will remain on the other side of any obstacle, the real you will always be there waiting for you to emerge closer to her. Sometimes it takes many years, lifetimes even to find her again, but she is always there. And as we release more and more and more layers, especially when we work with the moon energy, we move closer to her, that real Self, hidden in there *beneath the veil* of illusion.'

I was beginning to understand what Aunt Maeve was teaching me in a different way.

'Could it be like I am wearing lots of coats and jackets, many layers of them all on top of one another, but I am not the layers I am wearing. I'm actually always in there under all those coats and jackets. And sometimes, people have forced you to wear certain jackets, like Vincent and Finnigan always calling me slovenly? That was why when I got up late I thought I was slovenly. But it is just a jacket I've been wearing and sometimes you don't know that you're even wearing that jacket because it, well, kind of becomes you.'

'Exactly that, Clara! There are so many of those jackets that we have no idea we are wearing them, at times. We think that we are the jackets and the coats, but we are not. We are only wearing them, and *she* is inside looking out waiting for us to remember *her*. She is there.'

Maeve smiled with a sense of satisfaction, realising that she had taught me something.

'So, I guess this is what you're trying to get me to see. I have to let go of all those jackets and coats and shawls and jumpers and layers that no longer serve me, so I can find me in there.' I nodded, remembering that I was in there.

'Yes, Clara, you've got it. Remember it is not as simple as it sounds. Because some of those old jackets are very well hidden, and some, like the jacket of Granny Mary's you so love to wear, are very comfortable, they make us feel safe and warm and content where we are. But these too must go. All the layers of stories we have told ourselves, or other people have told us, to keep us safe and comfortable in life, all must go. For they keep us separate from our true Self.'

'Goodness me, Aunt Maeve, what's left when all

those jackets are gone then? If something makes you feel content and safe, why do we get rid of that?

'Because it is not real, Clara, that feeling is not real. It is quite hard to explain how it feels when there is nothing between you and the veil of the outside world. When there are no layers left, the Divine does not have to fight through all of that to reach you—it just does—it becomes a direct connection between you and the most Divine Light. When you feel it for the first time you remember that you don't need anything else to make you feel good or safe or happy, because it is all there … it is amplified beyond anything you could possibly imagine.' Aunt Maeve paused with a knowing peaceful smile which gently danced across her face and glistened into her eyes. She sat in the stillness of the moment and I let myself just sink into this feeling of calm that had landed in the cottage. After a few minutes, she looked at me and said, 'Yes, indeed, my Clara. You will teach me much. Now tell me, how did you go last night yourself?'

'Well, I'm not sure what happened. It feels all a bit of a dream. I fell asleep and then Sandy got me home sometime in the early morning hours. I was scared because you weren't with me, and it was so light. I thought I was scared of the dark, but it was actually scarier because it was so light, all these shadows kept flashing up and spooking me. When I calmed myself down, an owl came? Ah, yes . . . it was strange. It was just staring at me and then after I calmed myself down it came in real close and then talked to me, if you would ever believe that,' I shook my head, recalling the dream-like event with bewilderment.

'Ah, so she found you?' Maeve smiled seemingly impressed.

'Who?'

'The owl. She was missing last night. She is always there for the full moon. What did she tell you, Clara?' she asked, intrigued.

I tried to recall while resisting the temptation to laugh at the lunacy of discussing what an owl had told me while I sat alone on a rock under the moonlight. My life had certainly taken a very unusual turn since my life in the laundry of only a week ago which now seemed like a faint memory.

'I can't remember the exact words. It was something to do with the shadows, not being scared of the shadows, I think.'

'What do you think the shadows are?' Aunt Maeve asked.

'Well they are just a shape that isn't really there. We just think they are.' I struggled to get my head around it because I had never really thought about it.

'Indeed, they are, the images we see when the darkness is illuminated. And they are not real, but we trick ourselves into thinking that they are. And the more we focus on them the more real they become. I am exhausted because I danced with my own shadows last night, Clara. That is what the full moon is all about. The light of the moon allows us to look into the darkness within us. It gives us the chance to explore the shadow side, the part we keep hidden. All the stories that we hold onto that keep impacting on our life until we release them. And yes, they are painful to look at, sometimes when we release them it is not very pretty,' she motioned to the bucket beside her, 'but once free of these stories, they have no power over us. The memory is there but it just doesn't have the same feeling around it anymore, and that gifts us peace once again. The trick is having the courage to look into the most painful memories, the ones we don't want to remember and free ourselves from the hold they have over us.'

'And you've done this, Aunt Maeve?' I asked incredulously. 'Is this how you are so smart and calm and brave and how come you could speak up to himself Colin Stanley and Vincent and Mother Superior. I don't know how you did it, being so brave and all.'

'Clara, do you not remember that you did it too? You stood up to them in the church, you drew on the power of the woman you are, and you stood up to them and in turn you began to free yourself from them. But there is always more to do, and we have experiences that make us look even deeper within ourselves and free ourselves from that which we don't even know is still there. You see going to the laundry last week and seeing that woman again, brought up many painful memories for me. Memories which I believed I had healed, but for you to come into my care and me to serve you in the way that you need, I obviously needed to delve deeper into these memories and release any emotion that still remained there. And unbeknown to me, there was a great deal of emotion that I was still holding that I was unaware of, and now it sits in this bucket,' she laughed, her eyes looking brighter. 'I'm going to walk outside for a while, fix yourself some breakfast and tea and then we can talk some more.'

Chapter Twenty-nine

I busied myself, stoking the grange, boiling the kettle, buttering the bread and as I slowly ate I watched Aunt Maeve through the little window. As she walked about the garden she stretched her arms wide and leant her head back offering herself to the sun as she moved her hips back and forth. She seemed to be talking to herself. It was clear that my aunt was intent on teaching me her ways. She seemed more peaceful and content with life than anyone I had ever come across and I wanted to feel like that. I wanted to be free of all the heaviness that lay within me.

I had not thought about any of that old stuff since I had been here, nor while I was in the Magdalene

Laundry, as the nothingness seemed to keep it away from me, but this morning I could feel it inside of me. I preferred to not give it any attention and pretended it wasn't there, a great lesson I had learnt from my mother and all the woman who surrounded me growing up.

Aunt Maeve came back inside looking fresher with the colour having returned to her face.

'Now that's better. Sure, and doesn't a little sunshine make everything feel better. Let's take our tea outside.'

We sat companionably for a few minutes sipping our tea basking in the warmth of the sun.

'These next few days, as the moon wanes is the time to release what you no longer need, what's not good for ye.'

'How do I know what I no longer need, what I should let go of?' I asked.

'We are always doing it whether we realise it or not, which is why people can get so intense or crazy around the full moon. It happens without you knowing, because the energy of the moon is working with your energy almost behind your back. It becomes so much more powerful when you are clear on your intentions. If you look into the shadows within yourself, what do you see?' she asked gently.

I shrugged, distracting myself by patting Sandy who sat loyally beside me.

'I know you don't want to talk about some of these things, Clara. See, when we own our stories, particularly the most painful ones and have the courage to look at them and feel into them, only then we can release everything that is attached to them and weighing us down which is what is taking away our joy and light. I doubt you could tell me the last time you felt joyful, can you?'

'I can,' I countered, as the memory returned to me in a flash. Then I felt a mix of emotions zipping through me and I didn't like how it felt.

'Well, when was it?' she pushed sensing my discomfort.

'It was just before my First Communion. I went for a ride on Trinity and I met a Gypsy boy and we played and climbed trees and laughed and I was so happy and having so much fun. And then Vincent came and found me and then he whipped me in front of mother because father was away. He whipped me so hard that I bled. The blood that was on my dress at my First Communion day was from the wounds from Vincent whipping me. I was angry with him. I was angry at mother for not standing up for me. I wanted to shame them by showing everyone what they had done to me. But you saw how that turned out. Vincent had it in for me from then on. He hated me and has punished me ever since. So as far as I can see, my joy only created a lifetime of agony. Why would I want to be light and joyful again? I've no doubt it would only be after causing me a mountain of trouble all over again. I've no doubt at all.'

'Well if you believe that, you will create that,

Clara. But can you see that you have attached so many stories to that one beautiful afternoon and blamed everything that's come after it on that one experience. I don't know for sure, but I would say it was not so much that you were joyful or playing with your little friend that was the problem for Vincent. I'd say that Vincent was going to find a reason to beat you whether it was that or spilling milk at the table. It has more to do with Vincent and his need to show himself as a man, a dire representation of a man at that. He needed to prove himself to your own father and the other men of the village. And while you blame all your heartache on you having fun and being free, you prevent yourself from ever experiencing it again.'

I knew what she was saying to be true and a well of regret swelled inside of me.

'Have you ever thought by believing that your joy was the cause of all your pain and your reluctance to let yourself experience it again, might be the thing that attracted all the other pain and struggle that you have experienced from that point on?' she asked, treading ever so carefully.

'What …' I said, indignantly, 'do you mean that I am the one to blame for all the things that they did to me? That it's my fault?'

'It is not about blame or fault, that just adds to the story. It is about looking into your shadows, all those stories that are haunting you without you even realising it and taking responsibility for the part that you played in the story. I had to learn this too, Clara, it's not an easy lesson. Until you own your story and really shine a light into the darkest corners, you will remain a victim, while you remain a victim you keep yourself disempowered. You allow those other players in the story, the Vincent's, the Colin Stanley's, the Dempsey Finnigan's, the Mother Superior's to continue to have power of you.'

I flinched as she said each name. I preferred not thinking about any of them. They all brought with them memories that I didn't want to recall.

'Clara, the longer you avoid looking at them, the longer you give your power to them. When you stop being a victim in the stories, take responsibility for your part in the story and let go of all the blame by forgiving and viewing each story through compassionate eyes, then you reclaim your power. Then you are free and then you will allow yourself to feel love and joy again.'

Aunt Maeve was adamant that this was the path I needed to walk. I was not convinced because it didn't feel fair and a wave of anger and resentment surged through me.

'Why should I take the blame for what they did to me? Why should I forgive them and let them get away with it? I didn't do anything wrong. They are the ones that should be begging me for forgiveness. All of them, even you. You all let them do it to me. None of you stopped it. None of you cared enough about me to stop it,' I fired back resentfully as the rage brewed within me.

'Perhaps you were the one who didn't care

enough about yourself to stop it. Possibly you let them do it to you because you were too scared to stand up for yourself. Scared to be powerful and brave enough to have a voice and demand to be honoured and respected. Maybe all that rage that you are feeling for everyone else is rage at yourself,' she gently planted this seed.

I was not ready to hear it, but it landed within me nonetheless.

I stormed away, taking my rage to the cliffs, where I sat for hours, fiercely digging deeply into the ground as I watched the waves crash against the rocks, the waves of emotions crashing against my heart, mercilessly intent on cracking it open. My resistance was only met by more powerful surges of emotions. I was so out of my depth not knowing how to deal with all these feelings and all the stories that flashed before my eyes, creating even more agonising pain.

I fought hard to resist the torrent of tears. I would not allow them. I had learnt they were a sign of my weakness, I would not allow Vincent to see he had got to me every time he beat me or raped me, nor Dempsey Finnigan when he lay on top of me, nor Colin Stanley as he thrust himself in me. I would never let them know that they had hurt me, my tears were a weakness, I would not allow them. Not then and not now. I fought hard to stay in control yet all these feelings, the ache in my heart and the throbbing of my head screamed at me to let go. *Why wouldn't they just go away again? Why couldn't they stay hidden? Why did she have to go and ruin everything by stirring this up?*

I refused to go home to her, because I was so angry with Maeve, but I had nowhere else to go, so I could not run. The grass, the soil, the rocks, the trees, the water, the sun and the birds were all I had. I wanted to fly away with the birds like I used to in my daydreams, but they wouldn't let me. Every time I pictured myself soaring with them they would drop me, and I would land right back where I was. There was no nothingness to hold me, no guardian angel to wrap her wings around me, like once she would in the darkness of the night. There was nothing to protect me. I felt completely raw and more vulnerable than ever. I was drawn to the raging ocean and contemplated drowning my deafening thoughts and crippling anxiety, yet I knew that even if I tried she would not save me, she would keep me afloat, holding me as the waves pounded me until I let go. I was sure if I let go I would go under, drown in the intensity of it all. Why couldn't I let myself just sink into the unknown that implored me? I bellowed into the wind as I clutched the ground, beseeching something, anything, to take the inner turmoil that fought within me away. I howled as I fell to my knees and rocked myself as the wind carried my frustration and rage into the unknown of the world, and as it released, the torrent of grief I had so feared broke through the walls around my heart and I heaved from the depths of my being as the tears streamed from me. I gasped for a breath, I clutched the soil, arched my back as my heart cracked open even further, I was so outside of my mind that I could not fight it even if I tried. I rocked my body with each new wave of emotion as it ravaged me.

There was no *one* memory or person that elicited each emotion. I was beyond the awareness of both what I was feeling or why I was feeling it. I was in it. I was in the deep unknown of my shadows that I was so terrified of and yet I felt safer within it, moving with it, being it, than I ever had when I was running from it.

As the surges slowly began to ease, my breathing slowed, and I lay on my back with my arms spread wide to allow the exhaustion to engulf me. My body convulsed spasmodically as the remnants of energy drained from me and I gratefully fell into a comatose sleep as the sun and warm breeze cocooned me.

As the moon rose in the fullness of her glory many hours later, Aunt Maeve found me.

The confusion was confounding.

The light filled calmness appeased my anxiety.

I realised as I walked home in silence with my aunt and her protective arm around my shoulder that something profound had occurred—I was transforming, shedding who I was and becoming—while it was not gentle and graceful, it was indeed powerful.

Chapter Thirty

Goddess of the moon, divine light of the night,
She who holds the mysteries and cycles of the tides.
Ever changing yet ever powerful.
She who guides and lights the path we weave.
Guide me with your wisdom,
Infuse me with your power,
And hold me in your light as I dance with life.

Walking home with Clara, I prayed this prayer I offered every night.

I did not know what she had encountered. She felt otherworldly which left me in no doubt that she had battled the demons of her past. I had sat with her for some time on the cliff's edge before she woke from the deepest of healing sleeps. I felt reassured that she had allowed herself to sink into her pain and somehow release it. I had been nervous when she stormed away from the cottage, feeling she was ill-equipped to navigate her way through the storm that I could feel brewing, that which I had intentionally stirred. When I sensed the *wild wise woman* within her, I trusted that she would be guided by other forces, including her innate wisdom and the miraculous forces of nature that were ever present and ever wise. I trusted she would find her way as I had many years before. I had many dark nights of the soul and I had been able to move my way through whatever demons I was wrestling with. More often than not it was with my Self. The battle between the outer and inner Self is the most challenging relationship we will ever encounter, all difficulties we experience with others, is simply a reflection of the disharmony that exists within the Self. It took me a very long time, and much pain, to stop blaming others for my pain and see it as a gift, a lifeline to my freedom. In triumphing over my outer Self, I was able to find peace with my inner Self, my true centre of being, and a direct connection to the Divine Love that is awaiting all.

    I was relieved to have found Clara in peaceful slumber while the soul of the universe healed the pain of her past, taking her one step closer to reclaiming her power and releasing her from the victim story in which she had encased herself.

    As the night descended upon us walking back

to the cottage, I could see Clara settling as she became more grounded. Her eyes shone, and a curious spark expanded within her signalling a deep desire for more, a feeling that often accompanies profound periods of transformation, yet one which must be followed from an inner compass, rather than the desire of the mind to uncover the mysteries of the soul. The soul reveals herself when time and circumstance align, and when that occurs magic is created.

As Clara sat in silence by the fire, sipping her soup, she did not offer to share her experiences. There is something deeply personal and sacred in the healing of the soul, that when shared with others compromises its power. Clara was honouring her own healing experience. I sensed on one level she was profoundly confused by what she had gone through that day and her mind wanted to ask me to explain. Yet her connection to the wise woman within herself was strong—*she* told her that she did not need to understand—her acceptance of what was would allow her to move through it, and beyond it with far greater ease.

When she finished eating she asked if I could walk with her. Clara's body felt so awakened and I sensed her need to move. She needed my presence not my guidance tonight. We walked across fields and mountains, around cliff faces, along the beach, a slow silent meander through the night. The tide was low as we walked along the beach and I felt the calling to take her into the cave. A cave hidden within the cliffs towering above the sea, the

Beneath the Veil

tiny entry a deterrent for all but those who know of the blessed shrine within. We scaled the rocks to the entry. Clara did not ask questions. She followed me with an innate trust that can only come from one who knows she is loved. As we entered further into the hidden part of the cave, her face mirrored the magnificence as a shrine honouring Mary the Mother and Mary Magdalene was revealed. Together they were one, and their presence in her life would profoundly impact Clara, as they had me.

She reverently dropped to her knees before the shrine, immediately captivated by the majesty invoked upon entering this sacred space. Removing her beloved rosary beads from around her neck she began to pray her rosary.

This time it was different.

One week ago, in the Magdalene Laundry, Clara used her rosary to pray for survival. Here she prayed in a deep spiritual connection with the oneness represented by the two most blessed of women: Mary the Mother and Mary Magdalene.

I silently said my prayers.

I prayed for the wisdom to know when to hold Clara and when to let her go, for the clarity to know truth and the courage to live it. My calling to guide Clara and my fear that I may fail her weighed heavily on me. I asked to be gifted with the fierce strength of the Magdalene and the freedom to live fearlessly with the knowing I am always supported, combined with the gentle nurture of the Mother and the presence to live in the boundlessness of unconditional love. The last week had come with feelings of being desperately alone and I longed for the support of Cynthia, my teacher. Cynthia had passed from this earth two years ago. I had missed her dreadfully in the human sense, for she was my best friend, my mentor, my confidant and in many ways, I had become dependent on her.

While I had grown so much under Cynthia's guidance and was wise in the ways I sought to teach Clara, I was still learning my own lessons. I had come to the realisation that Cynthia had taught me so much, but there was just as much I had to learn without her. These last two years had been by far my toughest in terms of growth. There were many times, during those two years, that I wished Clara had come home with me after her Mary's funeral, because she would have been a welcome distraction from my own pain and struggles as I learnt to evolve without Cynthia to guide me. I understood that it was not the right time for Clara to come with me then, as we both still had much to experience and learn before we were to be brought to the time when we were to be reunited.

In my fear and doubt, I did not feel I was ready or worthy of being the teacher, yet I know that this was also true for Cynthia when I came into her life. As she often told me, 'the teacher awakens fully through her teaching.' As I walked Clara through the early steps of her journey into the remembering of the Divine within her, I could see my own remembering strengthening.

As my outer Self felt inadequate and vulnerable, I was challenged to stay connected to the Divine within. On that night, as I knelt before the shrine to my beloved Mary's, I offered my vulnerability to them and to all those brave, fierce and wonderous women who have carried their message here on earth, like Cynthia and Athena before her. I prayed that I may have the courage to embody their greatness and carry their message into the world. As I finally surrendered to my calling, peace and contentment flooded me and I could finally feel the presence of these great women surrounding us. Clara felt it too, interrupting her meditative state of prayer, she looked at me confused.

'They are here with us. It is grand.'

She nodded without needing to know more, her gift of acceptance of the unknown and ability to find peace in the not knowing was becoming stronger the further she allowed herself to sink into her new world. We allowed ourselves to be held in this space, absorbing the essence of love that permeated and the wisdom bestowed upon us because we were open, trusting and accepting.

The voice of my beloved teacher returned to me,

'You are ready, and we support you. She will move far quicker than you or I did, she already is. Do not slow her down for fear she will fracture. Her resilience is her greatest strength and she will always return to Grace no matter

what she must encounter on her journey home.'

My confidence grew knowing I was supported by the most powerful of all women and I allowed myself to breathe with an ease I had not truly felt for days. I now had a sense of knowing that Clara was on the path that would return her to freedom and beyond into the unknown of her own calling as a woman.

'Might we go, Aunt Maeve? I am awful tired, and we still have a long walk home.'

'Of course, my girl. I believe we have received abundant blessings tonight and a good sleep is exactly what we both need now.'

As we walked home across the moonlit sand and fields in joyful communion, I felt gratitude nestled within my heart for the blessing of Clara in my life, as both her teacher and her student.

May there be abundance.
May there be peace.
May there be contentment.
Amen.

Chapter Thirty-one

Each day became exhausting, between working hard helping Aunt Maeve complete her farm chores and walking for hours across the spectacular landscapes. I had not realised how frail my body had become from years of malnourishment, poor sleep and being trapped indoors. Aunt Maeve continued to feed me mountains of fresh fruit and vegetables, 'nourished with the energy of the earth itself' and my body hungrily absorbed the life force they shared with me. I learnt to offer gratitude to the food for its nourishment and the earth and sun for its growth. She made sure I spent hours in the fresh air, soaking in the rays of the sun refuelling my own vitality so that I had the strength to grow. I came to understand that my own growth was an ever-changing landscape, some days were blessed with ease and bliss, others I was tormented and struggled with a reason to continue.

Each morning as we sat drinking Aunt Maeve's specially brewed yarrow root tea, she would ask me more questions about my past. Questions that made me deeply uncomfortable and stirred torrents of emotions. I held back at first. I was shamed at sharing the secrets of my childhood and I feared she would judge me and in turn reject me for being dirty, as the people of my village had when I revealed my truths. But she never judged me—she just listened and probed where she felt I needed to go deeper—where she knew I was holding back.

I understood her intent, but every time I took myself into that barn and relived the sensation of Vincent near me and in me, my body screamed for me to close and to run away. But Aunt Maeve held me there. Guiding me to sit with the feeling of discomfort, connecting with it in my body and asking it what it needed me to hear.

When I became gripped by terror and froze she would tell me it was time that we walked, and that the movement was important in helping to release the shock. And as we walked in silence, I would feel the tension release and as I relaxed an avalanche of grief would wash over me and I would cry for the loss of me, the beautiful little free-spirited girl. It was a piercing pain in my heart that tore me open, and I could not find the words to explain it to Aunt Maeve. But she did not need me to explain, she simply cradled me in her arms and rocked me, as I grappled with this insurmountable loss of the curious, adventurous and joy-filled spirit that once inhabited this body.

When I realised how far removed I was from her, my hatred for Vincent violently tore through me. I hated him for destroying the little girl I once was and for stealing my life. I think I hated him most for making me believe that I was a sinner and dirty and forcing me to isolate myself from the world. I could not allow myself to connect with others, in case they saw my ugly truth. I had never allowed anyone to come close to me, in case they discovered my vulgar secret and publicly shamed me. He didn't say much to me in that barn and never spoke of it outside of the barn, almost like what happened didn't exist, yet somehow, he made me feel that I was responsible, that it was my fault and I was the dirty sinner. Perhaps it was the way he looked at me with repulsion and disdain, the way he constantly told me I was filth, the way he convinced me that no one would ever marry the likes of me. He made sure that I felt shamed every day and my filthy secret was never far from my own mind, making it impossible for me to open myself to anyone for fear they would discover what I desperately sought to hide. I wept for the loss of my mother and Aggie after realising that I had distanced myself from them because I was ashamed, I didn't want to let them find out what was really going on. My tears turned to fury for the loss of my life and what could have been if I had the courage to open my heart to my mother and Aggie, if I let them in. They might have said something or done something. How could she let Vincent do that to me? My heart ached for the love of my mother, her ability to withhold her innate maternal love bewildered me, but if I had told her, then perhaps it could have been different, maybe everything would have been different if I had not been so weak.

I don't know what was worse, the wretchedness that descended with the realisation that there could have been another way or the self-loathing for not allowing myself to trust those who I knew loved me. I remembered with regret how I turned away from Aunt Maeve after the funeral, fearful of the consequences should I leave, but also afraid that if I let her get close she would discover my truths and reject me. My fear of letting myself be loved and then losing it again was the truth of why I did not leave with Aunt Maeve that day.

I couldn't bare the awful realisation that it was not Vincent or Dempsey Finnigan or Colin Stanley that were responsible for all that happened after my mother's funeral, when I was married off. I was responsible. And while I desperately wanted to continue blaming them for their evil and depraved acts, I now saw that if I had found the courage to let Aunt Maeve love me, even if she rejected me when she saw my ugly truths, then none of what I went through would have ever occurred. It was my fear that created those experiences and my pitiful weakness that allowed them to disempower me in the most horrendous of ways.

The despair gripped me, as this truth rose to my consciousness and it was beyond any pain I had ever felt. I rallied between wanting to be held and comforted by my aunt and running to the edge of the cliff screaming in misery to the great winds that whipped me.

'Take it all away, please,' I begged of the wind. 'Take every last bit of it back out to the ocean and let her drown it all, because I cannot carry it anymore. I cannot keep holding it all in me. I am done with the suffering and shame. I am done with the tears and rage. Please take it all now.'

I opened myself as wholly as I could with my arms stretched wide and I allowed the wind to encircle me, cleansing me, and I begged my body to release it all, from within every cell of my being and I implored the great Atlantic winds to take it from me. The relief streamed through me as I felt the emotion lift and free me once again.

Aunt Maeve came to me and smiled with a look of knowing that I had broken through another layer. She allowed me to relish this feeling of renewal as we blissfully meandered through the beautiful rocky landscape, taking in the overwhelming beauty of the green pastures, rolling hills and the wild Atlantic. There was something untouched and magical about this land inhabited by wildflowers, trees, butterflies, birds and wild goats, and sprinkled with remnants of monasteries, holy wells and megalithic tombs and dolmens. I could feel the magic of these ancient lands reverberating through my feet as we walked barefoot in silence. Aunt Maeve stopped along the way to pick wildflowers and plants, I knew they held remedies of some sort, the vital ingredients in the tea she made me drink and the potions she rubbed into my body. She filled her jar with blessed water from the holy well, telling me prophetically that we would be needing this in the days ahead. I was naïve to what lay ahead, believing I had moved beyond the pain of my past.

Each day revealed another layer for me to shed and Aunt Maeve was determined to work within the cycle of the moon and use the powerful cleansing energy of the wanning moon to propel me forward. I was constantly exhausted and fell into deep healing sleeps at all hours of the day and night, she was always there whether it was in the midnight hours or middle of the day, never seeming to need her sleep. She was silent when I needed silence and she was ruthless when I needed to be drawn to free of something.

'Surely, I am done, Aunt Maeve, there cannot be more,' I whinged as we sat by the cottage one morning drinking yet more healing tea.

She laughed at me, sensing my childish reluctance to do the work I knew I needed to do. I was being lazy and wanted to stop, knowing that whatever lay ahead was probably going to be distressing. But she refused to let me stop what had already begun.

'Clara, if you stop now, you are only going to have to deal with it again at some other time. This is the time, it has been gifted to you, there is so much support surrounding you to help you move beyond your past, can you not feel it?'

I reluctantly nodded, for I knew what she was saying was true. I could feel a difference in myself, but I did not know what lay beyond here, and this felt good enough, compared to where I was.

'Do you not think you are pushing it a little far, you can see how good I am now, I am feeling well in myself, I am sleeping well, my skin is glistening, my hair is shinier, and I laugh with you. Surely you can see the difference yourself?'

'Indeed, I can, Clara. You are moving very quickly, which is why you must continue while this energy is here ready to support you in this way. And even though you have moved through so much already, the truth is until you can go into that barn or that bedroom or that church and feel nothing, you must keep honouring the pain. Whilst there is a flicker of emotion there—rage, shame, sadness, regret, guilt—whatever it is, while it remains we must keep cleaning. We must keep digging deeper to find the core of your pain, Clara. When we find that and release it then you will feel nothing around those memories and then you can return to peace. The truth is until you feel nothing in that barn, bedroom or church you continue to hand your power over to Vincent and Dempsey and Colin Stanley and all they represent.'

'I don't want them to have power over me any longer, but it feels so unfair that I have to do all this work, while they get away with it and don't need to do anything,' I stated righteously.

'It is not about who is right or wrong. It is about

freeing yourself, Clara. Whether they do anything to heal their part in the story or not, is not your concern, and whilst you keep distracting yourself with thoughts like that, you neglect your own work. Your judgement and condemnation of them only keeps you a victim to the stories. Nothing they do will free you, until you choose to free yourself. You choose whether you stay a victim or whether you rise. In forgiving them you become free, you rise.'

'Why should I forgive them?' I fought back furiously, even though, I knew Aunt Maeve had explained this to me many times before.

'Because they are a part of you, Clara. You are both feminine and masculine and while you continue to judge them, you continue to reject that aspect of yourself and that stops you from becoming whole. In honouring your sacredness, you honour all that is within you and within everyone, which means you get to the point of forgiving and allowing yourself to feel love for them and all that is,' she paused to allow me time to absorb the enormity of her words. 'It is not just about you anymore, Clara. You are doing this work for all those women who came before you and all those who will come after you. Those women who never had the chance to heal themselves and for all those women who will never have this chance. In rising in your power, you lead the way for other women to do the same. You can choose now, like I did, like Cynthia did before me, like Athena before her, to change yourself so that the world might change.'

I laughed in disbelief, 'Oh, Aunt Maeve! You are really pushing it now. Why don't you just leave, well, enough … alone? How can a farm girl like me in the middle of nowhere on the west coast of Ireland change the world? I think all your queer tea may be messing with your head now. Come on, let's just leave it be.'

Her tears welled as she replied, 'Never doubt how powerful you are to create change. You may feel like you are alone and small and unimportant, but you are so important, Clara. It may be slow to see the change to begin, but you must believe that what you do here on a farm on the west coast of Ireland will travel the seas and make changes all throughout the world. I see it like an unspoken message being carried across the oceans in the hands of the Goddess of the Winds, to land in the hearts and minds of women everywhere, to awaken a beautiful deep remembering of the power of the feminine and the harmony that exists within all. We cannot just talk it, we must live it and to live it in truth, we must heal the pains of the past, not just pretend it is not there or run from it by blaming the patriarch. Clara, there is much to be done, within you, within me, within all women, but as we allow ourselves to be guided by the Divine Mother and the most powerful of the Magdalene we move forward believing that what we change in ourselves, particularly as we return to harmony within ourselves, this change will in ways we cannot understand create change in all. Ultimately, to come back to oneness with the Divine, we must become one within ourselves and honour all aspects of who we are, so that one day, men and women will live in harmony as equals and will raise each other rather than suppress and dominate. The world you have lived in has shown you that. All aspects of nature work in unison for the greater good, the sun and the moon like a beautiful team flowing in the most peaceful cycle, never fighting for dominance, honouring the place each other holds.'

I heard the hope in her words and saw the beauty in the world that she described but still something within me fought it.

'I understand all you are saying, but I am not … not important enough to be one of these women like you and Cynthia who can change the world. I'm not special like you, Aunt Maeve. I am just a farm girl and I'm not so sad anymore and not so angry anymore and I feel safe here with you now. I think I am meant to just be this. Nothing more. Nothing special.'

'That is nonsense, Clara. I will not allow you to be so passive with your life any longer. You are running from what is next, it is as simple as that. You are being lazy because you don't want to admit something to yourself. What is it Clara? What part of the story are you not telling me, what part of the story won't you look at yourself? What are you so afraid of seeing?' Aunt Maeve was fierce in her attack and I met her with equal ferocity.

'Why do you keep forcing me to remember it? Can't you see I don't want to remember. Can't you see how painful it is for me. Can't you just leave me alone,' the rage erupted. 'You are just like them, forcing me to do things I don't want to do. Taking away my power, and my right to choose what I want to do.'

'You have every right to do what you want, Clara. I want you to start taking responsibility for your life. Stop letting other people dominate and control you. But you will never do that if you don't believe you are worthy of it. Why aren't you worthy of making your own choices?'

'I am able to make my own choices. And I am choosing to go now. I don't want to talk about this anymore. How dare you treat me so poorly. I stupidly thought you cared about me and perhaps even loved me. How stupid was I to think this would be any different to any other time in my life?' I stormed away in the depths of my victim story, and much to my despair Aunt Maeve did not chase me.

I was alone with my darkness again.

Chapter Thirty-two

I knew I had pushed Clara hard.

I wanted to push her hard, for until she was willing to expose the rawness, she couldn't start to grow her new skin. I knew that there was still much hidden within Clara that if she chose to ignore it then, eventually it would reveal itself and create havoc in her life. I understood that she did not want to keep digging, for I myself, had experienced the same exasperation and reluctance as I healed from my stories. Part of me wanted to share my story with Clara but I did not believe it would serve her, not yet. She did not need more fodder for her fire. She needed to focus on her own story and peeling back the final layers. She was holding fiercely to that final protective layer, but in truth it was not protecting her, it was limiting her. Of course, I had a strong feeling about what lay at the core of her pain, for it was not dissimilar to my own, or that of most women, but it was hers to own.

It was time to move as she had become stuck and I sensed that without a different stimulus she would remain hovering on the edge of a huge transformation yet hold herself back. The closer one gets to freedom, the greater the pull of fear and that is why the transition is often the most challenging part of any journey. My own pilgrimage across the ancient lands, brought me through many dark nights as I faced the demons of my past, and into a state that I can only describe as bliss. My days were long and hard but filled with peace as I felt myself move away from my past and into something wonderous and new.

We would leave tonight in the darkness of the new moon which beckoned with the promise of new beginnings and regeneration.

I packed for us.

I knew we would be nourished by the land and the people we encountered in whatever way we needed. I waited for Clara to return from where she had gone to release her resentment towards me for pushing her beyond her comfort. I knew that transitions were accepted more calmly at this stage of the moon cycle and all Clara's efforts to this point in time would grow visible. It was a time of spontaneity and instinctual action and I looked forward to allowing my wise woman to take the lead and guide us to where we needed to journey. The intensity of the waning moon had released, and it was time to embrace the freedom promised by the new moon.

The wonders of nature had cast their magical spell on Clara once more. She returned lighter and calmer than when she had stormed off. She was surprised and hesitant when I told her to freshen up as we would be leaving the cottage straight after supper and I didn't know when we would be returning.

'What do you mean we are leaving?' she queried bewildered, not accustomed to living impulsively.

'I mean we are going for a walk and I don't know where it will take us and how long we will be gone,' I smiled, enjoying watching her trying to comprehend such a concept.

'But we can't just leave and go for a walk and not come back. What about the dogs and the farm and the cottage and …' she stammered on, 'and where on earth shall we sleep?'

'Himself up there in the big house is well used to me leaving at short notice and he doesn't mind a bit. He is well able to look after the farm himself and lets me help out only because he knows I enjoy it. He'll keep an eye on the cottage. The dogs will come with us.'

'And where shall we stay, you, me, and two dogs?'

'We will sleep where we land, Clara. Under the moon, the stars. We will let them guide us,' I explained, amused by her resistance to the unknown.

'But where are we going?' Clara asked, becoming increasingly distraught by her lack of control.

'I don't know where we are going exactly. We will head to the coast tonight and where we go after that will depend on where we are called to go. I must take you into the world, Clara, away from your comfort. Whatever path lies before us will reveal itself and we will navigate it one step at a time.'

'They called me insane and locked me away, but this is insanity. You do realise this don't you, Aunt Maeve?'

'Come! Hurry along now. This is exciting, Clara. Magic belongs in the unknown, and you and I are about to step right into it,' I laughed, as she finally cracked and surrendered to my apparent insanity.

It felt good to laugh, as the heaviness of the past few weeks had begun to weigh heavily on me and I was relieved to feel a lightness return and I was keen to move in flow with the natural rhythms of the universe. I could see Clara felt it too and the spark returned to her as she washed herself and ate dinner. She didn't know that she might be without a proper meal for some days, fasting being a powerful tool to cleanse during this time of rejuvenation.

We walked in a companionable silence for many hours, neither of us tired enough to rest until the light of the dawn began to break. I was fuelled by the excitement of the unknown, and both our sleep cycles were disrupted by the intensity of the last few weeks. We created a small camp, laying our blankets, by a large rock, just off the path we had been travelling. We settled into a few hours of deep restorative sleep before being woken by a herd of wild goats who sought to reclaim their territory.

As we packed up our things Clara asked innocently, 'What do we do now?'

'I don't know. What do you feel we should do?'

I wanted to encourage her to listen to her own wise woman.

'I don't know either. Maybe we can eat something?' she suggested.

'Well are you actually hungry?' I challenged her to step outside of custom.

'Yes, of course, it's morning. We have not eaten since supper last night,' she retorted.

'Well if you are hungry you can eat, but I'm not hungry. Just because you always do something doesn't mean that is what you have to always do. Like last night, we didn't sleep until dawn because we didn't feel the need to sleep, so we just kept going. I don't feel hungry, so I know I don't need to eat. My body is always telling me what I actually need, as is yours, if you train yourself to listen to it,' I explained.

'Now you say that. If I feel into it rather than think about it, I'm not hungry either,' she smiled, proud of herself.

'That's grand, now when you are hungry be sure to let me know and we'll see what we can pull together, for we don't have much in the way of food, but the Divine will always provide what we need, we are never given more than we can handle and always provided with what we need.'

'Good, grand. I'm pleased,' she laughed.

'I feel the need to swim in the ocean. How long has it been since you've swum in the ocean, Clara?' I asked, remembering how much she loved the water when she was a toddler.

'Oh, I don't know. I know I have loved sitting and watching it while I've been with you. I can't remember the last time I actually swam in it. I must have been maybe eight or nine.'

'No, surely not. When you grew up living not a mile from the great Atlantic itself,' I exclaimed shocked.

'I wasn't allowed, Aunt Maeve. Not once Vincent took over things. He would go there with his friends in the summer and sometimes Aggie would join him with some of her friends, but I was never part of any of that and Vincent would never have let me go with them, not that I ever wanted to be around him anyway,' she lamented.

'Well then it is high time that you got yourself back into that water. Come on! We can make our way down a path about two miles along here. It is a little cove that I once stayed at for a whole week,' I remembered excitedly.

'You're after telling me that you stayed on a beach for a whole week by yourself!' she exclaimed.

'Yes, I did, but I didn't say I was by myself.'

'Oh, did Cynthia take you there to help you with your healing?'

'No.'

I strolled ahead sinking into the wonderful memories of that week on the beach.

'Hang on,' she gushed catching me, 'who was it then if it wasn't Cynthia?'

'A friend.'

'A friend, a man friend or a woman friend?' she asked, cautiously.

'Well if you must know, it was a male friend.'

'Surely not, Aunt Maeve! That's not allowed, surely! You cannot spend a week with a male friend on a beach.'

'According to their rules, Clara. Haven't you realised, I don't live by their rules, even when it comes to men, especially when it comes to men.'

Clara looked shocked. I knew that we had ventured into new lands. I didn't know we were going to go down this path quite so early in our adventure, but I trusted that this was exactly where we needed to go. I laughed with the comical wisdom of the Divine and relished immersing Clara into the wonderous new world, free of the rules and constraint of the patriarch. Not surprisingly, given Clara's propensity to call in her lesson's quickly, it was within an hour that the teaching had begun.

I stripped free of my clothes in preparation to

spring into the beckoning waves. Clara gasped as she realised that I was removing all my clothes.

'Aunt Maeve, what are you doing?' she shrieked.

'Going for a swim.'

I knew full well that my nakedness triggered her current moral compass as it contravened everything she had been taught about her body and the dangers of exposing herself in this way.

'But you can't go out there with no clothes on! What if someone is after seeing you. It's a mortal sin, you know that! The more skin you show the greater the sin, and you're showing all of it! What if a man comes along and he gets tempted and the like. You know it is your sin not his because you're after tempting him.'

Clara recited what she had been told a thousand times over from the pulpit from the likes of Colin Stanley, yet I sensed her doubting the words as they tumbled from her mouth, a recognition that they were not her truth. I left her be in her distressing internal battle.

I dived into the waves allowing them to envelope every crevasse of my body, the iciness of the water tickling my nipples as they hardened in response. I felt my body come alive and a surge of energy pulsated through my whole being in a way I had not felt over these last few weeks. I felt the release of tension escape from me as I dived under each wave and then thrust myself to the surface once again. I moaned with the ecstasy of it and relished the moment as I surrendered to the craving of my body to open and let go over and over again.

I returned to the sand to sit beside Clara feeling renewed from my dance with Mother Nature. She turned away from me as I approached in some way protecting my modesty, which I had no desire nor needed protection from. I gently patted her leg knowing her discomfort in my rawness, yet I was unapologetic and intent on demystifying the wonders of her physical body by exposing her to its true beauty and sovereignty.

Once again, we sat in silence and as I delighted in the freedom afforded me by my nakedness, I contemplated the expansiveness and power of the ocean that lay before us. As I surrendered even deeper I felt myself merge with it becoming one with the expanse while surges of unrestrained power surged up my spine. What must have been some time later, I emerged from my bliss induced state and found Clara staring at me with a look that spoke of confusion, admiration and heartbreaking grief.

'What is it, Clara?' I asked, sensing there was something of importance stirring within.

'Do you think I am dirty?'

Knowing exactly where she was going, I gently queried, 'Do you think you are?'

'Yes, I do, especially down there,' she muttered awkwardly and shamefully motioning below. 'I feel it all the time, I feel filthy down there, all the time. When I think about all the times that Vincent did it to me or Dempsey and even Colin Stanley, I don't really feel angry or sad or scared anymore, I just feel dirty now and it won't go away. No matter how much I try to clean it, when I was a little girl I used to scrub it so hard it would bleed, after that time with Colin Stanley I scrubbed it with a brush for weeks and even slept with chunks of soap in it, praying it would go away. But it never does. I can always feel it and smell it on me like there is something rotten in there and I think there must be mould or fungus or some sort of germ growing in me.' Clara paused in distraught but knowing she had come this far she took a deep breath and courageously continued, 'Sometimes this yellow gunk stuff comes out of me even when I am not bleeding and when I am bleeding, it is so heavy now and there are big clumps, and when I see it on the cloth in front of me, I just know that my soul is soiled and there is nothing I can do to change that,' she grasped at my hand willing me to believe her. 'Aunt Maeve, I can see that you are clean and free and can connect to what you call the Divine, but I am not you and there is no tea or potion or moon or tree or wind or sun or prayer or miracle from Mother Mary or Mary Magdalene that can ever change me. My soul has been stained for eternity.'

I saw a wave of relief wash over her as she finally expressed what she had always believed but never dared declare. I knew she desperately wanted me to agree that she was beyond redemption and that we should leave well enough alone.

'These last few weeks have made me realise that I let myself be dirtied by them because I was not brave enough or fierce enough to honour the voice that told me to stand up to them and speak up. So, you see it is my fault. For this very reason I am not worthy of the Divine Light that you seem convinced awaits me. No matter what you say or do, or what I say or do, nothing is going to change that. It just is. I have to learn to live in the darkness that I deserve.'

She did not storm away as she had in the past, instead she tightened her jacket around her and calmly walked to the water's edge, assured that this was as far as she was to go on this journey. I lovingly watched her knowing this was not the end, but rather the beginning of her next chapter.

Chapter Thirty-three

Maeve was different away from the cottage, the seriousness had melted away and she seemed younger, lighter and playful. She sang as we walked, some songs I knew and others I had never heard. She told me stories of her travels along these roads but unlike our conversations previously, I did not feel like she was trying to teach me or share her wisdom with me. I think she accepted that I was beyond redemption and heeded my plea to leave well enough alone. I was grateful for the reprieve, for the lessons had become tiresome and I had begun to feel intimidated by her knowledge and wisdom, believing I could never be so courageous, wise and open to new ways of thinking and being. I struggled with the ease in which she revelled in her physical body and sexuality, the deeply woven moral codes, fighting the urge to embrace these aspects of myself.

On the eve of our second night, my anxiety around where we were to sleep began to heighten, for I was tired and fearful of sleeping outdoors again. I was well beyond my comfort and it appeared Aunt Maeve relished this and propelled me further when we came upon a Gypsy camp. She laughed with delight as we approached. The sound of music, the children squealing, and the dogs barking flooded the otherwise peaceful land.

'Aunt Maeve, they are Gypsies!' I exclaimed as it became apparent we were heading in their direction.

'Indeed, they are. Travellers, the great people of the land,' she said with admiration.

'But we're never going to talk to them, are we, surely not,' I panicked as every story I had ever heard about their heathen ways flooded back to me, most significant the severe consequence of my own mistake in engaging with one Gypsy boy.

She looked to me, her eyes enlivened with playfulness contrasted her serious tone, 'Clara, we are going talk to them, we may eat with them, drink with them, sing, dance, laugh, sleep and pray with them.'

'You mean we are going to stay with them the night?'

'Tonight, and as many other days, and nights, as we are called to by the Divine Mother.'

She infuriated me by not stopping to appease my

apprehension. I stopped where I was and refused to take another step.

'This is insanity, Aunt Maeve. I will not be drawn into any more of this nonsense talk. Let us just turn around and head home to the cottage. It is safe there and this, well, this is ludicrous, and we cannot trust these people. You know that!'

'Clara, I can trust these people. They are my people, they are your people,' she said as she walked back to me no longer teasing me. 'Look at us right now, two women on a journey with nothing but two dogs and a bag between us. We are Travellers Clara, exactly the same as these people. You will discover as you spend time with these people, that all you have been told of them are lies that have come from fear. These people do not live by the rules prescribed by religion, government or society, they live in harmony with the law of nature and are deeply connected to the spirit world, blessing them with great power. It is this which is what those who so viciously condemn them fear most.' She looked deep into my eyes, seeking my trust.

Fear told me in that moment to turn away from my crazy aunt and make my way to the nearest town and find refugee with normal people, but the love I felt in Aunt Maeve's eyes convinced me to trust in her and walk beside her into the other world.

I took her outstretched hand and walked towards the world I had been convinced my whole life was filled with darkness and evil. A strange feeling engulfed me as I merged into the unknown and I began to feel more empowered with each step, knowing that my trust in Aunt Maeve was unshackling me from a world that had proven to be controlled by the very evil I had been told to fear.

The sounds of a mystical beat lightly danced on the edge of the wind and echoed across the lands. I was immediately captivated by the vision of a girl dressed in a white floaty dress playing a harp. The sound was mesmerising to all those around her and they moved in dramatic swirls of brilliant colour around the fire. The mess of carriages, the squealing of the children and the barking of dogs that I first observed, now blurred into oblivion, as I was drawn into the magical world.

'I remember my first time as well,' Aunt Maeve whispered. 'I thought I'd stepped straight into the faery kingdom. Yet there was not a faery in sight, only other people just like me.'

She was right. Once I allowed myself to see beyond the wall I had created, I felt the magic, a sense of familiarity that both confused and comforted me, stirred within my core and I felt every cell in my being awaken as my soul remembered her home. Aunt Maeve squeezed my hand and our tears welled.

'This is the ancient home of your ancestors. You have lifted the veil and seen what lies beneath and now they call you to come home.'

The most glorious old woman approached us, her white hair flowing down her back was adorned with a crown of wildflowers.

'Welcome home, my daughters.'

She embraced Aunt Maeve with the love of a mother before placing her hands on my cheeks, looking deeply into my eyes and examining my soul.

'I see it has been a long road that you have taken to arrive here, my child.'

She placed her hands on the top of my head and whispered words whose origin mystified me and I felt a tingle flow from my head right through my body. She removed her hands and smiled. The beauty emanated from her sapphire blue eyes and every crease etched in her face made me gasp in wonder that someone so old could be so exquisite. Her face emanated light that shone even brighter as she grasped both our hands with delight.

'Now we celebrate, for you are home, Clara. We have been waiting.'

As we entered the inner sanctum of the circle, I wondered how she knew my name. Aunt Maeve had not introduced us. I decided I didn't need to know the answers, it just was and as there was much I did not understand there was an extraordinary freedom that came with not bothering to seek to understand. I was in an unknown world and I chose to surrender and open to the magic.

She guided us to our place around the fire and as I sat on the blanket, my legs grateful for the reprieve, Aunt Maeve began to dance, embracing people as she moved rhythmically around the circle. The warmth and joy in which her presence was received showed me how loved she was by these people. She threw her head back in reckless abandon and as the flames of the fire illuminated her face I witnessed her breathing taking light. I saw a girl who was free as a bird soaring into the sky beyond the cliffs and I remembered my desperate longing as a child to be a bird, so I could be free. There were so many years, I lay in bed terrified by life yet pacified when I could take myself to the edge of those cliffs and soar with the birds. I realised how restricted Aunt Maeve must have felt with me these last few weeks, now I saw her in this way, I felt a combination of guilt and envy, for I wanted what she had.

'You can, whenever you are ready. It is waiting for you,' the old woman spoke quietly, as she sat down beside me and placed a bowl of steaming soup in front of me.

'I know,' I murmured, so mesmerised by Aunt Maeve that I didn't even have a chance to question how she knew what I was thinking, nor how I knew that the light I saw radiating from Aunt Maeve was being offered to me. I ravenously ate the soup, having not eaten since a light supper the previous night and I felt it nourishing not just my body but my soul. I felt her rising in me, as my mind was stilled by the hypnotic movements of Aunt Maeve and her friends in harmony with the sweet melodic sounds of the harp.

'Go on then,' she instructed me as she took the emptied bowl of soup from me, 'listen to her and be free, child.'

As I rose to honour my soulful calling I felt a sudden sharp pain in my heart that brought tears, not those of pain, but of a joy so wonderous as I felt her within me and I knew that she had cracked open my heart and shards of my past shattered to pieces in that moment. My body began to move as one with the music and I immediately lost myself only to rediscover my true Self. I was unaware of the hours that passed and oblivious to the world outside and it was only when the music stopped, and I felt Aunt Maeve's arm around me that I became aware of my surrounds. Her face was flushed, her eyes beamed as she looked at me with admiration.

'Clara ...' she kissed my forehead and held me close to her chest, '... never have I witnessed a more beautiful vision than you here tonight.'

A slither of fear darted back into my peaceful consciousness

'Was I after embarrassing myself?'

'Never, no one is ever an embarrassment when they dance with the Divine!' she assured, immediately dispelling the fear that threatened to take this moment from me. 'The difference with these people, our people, Clara, is they live from a place of love so there is no judgement of others, just a wonderful acceptance of all that is. If it rains, it rains. If someone is angry, they are angry. If there is no food, there is no food. If they get moved on by townsfolk, they move on. It is a very peaceful way of being, one that is in harmony with the world around them.'

'But when you just go along with things and not speak up people take advantage of you. Look what happened to me when I didn't speak up and just went along with life.'

'I thought the same thing when I first came to know these people. I adored them, and I became worried because I knew what people thought of them and their way of life. I feared that people like the McDermott's and Colin Stanley's of this world who are threatened by what they cannot understand, and control would destroy them. But these are ancient people who have walked these lands and lived in these ancient ways for millions of years. They know how to survive. They are fearless and wise. Knowing when to be silent and when to speak up. When to stay and when to go. When to let go and when to fight. Everything has a season, Clara. These people move in harmony with the cycles of life and the wisdom of the Divine, the Divine Mother and the Divine Father. They are gentle loving people but when they must fight for truth and to protect the tribe, they are wild and fierce, and their power is immeasurable, because it comes from love not fear.'

I finally understood Aunt Maeve because she belonged to these people and lived her life in this way.

'This is how you got them to let me sing at my mother's funeral. And how you got Mother Superior to let me leave the laundry with you.'

I looked at her with awe as the realisation of the

depth of her love for me descended.
    'Love is powerful, Clara.'
    She knew, I finally understood.

Chapter Thirty-four

Aunt Maeve was gone by the time I woke. I was surprised I had been able to sleep through the hive of activity within the camp. I was nervous seeing it in daylight and felt exposed without Aunt Maeve there with me, but I was relieved to see the old woman sitting nearby surrounded by roots and leaves, wildflowers and crystals. There were three little girls sitting with her. They were listening to her intently as she explained the healing gifts of the ingredients she placed into the crucible.

'Come, Clara, join us,' she said, without even looking to see I had woken.

'Marigold, would you mind pouring Clara a cup of the tea?' she asked the little girl who last night had played the harp.

I was surprised to see her sitting there looking like a normal little girl for I was convinced last night she was an angel. She dutifully poured the tea, her respect of the older woman evident and as she handed it to me she smiled shyly as her eyes caught mine for a milli-second and in that moment, I felt I knew her. She sat down beside me and turned her attention back to the older woman. I could feel her presence intensely which calmed me.

I drank my tea, a brew of sweet florals and listened with intrigue to this mystical woman, the carrier of ancient sacred knowledge, who shared it passionately with her captivated audience.

'Ma Ma, why are you making this remedy?' Marigold asked, curiously.

'Because Clara needs it,' the older woman assured her.

'How do you know when you're just after meeting her last night, Ma Ma?' One of the other girls queried.

'A woman knows, you will all grow to know. You listen and watch and learn and over time you will start to know as well. As we sit here, I can feel Clara and I know her pain and so we prepare. All five of us, as we sit here in this circle are surrounded by our ancestral mothers and the wise women who have gone before us and as we connect with their spirits we prepare to bring Clara home,' she looked at me unapologetic for the fear she elicited as I contracted to hide my vulnerability.

The girl's eyes shone with excitement at the

magic unfolding and honoured to be invited into the mystical world of their matriarch.

'It is a powerful gift we offer as women when we come together to help others to rise. Never doubt the power you have when you combine your energy, my daughters, and never fear it, even though others may seek to destroy it. As you remain in your power and unite, nothing can touch it. Nothing! For it is beyond this world and they can never access it should you honour its sacredness.'

The children listened mesmerised while I shrunk further into my discomfort as the power of her message striped away more layers and left me feeling even more exposed. Sensing my distress, she advised me to drink more tea and invited me to walk with her on the premise of collecting more wildflowers and plants.

'Marigold, you can come with us. Go and grab your basket.'

As the children ran off in their separate directions, she spoke to me earnestly, 'Clara, you do not need to be afraid of me or what is to come. The children call me Ma Ma but my name is Athena. I understand you met my owl on the full moon,' her eyes twinkled playfully, knowing she was pushing me further into uncomfortable intrigue.

'I was Cynthia's teacher and that is why I have such a great love for Maeve and in turn for you. The passing of Cynthia has been very hard for all of us, for she was deeply loved and an important member of our community and a teacher for many, but especially for Maeve. She always knew you would come to live with her and that she would become your teacher, and now she brings you to us, so we may all bring our gifts to your healing and bring you home to the Divine within you.'

A million questions filled my mind and my head began to throb under the pressure of uncertainty, yet I could not find the words to ask Athena. I followed her lead in silence as we began to walk beyond the camp and into the wilderness that was The Burren. I wondered where Maeve had gone and whether she would be concerned that I had left, but I felt she had entrusted me to Athena.

My fears abated as we meandered through the fields awash with wild plants and flowers. Marigold ran ahead picking the occasional flower and running back to Athena for clarification of its name and use. She absorbed every word, knowing that one day she would be the sole carrier of this ancient knowledge and it was her responsibility to pass it on to others, as well as use it to help her people. Athena explained that Marigold, much like herself, had come into her gift very early and it was essential that it was gently nurtured, so it was neither lost nor became a burden for her.

I watched Marigold. Her spirit so vibrant and free and I realised I was so drawn to her because she represented the child I once was. But I had lost my gifts and any awareness of them, because I did not have people around to guide and nurture me. I felt the weight of this loss weigh heavily on me and Athena sensing my despair offered sage reassurance.

'All is not lost, Clara. The last of your layers will be revealed soon, no matter how hard you resist and when you finally surrender, you will reconnect to the magic that lies within you.'

'I don't think I'm magical at all, not like you and Marigold. I'm just a normal woman, a farm girl,' I reflected sadly.

'Weren't we all, Clara,' she laughed, 'until we discovered that we are so much more than the farm girl, the wife, the mother. There is magic waiting in each of us, but most are too afraid of its power. 'Who am I as a woman to be so powerful?' they ask. 'Who are you as a woman, to not be so powerful?' I ask in return. Magic belongs to those who use it. We all have the choice, if we use it, and how we use it.'

I pondered her words as I strolled around the rocky terrain, leaving Athena and Marigold to their sacred task. While my mind couldn't comprehend the magic she spoke of, I could feel it around me and knew I had accessed it the previous night. I wondered whether I would ever be able to connect with it again. I knew I wanted to because I had never experienced such freedom and I loved how it felt, but another part gripped at me and told me I did not deserve this light and warned me against indulging in their wicked ways. But their ways did not seem sinful, they were pure and flowed with a natural rhythm of life and I wanted to live my life in this way but something within me fought to hold me back. The internal battle between my mind and my soul, lies and truth, fear and love, exhausted me and I stopped to rest on a large boulder. I lay back and stretched my arms wide, opening myself to the warmth of the sun and I prayed—to whom or what I did not know nor care—for my struggle to end, so that I may have peace.

The magic that surrounded me was more powerful than my fear fuelled darkness that had held me captive for so long and an aggressive force immediately took hold of me. My breathing became laboured and I panicked as I once more fought what was beyond my control, the more I resisted the more difficult it became to breathe. An impending doom threatened as I suffocated. Marigold was soon by my side having heard my desperate coughs as I grasped for air and she immediately took me by my hands and pulled me upright and firmly instructed me to slow my breathing. She knelt behind me and reached over my shoulders to place her hands on my chest and whispered, 'Breathe with me, Clara, as I feel into ye.'

A surge of heat pulsated from her tiny hands through my body, which instantly calmed my whole body, but also terrified me as my mind was challenged with thoughts of witchcraft and curses and spells and sorcery. Every story I had been told of these people and their wicked ways fought for supremacy and urged me to run from the Devil's playground back to Maeve's cottage, where I was safe.

'You cannot go back, not now. You have come

too far into the other side,' she whispered to me with a wisdom beyond her years. 'You cannot stay in the in-between, Clara. It is too painful. It is time to let go and become,' her words taunted me and I spasmed with resistance, for I did not know what I was to become.

'I see you. I feel you. I lean into you. I am you. I see you. I feel you. I lean into you. I am you,' Marigold methodically repeated.

She was like a mother soothing her child and as her words seeped into my being I sank into her arms, knowing I was held and supported and loved in a way I could never seek to describe. I remembered I was not separate from the Divine, I was not separate from anyone or anything, most importantly there was no separation within me, between my conscious Self and my soul Self. I was whole, and the fighting ceased.

Nature had taught me that everything has a natural cycle of life and death and I had come to the completion of this cycle. I had fought the finality of it, not believing myself deserving of the next phase that lovingly beckoned me. My resistance to this inevitable death had depleted me and I had to choose. I either kept fighting and be taken from this life or I surrendered to the force that ravaged my body, determined to obliterate the thorn that was rooted in my soul and burn a pathway for rebirthing.

My wise wild woman begged me to rise in her sovereignty, so she may once again frolic in the ocean, dance by the fire, sing in harmony with the winds and howl to the moon.

    I surrendered to her.

    I died as Marigold cradled me in her arms.

Chapter Thirty-five

I waited until Clara had fallen into a deep sleep, the walking and dancing ensured it did not take long.

I left her in Athena's care and returned to my lover. It had been two years since I had seen him, as he was known to come and go. He belonged nowhere and to no one yet seemed to belong everywhere and to everyone. I wasn't surprised to feel his presence as we approached the camp—our powerful connection remained—we were contracted to support each other in our ascension. Always drawn back to one another when we were needed. I sank into his arms to be held again and let go as I remembered that everything was exactly as it was meant to be. There was this moment and no other. I joyfully became one with it.

While much of this journey was about Clara's rising, I was also walking this path to awaken another aspect of my soul. I had danced around my gifts for many years and walked away from them completely since the passing of Cynthia, for I doubted myself without her. Now it was time. As Clara edged her way further into transition, the calling for me to step into my gifts grew stronger. Reconnecting with Dòmhnall was pivotal to my transformation, as it had been when Cynthia first brought me to her people. I was wary of him to begin with even though he was Cynthia's son, the unborn child she had carried with her when she courageously left her husband and son all those years before. She was determined she would not raise another child under that roof, having seen the dire impact her husband's behaviour had on her beloved son, Padraig, who at an early age demonstrated a propensity for disrespect and violence. As heartbreaking as it was to leave her son with this beast of a man, she was left with no choice but to save herself and her unborn child, when he mimicked his father's actions and hit her in the stomach after he challenged her integrity around the father of her unborn child. She knew what her son was becoming and felt powerless to change him. Cynthia reconciled within herself that she could not risk another soul, whom she had been chosen to mother, whether it be a male or female to be destroyed by this man and all he represented.

I had grown up with Padraig and remember ever

so clearly when Cynthia, who was my mother's best friend, ran away. His contempt for the girls in the school, fuelled by his father's hatred of women, intensified after Cynthia left and he mercilessly berated the girls in the classroom and dominated them in the playground, first physically, then, as we got older, sexually. He had little if any regard for women only showing respect to the nuns who taught us in the little school, because old Father O'Brien threatened to beat the boys with his shillelagh if they acted out of line.

Dòmhnall proved to be nothing like his father or brother in looks or nature. He was like no other man I had ever encountered. I initially preferred to stay close to Cynthia and in the company of the other women, because my trust in men had been destroyed. Yet I remained intrigued by Dòmhnall, he was younger than me yet felt so much older. A favourite with the children because of his gentleness, yet strong, muscular and fierce in his protection of those he loved. He had a way with words that would hold you with a story, weaving wisdom with humour and keeping you wanting more. He would immerse himself in the community, a central figure that everyone seemed drawn to, and then remove himself for days, weeks or months at a time to seek solitude. He confused and fascinated me as I tried to make sense of his contradictions, until I understood that he was a true manifestation of masculine in human form.

I did not move through my pain and transform as quickly as Clara did and it took many months for me to let go of my resentment towards the masculine, move beyond my fears and open myself to Dòmhnall. In welcoming him in, he became a pivotal part of my world, helping to activate aspects of myself that had remained hidden. We rode our horses for hours exploring ancient terrains, we hiked through gully's and across mountains and he told me stories of faery folk and historic battles on this land. He spoke of Celtic Gods and Goddesses and we danced with them under the moonlight. He taught me to move my body listening only to the rhythm of my own soul and I discovered the most wonderous worlds within myself as we shared this space.

    I felt the stirring of embarrassment and shame as he stripped naked to swim in the secluded cove we had discovered. My beliefs shying me away and closing me down again and again. It took but one breath for me to remember that they were not my thoughts, nor my feelings, they belonged to others and as I released them, I saw him in truth, not as man, but in the purity of his magnificence. I felt him as he dived through the waters and I heard my soul call to join him. As I took my clothes off, I sacrificed the fear that had kept me separate from oneness my entire life and I lost myself as I dived into the water and the unknown. I opened myself to the vulnerability and moved with the flow of the water and the natural harmony of our bodies as they met, our souls merged into one through the physical. The power of the Magdalene, whom I had once feared, joyfully surged through me, meeting his masculine and awakening the feminine I had veiled for so long. He honoured her. Exploring my body like a sacred flower, he brought her to blossom, and I, in turn, remembered the mystical power that she held.

Dòmhnall reconnected me to my maiden, an important rite of passage that I, like so many other girls had missed, transitioning straight into woman, an underdeveloped woman for loss of the important lessons through the maiden. It was here that I learnt how to use my sexual energy as a creative force to bring abundance, peace and contentment into my life and those I shared it with.

The sudden passing of Cynthia had shocked me so much that this part of me had remained dormant for almost two years now. When I heard news of Clara being held in the Magdalene Laundry, I knew it was time for me to reconnect to this powerful energy, to be a warrior and rescue Clara. While it was challenging for me to step into the huntress, to protect those who were vulnerable from the likes of Mother Superior, who thrive on abusing their power on the innocent, my love for Clara drew me into this power. Love is the most powerful force and I prepared myself before arriving at the laundry by filling myself with strength and conviction. I was prepared to fight for my Clara and when she resisted my demand to bring her home with me I rose in my potency, poised and ready to strike, towering in power, holding my truth yet leaving her in no doubt that I was willing to do whatever it took to end Clara's unlawful imprisonment.

Beneath the Veil

She was caught off guard and shrunk in fear, revealing her cowardice nature and immediately conceded to my demand. It was at first exhilarating, the surge of power stimulating my being, but I quickly became aware of how much it depleted me to rise in this way, because I had not activated this energy for so long.

Athena had signalled to me when we arrived at camp that Clara's death was imminent, I needed to prepare myself to bring her through the other side. She had powerful insight and an ability to read others energy and I implicitly trusted her wisdom. It was time. I was being called to rise as warrior, huntress and healer and Clara's soul experience depended on me accessing the potency of my highest potential and using the gifts I had long avoided for fear of their power.

Dòmhnall had been away these last two years to deal with the loss of his mother in his own way. Now he returned for this momentous occasion, to support me in reawakening the power of my feminine.

I opened myself to the beauty of the night and I rose into my sovereignty through dance and song. The Magdalene surging through me which reminded me once again that I did not *need Dòmhnall to access this energy, but I delight*ed in reconnecting with him regardless as we held each other in the deepest of love and united in body and soul.

When I saw Ceallach, the son of Dòmhnall carrying Clara in a state of unconsciousness across the fields the following day with Athena and little Marigold following, I knew it was time. I was not worried, accepting that she was now deep in the final stages of her transition just as Athena had foreseen. I was ready to support her as she released the final remnants of the past and burst into her new life.

The women gathered in a circle in the paddock adjacent to the camp, Ceallach placed Clara in the centre on a bed of wildflowers, kneeling beside her, he gently brushed her hair from her face. He remembered the fiery free-spirited little girl he once climbed a tree with whilst pretending to be a dragon and she a bird. His faced appeared wrecked with worry by her fevering body. He took her hand before he offered her a blessing to unite their souls.

Ceallach said,

'You are the star of each night,
You are the brightness of every morning,
You are the story of each guest,
You are the report of every land.
No evil shall befall you, on hill nor bank,
In field or valley, on mountain or in glen.
Neither above, nor below, neither in sea,
Nor on shore, in skies above,
Nor in the depths.
You are the kernel of my heart,
You are the face of my sun,
You are the harp of my music,
You are the crown of my company.'

He kissed her forehead before leaving and whispered, 'I'm sorry.'

I took his place beside Clara and as I inhaled deeply I sought Athena's counsel. Part of me secretly wishing she would take over and bring Clara through the fever with her herbal potions. Athena's eyes told me it was not her place. Clara needed my gifts, this was my time. I immediately felt the power of her love supporting me and that of all the women who encircled Clara. Placing her hand in mine, I closed my eyes and lowered my head and moved outside of my physical and into my sovereignty.

'My beloved sisters, as we cradle Clara in our hearts and move her into the new world that beckons her, let us remember we are the givers of life and the conduit of change. As we rise we invoke the healing power of the Divine Light to hold us in the most sacred of spaces.'

Marigold stepped into the circle holding a basket and reverently sprinkled the wildflowers around Clara's body before placing the herbal balm that she had earlier prepared next to Athena.

'The fruits of our Divine Mother Earth,' Marigold whispered, before she returned to her place in the circle.

Athena stepped forward. 'The wisdom of the Divine,' she said, placing the feather of an owl.

Another placed the statue of Mother Mary, 'Our Divine Mother.'

Another the statue of Mary Magdalene, 'Our Divine Wild Woman.'

A small girl placed her rosary beads, 'The power of the Rosary.'

The girl's mother laid the St Brigid's cross, 'The Goddess of Fire.'

Another placed a jug of water from the holy wells, 'The Goddess of Sacred Waters,' and her daughter sprinkled dirt, 'The New Earth.'

A young mother carrying her infant placed the sword, quietly saying, 'The Huntress.'

An older woman carried forth a candle, 'A light to call home the great ancestral spirits of this ancient land and our sisters who have transitioned from this life,' she paused, holding the light above her head.

The lightest of touches on my shoulder shot a shiver through my being and I knew that Cynthia's spirit was present. She was comforting and empowering me. I felt the touch of another hand on my other shoulder but as my head was lowered honouring the energies invoked into this most powerful and sacred circle, I did not see her face.

I did not recognise her voice as she spoke, her words revealing her truth, 'I bring this rose and call on the spirit of my mother, Róisín, to honour her daughter, Clara, as she is reborn, as she was not able to do in life. I call on the spirits of our ancestors, the wise wild women who reside within us to stand in their power now, that we may rise together, so that those who come after us, our daughters and granddaughters, might know their power and honour their sacredness.'

I held her trembling hand on my shoulder as the tears streamed down my face, the power of her words obliterating the shame of all those women who believed they had failed their daughters. The whispered cries of the ancestral spirits echoed around the circle.

> *'Forgive me for not raising you up.*
> *Forgive me for holding you back.*
> *Forgive me for failing you.'*

'Ma-ha-la,' the sound danced with my breath as though it came from the unknown. I inhaled deeply and sang louder, 'Ma-ha-la,' calling these spirits to come home, assured they are forgiven, 'Ma-ha-la. Ma-ha-la.'

I heard the sweet sound of Marigold's voice joining me as I sank into prayer, followed by a chorus of women echoing our prayer for all women. I squeezed the hand of my niece, astounded by her presence and I felt the spirit of my sister, my beloved mother and grandmothers surrounding me with a boundless love that infiltrated every cell of my being.

The chant began to fade.

Aggie spoke once more, this time her voice choked with emotion, 'Here is the veil that Clara once wore and courageously sought to show her truth. She remained hidden, shadowed beneath and now we free her to reveal what lies *beneath the veil.*'

Aggie took the candle that burned passionately to the veil, settling it alight, invoking the power of St

Brigid, the Goddess of Fire and igniting the light for me to begin my work.

I embraced the honour.

Chapter Thirty-six

Clara moaned through her delirium as I gently removed her clothes already damp from her fevering body. She lay naked allowing me to place my hands on the rawness of her physical body. The gift I had run from for so long lay in my hands, I trusted the Divine to work through them to unlock the final chambers of torture that Clara had fought so hard to conceal. I placed some of the healing balm on my palm, as I rubbed it in I felt the heat exude. The herbs Athena had intuited Clara would need were intense and would burn through the barriers Clara's fears had constructed.

Placing my hands on her back, my mind devoid of awareness, I became one with Clara. My hands were immediately drawn to the tension through her spine that widened as it reached her lungs, spreading across her back and squeezing, like a vice holding her trunk and slowly suffocating her. I could feel the infectious energy raging and taking a deep breath I allowed myself to see into her body, a dark parasitic presence engulfed her core and from it eight arms, which looked like the tentacles of an octopus, wrapped themselves around Clara's lungs threatening to crush her. My awareness recognised the threat, but I did not fear because I knew that this parasitic energy had been gifted to Clara as a reflection of the darkness in her soul that was now surfacing, ready to be released. The eight arms whilst menacing in appearance, were a sign of hope, the number eight representative of new beginnings and rebirthing, but it was imperative that the darkness at the core of Clara's being was now honoured to enable it to be released, or it would suffocate and kill her.

My being felt the intensity of Clara's presentation, but felt assured that as she lay in this circle of the most powerful feminine energy that she would return to us. I would play my part and then allow the innate wisdom of her body to heal her. I followed the tension with my hands to the base of her spine where it didn't feel as restricted, yet the heat radiating from this area amplified radically. I gently moved my fingertips around this space, and felt it quickly spread ferociously through her pelvis. I steadied myself before sinking deeply into it, and looked into her uterus and vagina, where I saw a mass of churning putrid liquid containing puss filled globules that popped and shot toxicity up through a cord connecting it to the growth that was encapsulating Clara's lungs. It was here, in the core of her trauma that was fuelling Clara's fever and lung infection. I explored with both my hands to ascertain if it had spread to any other parts of her body.

My fingertips delicately traced a line of fire from the pelvis to the heart space. There was no tension as my fingers carefully followed this thread and when I tuned into Clara's body I could not see it, but I was certain there was something there because I could feel its rage beneath my fingertips. I paused. I felt my mind seeking to understand the nonsensical and knowing that my mind would only confuse me more, I let go of needing to know what was refusing to be seen. As I relaxed into the unknown I witnessed a fierce blaze rip through Clara's body and land in the centre of her heart. She screamed from her unconscious state and clutched at her heart. I placed my hands upon hers knowing that she must hold in this place and listen to the wisdom of her body that was aggressively demanding her attention. As the conduit for Clara's healing I honoured her pain by asking what it sought to share, and I listened through my hands to the truth of her pain.

> *'I am not going away because she does not want me to go away. I have taken her lungs and now I have her heart, and the more you expose me, the more toxicity I will pump into her heart and through her body.'*

I was shocked by the intensity of her pain and asked it why it was so intent on destroying her now.

'She told me she would never forget, and I have reminded her of my presence every day. She shut me out when the nothingness came, she could not feel me, but I had not gone away, no matter how much she has released of me over these last few weeks, I remain.'

'Who are you that remains?' I silently asked.

'I am the core of her pain, the darkness she vowed to hold for eternity. And I would have remained hidden, subtly destroying her life, if she had not danced last night. As she moved her body, forgetting herself, she awakened the darkness and unlocked the doors that kept her safe.'

'She doesn't want to be safe. She wants to be free,' I spoke for her, knowing her truth.

'You know nothing. You have made her think she wants to be free, but she forgets she cursed herself by declaring 'I am not worthy of freedom because I am a sinner,' and I am tasked with holding her to that decree.'

'When did she make this declaration?' I probed sensing I was getting closer and knowing if I could isolate the memory that forced her to make such a drastic vow, then I would be able to help her to heal it, even though I did know how, I trusted I would be shown.

'Every time she was violated, she demanded to be punished for doing wrong, locking the door

on happiness and ensuring she became a victim to her past. But once she vowed she was not worthy of freedom she threw away the key and imprisoned herself.'

'What happened that forced her to make this vow?' I asked, again.

I sensed a reluctance to expose the enormity of this truth. I breathed deeply calming myself and releasing the tension in my hands, respecting the sensitivity of the moment and knowing the implications of forcing the release. I would not force her. She had been forced from her power for most of her life and her darkness deserved to be respected because it was as an important teacher and imperative to her growth.

Once again, I surrendered into the unknown and channelled Divine Light into the darkness that pulsated within Clara's pelvis. She stirred with irritation, murmuring in distress before thrashing her arms about, knocking me away and throwing herself onto her back. She spread her legs wide revealing the sacredness of herself before suddenly sitting upright and staring, eyes glazed, at the women before her who held her with love in a vortex of light.

'I-am-not-worthy-of-freedom-because-I-am-a-sinner,' she spat each word with ferocity to be sure no one would be in any doubt of the certainty of this statement. 'He forced himself on me, Colin Stanley. He pushed himself into me over and over and over again,' she paused. Her face contorted in spasming pain, 'And my filthy heathen body relished it. I moaned and arched and thrust myself at him like a brazen whore!' she screeched in hysteria, her glassy eyes evidence she was speaking outside of herself, her darkness finally exposing her truth.

The heaviness hung heavily in the air before it was broken, by the sweet voice of Marigold, 'Ma-ha-la.'

The women, past and present, echoed Marigold's chant. A chorus of love and forgiveness calling Clara home flooded the circle. The men could be heard across the field singing in unity a prayer for Clara and a prayer for all, that we may come home as one.

As the song echoed around me, I gently turned her face to look at me directly in the eyes, hers remained glazed and devoid of life.

'I see you. I hear you. I honour you. I love you,' I repeated each phrase quietly as I stroked her face, imploring her to return. I held myself with the Divine Light as I cradled her in her rawness, not allowing the fear that threatened to invade my mind, knowing that love was my greatest gift, the most powerful healer.

The sun had set.

The moon had risen before Clara broke through her fever, finally.

Her body settled, no longer needing to fight the battle. Her pain no longer blazing as I placed my hands over her body. The tension had released from her spine as with the spasming around her lungs. Looking within I saw that the mass within her core that had extended beyond to her lungs had been destroyed. The thread that threatened her heart had dissolved and no longer held power over Clara. The putrid mass remained through her uterus and vagina, but it was contained in this area and would expel from her body in the days ahead. The release of its toxicity would be unpleasant, but she would then be free and her Divine Feminine could return to her throne within her woman, reviving the essence of her being, her soul.

Clara's trauma had created chaos that stripped her bare and, in her rawness, she battled her inner demons, revealed her hidden secret, freed herself from her self-imposed prison and left behind all that no longer served her.

She died.

She rebirthed.

Now it was her chance to start again. A time for renewal and growth within a different landscape, one not littered with fear based patriarchal beliefs. She was free to live by her own rules, to write her own story and honour the sacredness of her soul. Nature is always teaching us this, the chaos of fires and floods, strips the landscape and gifts it with the opportunity for renewal and nature never says no. She is reborn and rejuvenates stronger because of the chaos, calmer because of the storm.

Clara stirred and as she opened her eyes, a calmness encircled her appeasing her confusion as she contemplated her surrounds trying to make sense of the circle of women, her nakedness and the chanting that was now accompanied by a distant drumming. She smiled with an exhausted acceptance, knowing all would be explained when the time was right.

She took my hand, closed her eyes, and murmured, 'What does it mean?'

'What does what mean?' I whispered.

'Ma-ha-la?' she purred.

'I don't know, Clara. It came to me from the Mothers of Mothers as they came home to us. I don't know, it just is,' I replied wearily, happy to relinquish my need to know and understand that which was beyond the capability of my mind to know and understand.

Freedom lies in the unknown.

Chapter Thirty-seven

I have no recollection of what happened after I collapsed into Marigold's arms in the fields. Everything was a blur for many days. Even in the moments when I woke, nothing would make sense to me. I was confused and felt like I was in the space between here and there. It was peaceful when I allowed myself to surrender to it and my exhaustion ensured that I let go of any sense of control as I slept through most of this deep transitioning of my soul.

That is what it was. A most profound transitioning of my soul. And while I was removed from it, easing the experience, my body did not transition with such grace. While I broke through the fever that first night, alleviating the intensity of the threat on my life, my body took many days to release the parasitic infection that had taken hold of me. The repugnant emotional toxicity spewed from my body with ferocity gripping me with bouts of vomiting and diarrhoea coupled with intense coughing episodes that released masses of thick vile mucous. A cloth lay between my legs absorbing the bloodied puss filled discharge that had intoxicated me with shame, guilt, disgust and self-hatred. The smell was abhorrent, and I was grateful to have been consciously removed from it. My humiliation of my gracelessness would have only set me back.

On the fourth day, I woke just as the dawn broke and knew I was back. I breathed deeply into my body and felt the breath pass through my whole being, no sign of the congestion that had plagued me acutely for the last few days and chronically since I was a seven-year-old. There was no wet cloth between my legs and no smell permeating the air. I was clean and the air surrounding me fresh and inviting. My mind slowly reconnected me to my surrounds and while I tried to remember how I ended up here lying on a makeshift bed, under a tree with the radiant blue sky, sprinkled with golden tipped clouds above me, it simply didn't exist in my memory. I trolled through that space in my mind where my memories reside, so used to living in the past and reliving my stories. They would not come to me. I could feel them but when I went to grasp them they disappeared seemingly unattainable. I thought of my brother and while memories came to me and I attempted to connect with them, there was no longer anything there for me to attach, they had flitted away. Curious, I sought to connect to my life with Dempsey Finnigan, I saw snapshots of him lying on top of me, but I felt nothing in response to what I witnessed. I sought memories of Colin Stanley, I saw him standing at the pulpit and before me at the altar, his head between my legs examining me, shoving me towards Mother Superior in repulsion and while some part of me wanted to be enraged, I grappled about pointlessly endeavouring to latch onto these emotions, the hook had been removed, there was no charge able to pull me from this most interesting place of peace in which I had found myself.

'I think ye might be back for good now, Clara,' a little voice whispered.

I turned to see the elfin face of Marigold lying right beside me, an excited spark twinkled in her eyes.

'What are you doing here?' I whispered back.

'I've been here the whole time, Clara. I would never leave ye, I love you so.'

Marigold squeezed my hand tightly, closed her eyes and sighed with deep relief. I was overcome with such an intense surge of love that it brought tears to my eyes.

'And I love you little one,' I whispered returning the squeeze of her hand, realising that this was the first time I had ever truly felt love in this way, the love of another for me and my love for another. What a wonderous moment! I smiled with the purity of it, and lay there, sinking its magnificence.

I saw this magnificence in everything that day as I re-emerged into the world. There was a sense of joy and celebration in the air and I was surrounded by love from these people who in many respects were strangers, but in some other way felt like family as my connection to them was so strong. Aunt Maeve watched me from afar, allowing me to find my way, her part in my journey was now complete. She too had a renewed vibrancy about her and I watched as she shone like never before as she spoke with a man. It was obvious he adored her being. I didn't know who he was, but their intimacy told me that he knew my aunt far better than I did. The pang of jealousy was quickly extinguished by the joy I felt for Aunt Maeve. I knew she had experienced her own pain and had sacrificed much while waiting for me to meet her on this journey.

Marigold never left my side. I saw her in the beauty of her humanness, a little girl who was at once smart, sassy and sweet, whilst also carrying the wisdom of an incredible old soul with much to share with the world. At different times, I felt her as one might a little sister, best friend and daughter, uniting the child, maiden and woman of my Divine Feminine, who had finally awakened.

Little did I know how much more she would be awakened once he appeared.

Ceallach, like his father came and went from the group, seeking adventure and solitude in equal doses. He had left once I had moved through my fever. It wasn't until a few days after I had recovered when I had settled into daily life on the land and freedom that he returned.

I was sitting by the fire, braiding flowers through Marigold's hair. People were chattering and preparing food when Ceallach sat himself beside me. He leaned forward and nudged Marigold who jumped into his arms and squeezed him with delight. I was a little affronted by her show of affection for him, because for the last few days Marigold had not been separated from me, even sleeping beside me each night. I had learnt that Marigold had been abandoned as a newborn. Cynthia and Athena discovering her early one morning, wrapped in a shawl, beneath a tree that was close to the camp. She was only hours old and still covered with the remnants of her birth, her mother most probably a young girl from the nearby village, who had hidden her pregnancy and took herself away into the fields to deliver her baby avoiding the shame she would have brought upon herself and her family should she have delivered a bastard child. Cynthia and Athena tended to the newborn and named her Marigold because of the golden light that shone on her face that very morning. They did not seek out the mother. Having seen this happen before, they took the infant into their care raising her as their own. Ceallach was like a big brother to Marigold as he was the grandson of Cynthia. Since her sudden death he had taken her under his wing more than ever becoming more of a father figure.

'Where have you ever been?' she demanded of

him, feigning her displeasure.

'Were you after missing me then?' he teased.

'Not at all, sure and haven't I had Clara here all this time, while you've been off traipsing about like an old gypsy,' she teased knowing his sensitivity to the name. He frowned with mock displeasure at her taunt, even though he knew he couldn't deny he had the soul of a Gypsy.

'Ah, Clara,' he said turning to me with a broad grin. 'So, you're after filling my shoes while I've been away doing my gypsy thing?'

'No, just walking in my own shoes,' I smiled back at him.

'I am glad to see that you've finally found your way back into your own shoes,' he smiled knowingly at me. His meaning was not lost on me.

'Yes,' I breathed deeply, closing my eyes and appreciating the wonder of being me once again and when I opened them again, he was staring and smiling admiringly. I felt a flutter in my stomach that unnerved me momentarily until I convinced myself it was just hunger.

'How long has it been then?' he asked, noting my fleeting wobble.

'It's been three days now since she came good,' injected Marigold, misconstruing his question. 'It was magical, Ceallach. The circle and the healing. Maeve was after rising and she could see into Clara's body and moved all the stuck energy about. It was beautifully magical. Did you hear us sing?'

I blushed with embarrassment, feeling exposed in the rawness of my healing, yet appreciating the awe and wonder Marigold expressed about my transition. He watched me carefully, navigating how far into my discomfort the conversation was taking me, knowing it was important I learn to sit in my unease, but appreciating my vulnerability.

'I did hear the singing,' he said, turning to Marigold. 'Was it you who led the chant?' he asked, curiously.

'Yes, it was,' she said a little sheepishly, knowing she had followed her intuition, but slightly unsure as to whether she had overstepped her place in the circle. Sensing her unease, I grabbed her hand and squeezed it tight.

'You know I cannot remember much of what happened over those days, especially not in the circle, but I do vaguely remember hearing a chant or singing at some point. I didn't realise it was you who led it.' I pulled her into a huge embrace, 'You certainly amaze me my beauty. I wish I had your courage when I was your age.'

'I think you did, you just can't remember,' Ceallach whispered.

'What did you say?' Marigold demanded. 'You can't be after keeping secrets from me! I'm the one that knows ye both, so you should be telling me the secrets, not each other,' she laughed despite her righteousness.

'Here then,' he said, taking her onto his lap and whispering in her ear.

'You never did!' she exclaimed and ran off to find Athena.

He laughed at the beauty of her innocence, knowing in her wild imagination, she would be in no doubt that the snow white feather he had earlier gifted to Athena was in fact the wing of some extraordinary mythical creature.

He turned his attention back to me, explaining the secret which had resulted in her swift departure. While we laughed at her, I felt a sudden intensity land between us now that we were alone that took my breath. I steadied myself to maintain my integrity and noticed a similar change in his demeanour, that in some way calmed me, knowing he had felt it too.

'So,' I began with an unfamiliar confidence, 'what is it I can't remember?'

'You cannot remember you and how courageous you were as a child, just like our Marigold. I saw her again the other night when you arrived with Maeve and danced. I had almost forgotten her.'

I felt another quiver in my stomach at the thought of him watching me dancing, seeing me so free.

'What do you mean you had almost forgotten who I had forgotten?' I giggled with the absurdity of the question, noticing how relaxed I felt with him, a male and a stranger, whose name I didn't even know.

'I don't know even know your name.'

I surprised myself with my sudden assuredness. I had never been spoken to men in this way—as my equal—and when I realised this I began to recognise the enormity of my transformation.

'Ceallach,' he smiled. 'My father liked to keep the tradition of old Irish names,' he explained, but I was not listening as I was searching my mind for a memory, because the name was so familiar, but my memories were now so vague that I couldn't immediately grasp it.

'I knew you couldn't remember,' he declared interrupting my search. 'But I remember you, Clara. You were a bird and I was a dragon, and I beat you to the tree,' he looked at me tenderly willing me to remember.

The memory of that afternoon came flooding back and I stared at him aghast, 'That was you?' I finally said, laughing.

'And I still believe in dragons!'

I reached for his hand and turned to him in amazement, 'It never was! I can't believe it! You're him.'

I felt him, that little boy who had shared my joy, and even though I became aware that I was holding his hand, I did not pull away because something in me desired so strongly to be connected to him because he was a link to her. He knew me before, before everything changed, and I lost her. I felt the wave of emotion roll over me, stripping me bare once more.

'Do you remember her?' I asked, as tears filled my eyes causing me to shy away.

He gently stroked the side of my face and

whispered, 'I remember you.'

I may have died again in that moment, because my breath left me, and the world seemed to stop. There was only him.

I cradled my hands about his face, 'I remember you!'

I traced the line of his cheek staring into his eyes and saw the same impassioned expression that had danced when he spoke of dragons and his people and being free. He took my hands from his face and clasped them in his own and lowered his head to hide his emotion, but I could feel the shame and sadness rising in him.

'What have you to be ashamed of?' I whispered.

His eyes were pained as he returned them to mine.

'It was my fault. All your suffering was my fault. I should have stood up to him. I should never have let him take you home. I should have protected you. And when I saw you in church that day, with blood all over your dress I knew what he had done to you and it was all because of me. And you were so courageous, standing up to them in the way that you did. I saw you give in to them and I should have stood by your side. I was not brave enough to face them. I knew what they thought of me and my people and I wasn't sure enough of who I was to stand up to them and stand by you. You suffered because of me and my weakness, Clara. I have never forgotten *that,* and I promised myself I would never let anyone disempower me again and I haven't,' he paused allowing the purging of his words to settle before he took my hands to his heart. 'I'm sorry, Clara. I failed you. But I promise you … I will stand by your side and will never fail you again.'

A million thoughts tried to demand my attention, but they couldn't reach me. I saw him in me. I felt him in me and I let go and leant into him and we became one. We remained in the sacredness of this intimacy, relishing in the deep soulful exploration of our oneness, and I felt its magnificence rising through my body, and my soul moaned with relief in the discovery of this hidden aspect of her being. She rose, the most Divine Goddess of Light. I felt him rise to meet her here and again dived deeper into the connection, ecstatic in uncovering the innermost sanctum of being. We merged deeper into oneness and drifted into a vast expanse of light where we lost ourselves completely in the Divine Love that had been longing for us to return Home.

Love called me Home.

Chapter Thirty-eight

I watched from the other side of the fire, and although their enduring look only lasted a few seconds, I felt the intensity of their connection. I chose to look away, not wanting to impose on their intimacy, for it was so pure and beautiful. I took Dòmhnall by the hand and traced the fine lines of his fingertips, adoring every aspect of him, knowing that Clara had just experienced intimacy in this way for the first time. It is something so sacred and hard to place in words, it is just the being with another whose very presence takes you into yourself and into love.

'Thank you,' I whispered to the Divine, overcome with gratitude for blessing me with Dòmhnall who had helped me discover this within myself. He felt me expand into my gratitude, disengaged himself from the lively conversation surrounding us, turned to me with a curious smile, and noticing the tears in my eyes, I know he could feel the joy I was experiencing.

'You right there, Maeve?'

'Indeed, I am. I am filled with joy and gratitude.'

'I see you are!' he laughed, pulling me closer, kissed my forehead and held me.

His presence centred me more than anything else in this world and while I lived fully in my wholeness for long periods without him physically present in my life, I treasured the sanctity of our connection, as I knew he did.

'I see Ceallach and Clara have met. He got back from taking Aggie back up north this afternoon, took a detour for a few days he said, you know how it is,' he commented casually and then paused, as he watched Ceallach and Clara more closely from across the fire. He sensed the intimacy of their connection, even though they were now just talking, Marigold had joined them. He turned his attention to me, and gave me a knowing look, 'Did you see that then?'

I nodded, tears filled my eyes once again, 'It happened. Just sitting there on the rug, I felt it all the way across here, it was blessed and exquisite. You can see it in them can you not?'

He laughed, 'You cannot miss it! Lucky little Marigold is there with them now to keep them grounded because they would both be away with the faery folk if she wasn't. They may just be anyway.'

Together we laughed knowing the otherworldly feeling that comes with the intensity of such a sacred connection. A feeling that can come sitting on a rug and looking into another's eyes, or through the intimacy of a sexual union or even while thinking of another while they are on the other side of the country. Dòmhnall and I had many experiences where we had been able to intimately connect without being physically present with one another, our souls meeting in the ethers and reuniting in love. The most magnificent magic can happen when we remember that we are not separate from our beloved, our family, friends, trees, birds, leaves, water, dirt, when we remember that we are not separate from the Divine, because the essence of each one of our beings comes from the Divine, we are all one.

Dòmhnall taught me that the masculine does not live outside of me in the form of a man, it lives with me, the same as the feminine does not live outside of him, it resides within him. When I learnt to look at the world in this way I did not reject the masculine. I embraced it. I knew it was part of me. I adored my soul being, all parts of her. And in honouring myself I was able to look to those who had abused the masculine and made me fear it with compassionate eyes. I saw myself in them, because of my unbinding love for myself, I was able to love them. When you love another, you do not punish them, you open yourself to forgiveness and you no longer become a victim to them or who they represent.

This was Clara's journey now, discovering the Divine Feminine within her but also learning to love the Divine Masculine as Ceallach would model to her, just as his father did to me. I knew I would need to speak to Clara about sexual intimacy, because it was a beautiful and powerful way to express their connection. Her past experiences with the sexual act, had not honoured its sacredness and while she had released the trauma and shame around these experiences, she needed to be prepared so the memory of past trauma was not triggered when she united with Ceallach in sexual intimacy. I was to teach her about these divine parts of her physical body, so she could be empowered by them, not ashamed, as she had been taught in the past. Cynthia had passed this wisdom to me, and Athena to her, each of us needing to be taught the truth about the most intimate part of our bodies.

I looked at Marigold and celebrated that she would not have to unravel the untruths about her body, for she had never been made to feel ashamed of her body and was already being taught to honour its divine sacredness. I could see in her an innate confidence, something that Athena, Cynthia and I had to cultivate, and one that Clara was growing into as each day passed. The experiences she was to have with Ceallach in the days, weeks and months ahead would only help her to grow assured in expressing her true Self in the world.

I could see the future they were to create, and I

was excited for them. It was joyful and abundant. Yet a quiver of unease flickered in my stomach and I was not immediately sure what it was, so I sat in its discomfort letting it speak to me. Tiny surges of panic shot through me and I felt it between my eyes and I realised that I could not *see* what was next for me, where my own life was to go. I could *see* this with such clarity for Clara and Ceallach and Marigold, but when I felt into it for myself I couldn't see anything. I didn't know what that meant. A sense of impending doom landed, as I feared there was nothing more for me to do in this life, for it was true I had been waiting for Clara for so long to fulfil my purpose, to help her overcome her past and bring her to this exact point within herself.

I knew that there was more I was to teach her, but I was never to be like Cynthia and Athena and be the matriarch of this community. These were my people, but I had always come and gone, a welcomed visitor who shared in their life and their ways, but I balanced it with the solitude and stability of my life in the cottage.

I stared into the fire willing it to show me what was to come next, for my innate sense of knowing had been a loyal companion for some time and I relied on it to guide me.

My thoughts were interrupted by a whispered, 'You don't need to know. Just allow it, my love.'

I looked to Dòmhnall who was smiling tenderly at me, 'I know it's been big for Clara but for you also. Everything is changing. You are changing. And while you're here in the in-between nothing is going to be clear,' he reassured me.

I hadn't realised the enormity of my own transformation, my focus being consumed with Clara's transition, and I realised why my future was a mystery.

'Let's enjoy the mystery,' he mused, 'there is freedom in the unknown.'

He mockingly reminded me of the very wisdom I often shared with others but had momentarily forgotten. Taking a deep breath, I surrendered into the mystery of my life, trusting that I would land where, when and how I was supposed to. We sat in the silence of surrender, remembering the freedom of not being in control.

'Wherever you do land,' he began, with an unusual sense of seriousness, 'I promise to be there with you, if you'd have me? I am a free spirit that's for sure, but I don't want to keep wandering through life without you, Maeve. I want to share my days and nights with you. I want to walk by your side every day and discover new worlds with you. What do you think?' he nervously stroked my hand that he gripped in his while staring intently into my eyes.

The unknown was certainly full of mystery and surprises, none more than this. I paused in gratitude for the blessing of the Divine in my life and then laughed with her at this unforeseen magical twist, which I don't even think Dòmhnall knew was coming as he sat beside me that night. Who was I to resist the Divine and her mystical plan of travels, adventure and exploration of unknown lands, both within and outside of me. I cupped his face, adoring the vulnerability in his eyes, the defined line of his cheek, the strength of his squared jaw, the mess of his wild, silvering hair, the magnificent radiance of his soul and vowed, 'Wherever I land, I land with you.'

'Yes,' his soul sighed in anticipation of the wonder that lay ahead. 'Let's soar beyond all that we know. Beyond here, beyond you, beyond me, into the infinite.'

I trusted the adventures that were awaiting me, in sharing my life with this wild, free spirit, who would take me to places I would never have even dreamt of.

Chapter Thirty-nine

I did not notice the passing of days as I was consumed in the present. My heart centred me in the extraordinary beauty of my true self, whom I was growing to love. Marigold showered me with love and adoration. Ceallach opened me to a type of love I had never known. From the moment we connected by the fire, we were inseparable, seeking to know and understand one another so there was nothing between us in our human experience. We knew there was nothing between our souls, for we had both felt the oneness, and we sought that same experience in our physical.

I shared with him the story of my life but was

surprised that I did not wallow in self-pity as I so often had in the past. I realised that I had been resisting Aunt Maeve's guidance for all these weeks because I didn't know who I would be without my victim story. But now that I had moved beyond my past and detached from the identity I had created as a victim I was able to tell these stories from a place of truth. A truth that surprised me in its power, for I spoke with a love of myself, and compassion for others. I did not need to be a victim to my past, because my present offered me love.

I felt Ceallach tense as I detailed the intimate details of my trauma, but I knew he needed to know the whole truth. He needed to let go of his guilt, for he believed it was his fault that my path had been so challenging. He cried when he told me that he thought of me every day for years, reliving that moment with Vincent in the paddock and seeing my blood-stained dress. He knew he loved me then, yet could never make sense of it, trying for years to convince himself that it had been nothing more than two children playing a silly game.

He did not want to go to the church the day of my First Communion, but his father was insistent that they go, as he always had whenever they were in these parts. Dòmhnall did not abide by the traditional view of the Gypsy lifestyle. He took his son, across the country and across the sea. He was well-educated, Cynthia making sure of that, and had been able to secure teaching positions in Ireland and abroad. He inspired people with his philosophical way of viewing the world and had become a sought-after scholar, albeit a controversial one.

He always returned home to these people who were his kin, most especially his mother, whom he adored, and brought with him an insight into the world beyond. Yet whenever they returned home, he would insist on taking Ceallach to the church, even though he was not religious himself. It took many years before Dòmhnall would explain that he needed to go so he might observe the man he might have been had it not be for the courage of his mother. He would sit at the back of the church and watch Padraig McDermott, his older brother, whom he had never met. Cynthia had told him the truth of his story from the time he was old enough to understand, and his curiosity about his father and brother only grew as he got older. He never sought to meet them, his purpose in watching them, was to strengthen his own sense of Self, by shining a light on who they were. He was aware that who they were existed within him, deeply woven into his cellular structure and he was determined he would not become them. He needed to know who they were, through observing their behaviour so that he could recognise that which he did not desire to be within himself.

He did not know that Maeve also sat hidden in the back pews of the church that day, because at that time, she had not connected to Cynthia. I was astounded to find out how much else was going on in that church that day. I was young and oblivious to anything but my own story, it all made me realise that life is not always what it appears, when we rise above our story and view life from a higher perspective, there is much to be seen.

Ceallach had a unique perspective on life, having been educated both in the classroom and in nature. He was more reserved than his father in expressing himself. Dòmhnall able to stand in lecture theatres and in halls across the country and share his wisdom, while Ceallach preferred to fly under the radar gently radiating his power and wisdom into the hearts of others. He was everyone's friend, easy to be around, able to engage in light banter and draw you into deep conversation, sharing stories of his travels, planting seeds of expansion in those he connected with. He travelled in solitude, and moved from town to town working on farms, sleeping under the stars or in barns, connecting with people everywhere he went.

Like his father, he always came back to his people, valuing the purity of their way of life and the love that engulfed him whenever he arrived. But he knew he was different to them in ways he found difficult to articulate without offending, and his father was the same, but unlike Ceallach he was untroubled by being labelled, rising above the judgements of others. Ceallach struggled with his identity for much of his youth and sought counsel in his beloved grandmother, Cynthia, who suggested he was not alone in resisting being labelled in accordance with whom he associated. She explained that anyone who has a strong sense of Self, cannot possibly see themselves categorised in this way, for they know they are spectacularly unique and unbelievably expansive, bigger than any box. She encouraged him to see labels as simply the perception of those who could not understand, nor attempt to understand those who chose to live a life outside the constraints of societal ideals. Cynthia knew this, too well, as she had been ostracised, publicly declared dead and never to be spoken of again, all because she chose to live in alignment with her truth.

Ceallach had created his own identity but admitted he was still challenged from time to time when he was called a Gypsy suggesting to him that he was still missing something within himself. Something that he had not found with his people, nor in the vastness of his travels. The closer we came over those first few days together, the more he opened to me and admitted that he had finally found that missing piece when he connected with me by the fire, yet it had nothing to do with me. He did not need me to complete him, rather in our connection he was able to remember his truest expression of Self and no longer felt alone. He discovered a new sense of peace and knew he no longer needed to keep travelling and searching for something that was within him all the time.

One day, as we sat on the branch of a tree, just as we had many moons ago, he asked me what my plans were given Maeve and Dòmhnall were to be wed. I had not thought of the future and a momentary sense of panic overwhelmed me as I feared I would be left alone when

Aunt Maeve married. This moment passed surprisingly quickly as I remembered my truths—I loved and was loved, I was worthy of loving and being loved—I was never alone. I had more love surrounding me and within me than I could ever have imagined, however, my future turned out, I knew it was to be blessed.

'I don't know what it looks like exactly. I just know that it includes Aunt Maeve and Marigold and you,' I was not shy in speaking my truth, not with him, because there was no separation between us, so I did not have to hold back for fear of him rejecting me. I just knew that I loved him like no other and he would be an integral part of my life.

'I don't need to keep travelling. I would like to settle down somewhere, with my own piece of land and live a simple life,' he stared beyond the horizon with a dreamy look in his eyes. After a few minutes he looked at me with an excited glint in his eye, 'Would you ever?' he stumbled. 'Do you think you'd ever want to settle down somewhere with me? I can see it, you and me and Marigold,' he smiled with the memory of the vision he had just received. 'And one day, if you … well, maybe, one day we might even be blessed with another child, if that was something that you would consider.'

I didn't need to consider. I had known from the moment our souls connected by the fire, that we were meant to be together and that included Marigold. I wasn't sure if I would be able to bring a child into this world given my past, but I decided then and there, sitting

Beneath the Veil

in a tree, that I would not allow my past to dictate my present. I empowered myself to write a new story, one where I was more than a vessel to impregnate.

'I know that we will love Marigold as our own and if we were to have more children, they would come from love, our love.' I was in awe of the confidence with which I spoke of things I had believed, until very recently, were unspeakable especially to a man. 'You will have to teach me,' I added quietly.

'What if we taught each other?' he replied, gently. 'A dragon must learn the way of a bird, and the bird the way of the dragon.'

I felt that familiar stirring in my stomach, a yearning that Maeve had explained to me was not hunger, but was desire, a longing of a different form. I could feel it in him as well and I wasn't sure what I was to do. I had suppressed this feeling sporadically for days now and while there had been moments of deep intimacy, similar to that we shared on the first night, none had been through our physical connection.

He jumped from the tree, looked up to me, took me by the hand and helped me down. We stood under the tree, the remains of any nervousness having dissipated and replaced by a shared longing for oneness. I had never felt desire nor been desired and my heart raced in anticipation, my lip quivered as he traced his finger along it ever so gently. Nobody had ever touched me sensually, I didn't know if I could handle the intensity of it. He held my cheek and ever so slightly titled my chin and ever so softly moved his lips onto mine. The touch alone sent waves through my body. I shivered, he drew me closer, wrapping his arm around my waist and I felt myself lean into him, sinking into all of him, as he tenderly kissed my lower lip.

I had been married but I had never been kissed. I had been touched but I had never been held. I had had sexual encounters, but I had never made love. It was new, it was my first time, no memories of past experiences were trigged to taint it, because it did not remind me of those experiences, it was completely different. He honoured every part of me and lavished my body in sensual touch that aroused me and stirred my longing to be completely lost in him. I took his face in my hands and brought his attention to my eyes and we sank deeper into one another's soul. He responded to my passion, kissing me deeply with an intensity that matched my fervent desire, his hands grasped at my body beneath my clothes and I began to pull at his shirt needing to feel the rawness of his body.

I drew my hand across his chest, astounded by the hardness and grasped at his shoulders that were broad and defined. I was taken by the beauty of his powerful muscular body that was hidden beneath his clothes. I eagerly removed my blouse and undergarment needing to feel his rawness and I savoured the sensation of his solidness against my softness. I explored the ridges and lines across his chest, shoulder and stomach. I lightly traced my finger tip in a line from his core to his nipple and marvelled at it as it responded, hardening in anticipation. I circled it delicately, teasing him and further arousing myself, the desire growing stronger in me. I drew a line from his chest across his jaw to the edges of his mouth, my fingertip tracing the delicate line around his lips which trembled. There were no barriers, no limits to the depth we could feel within the other, in our oneness, and we surrendered into it, disconnecting from all time and space, allowing our bodies to meet in this place.

    The innate callings of our souls for more, more depth, more connection, more oneness mirrored as our bodies sought more of each other and my body opened to him, hungrily taking him deeply within me. The sacredness and intensity of our physical oneness filled me, every cell in my being infiltrated with him and I moaned in ecstasy as I felt each cell expanding in pleasure, swelling in me, surging as they sought to explode. My being quivered as my body lingered on the edge of the unknown and I let go and leapt into the expansive nothingness of my own being. The nothing was everything, there was no separation and I soared through it as my cells released with a euphoric eruption that shattered the last semblance of my illusion.

    I was not her. I am.

Chapter Forty

He the dragon.

I the bird.

A Divine union.

A sacred marriage of perfect balance that gifted us with home, unity and love.

I was the earth to anchor him. He the Heaven to take me beyond. We honoured the balance of masculine and feminine in each other. Ceallach was strong, passionate, honourable. He cared for and protected me. I adored his strength and vulnerability and nurtured his earthly sensitivity, grounding him in this world and bringing out the best in him and in turn me. Our love was both serene and passionate, the need for one another chosen, not for survival but to be. To be in our eternal truth.

We moved within our sacred love story, travelling from the camp back to Maeve's cottage after the next new moon, bringing Marigold home with us to begin our family life. Maeve and Dòmhnall had left to explore their relationship and new worlds, assuring us that they would return when the time called. I surprised myself by being filled with nothing but joy as I waved goodbye to Aunt Maeve. Once I feared her abandoning me, as so many others had before, but now I knew differently. Now I knew that I was never alone, and my heart sang as I watched her transition into her new life with renewed vitality and passion. Dòmhnall held her in such high regard, something I know she found hard to accept, for she was so grounded in herself that she failed to recognise the depths of her own magnificence. He adored her, even though, he was a man who had garnered much attention and glory in his travels, he was humbled in her presence. He revered her because he knew her sovereignty which she obscured beneath her shawl, not because she feared her beauty or power, simply because she did not need the world to bear witness to it. She would remove the shawl when called, as she had done to support me in my transitioning, but she held the sacredness close to her, only sharing it through her gifts when she knew it was her Divine duty.

Aggie stood beside me as we waved farewell to our aunt, hand in hand, similarly touched by the transformational role our aunt had played in her life in recent months. When she courageously came to see me at the Magdalene Laundry, she opened a door not only to my freedom but to her own and her life had been shifting with rapid speed since that time.

She dared to speak to a Gypsy who was passing through the village, telling him to send Maeve for me, and as chance would have it, that 'Gypsy' was Ceallach. He returned to the village to tell Aggie that Maeve was planning to head to Galway, but first she wanted to see her. Aggie told Vincent she was going to Dublin to stay with an old friend, while he objected and tried to stop her from going, she stood up to him, knowing it was imperative that she meet with Maeve. Aggie stayed with Maeve for a week, before Ceallach took her to the camp where she spent another week with Athena. She underwent a profound transformation as she immersed herself in her healing, absorbing the teachings of Maeve and Athena. She had demonstrated that she was ready to change and move beyond the life she was living when she broke the rules and went to the laundry to see me without the permission of Vincent or Colin Stanley. Her wilful defiance of the patriarchal structure continued when she returned to the farm a different woman, an empowered woman, who was intent on reclaiming her life and living by her own rules, not those prescribed by her brother, the church or the small-minded people of the village.

I had always admired Aggie's confidence and ability to push the boundaries without stepping over them, keeping both herself and those in authority happy. However, since I had married Dempsey Finnigan and moved from the farm, the restrictions Vincent placed on her had become tighter and she felt herself losing more of her freedom as each day passed. She couldn't see a life beyond the farm should she continue to live that way and her nagging feeling that something had to change spurred her to act.

I didn't know she had been a part of my healing circle, for I remained oblivious to most of what transpired in that space. Ceallach had gone to the farm and brought Aggie back without Vincent's knowledge and she remained overnight until I broke through the fever. She returned to the farm the following day and feeling more empowered than ever she told Vincent she was moving to Galway to live with our father's sister whom she had reconnected with when she came to the laundry. Ceallach had waited for her in the village as she had told him of her intention and he took her to Galway and waited about a few days to ensure she settled. She quickly got a job working alongside our cousin Adele in the family horse breeding business. Within days she had met Seamus, the son of a wealthy horse racing family from Dublin, the man who would fall in love with her and within weeks ask her to marry him.

I was both excited and nervous as I prepared for Aggie's wedding. Aunt Maeve had given me an exquisite dress, brought back from her travels, which hung delicately across my beautiful burgeoning bump, the most magnificent expression of new life and love growing within me. I had not returned to the village since being sent away to the laundry, I felt my heart racing in anticipation of what lay before me. I was reminded of the glances and whispers when Aunt Maeve walked into the church at my mother's funeral and recalled how she had held her head high, rising above their small-minded gossip. I intended to do the same. I knew I was not alone because my family would walk beside me: Ceallach, Marigold, Maeve, Dòmhnall. I knew with their love and support I would be strong enough to rise to any challenge.

I held hands with Ceallach and Marigold as I walked down the aisle, the mantilla veiling my face. I saw them coming towards me, aggressively intent on blocking my path and shaming me before the congregation. I would not allow them to disempower me, so I stopped before they reached me, I sensed Ceallach flinch as he sought to protect me. I squeezed his hand to assure him of my confidence. I pulled my shoulders back, raised my chin and looking straight ahead I lifted the mantilla veil. I would not hide *beneath the veil*.

I could feel their rage at my blatant disregard for the strict rules of the church, cursing me to Hell for daring to reveal myself.

'How dare you set foot in this most sacred home of the Lord Jesus Christ, you are a sinner, you and your kind are not welcome here,' Colin Stanley spat at me.

I chose to remain centred. I would not allow their judgement, their name calling. Nothing would dethrone me, for that is what they desired.

'I come with my family to celebrate Aggie's

marriage, nothing more,' I spoke with a gentle calmness that further incited his fury.

'Are you married, do you carry a bastard child?' Colin Stanley said, full of condemnation.

'She is not married. They are living together and breeding outside of wedlock. The most mortal of sins,' Vincent declared vehemently.

I could feel Ceallach stiffening. Dòmhnall bristling behind me. But I did not need them to stand up for me. I would not fight. I would not descend to that level. I spoke from truth and from the place of love that I was blessed to feel every day.

'I am married. It is in a way that you do not understand. I am not married unto rules. I am married in love, the union of two souls, and our child is a creation of our Divine love.'

'What nonsense! Married in love. You are either married in the eyes of the church or not! Anything else is a sin in the eyes of the Lord our God,' he bellowed in outrage.

'That child will be condemned to Hell. A child conceived out of wedlock is not of God's creation,' Padraig McDermott said, as he stood from his pew and joined Vincent and Colin Stanley in the aisle.

I could feel the tension building and McDermott seemed intent on escalating an already volatile situation.

'I am not here to argue with you nor do I seek your approval. I forgive you for the pain and suffering you once caused me, I thank you for the lessons I have learnt from that pain and suffering. I am who I am because of these lessons and through all I have experienced I have found love within myself, within others, within all of life. I accept where you are in your own spiritual homecoming and I pray that one day you may be blessed with experiencing life in this way, too.'

I said all I needed to say. I would allow the power of my words to speak to them and I took a step forward to take my place in the pew Aggie had allocated for us at the front of the church.

Padraig McDermott stepped forward to meet my advance, 'I do not want the likes of you or your Gypsy folk praying for me.'

The pains of his past rousing him. I ignored him and continued to walk and with each step I felt myself rise further into my radiance. Vincent and Colin Stanley moved out of my way. As I moved past McDermott he raised his hand to strike me. I did not flinch as once I might. I knew I was loved and protected. Dòmhnall moved at lightning speed and caught him by his arm and stood directly in front of him.

'A real man would never strike a woman. Our mother prayed every day that you would not turn out like our father. There's still a chance for you to change if you'd ever let yourself look at life from a higher perspective,' Dòmhnall said, as he dropped McDermott's arm.

He ignored the startled look on his face at finding out that Dòmhnall was his brother, and gently guided Maeve and Marigold past him.

I stood before the altar in my truth. I was worthy of a place at the table. I had just claimed my place. I felt the presence of Mary Magdalene at the altar, standing at the table, radiating pride and compelling me to share my story so other women may be inspired to rise and claim their place in truth, in the Divine.

Chapter Forty-One

As the ship sailed from the shore of the land I called home I did not turn to mourn. I knew that stage of my life had fallen away. My past had empowered me with knowledge and wisdom which I carried into the tomorrows that beckoned with expansive possibility.

I looked to the horizon, excited by what lay beyond. I opened myself to whatever it would bring to me and my beloved family. It was a time of new beginnings. New lands lay ahead to explore, new opportunities to embrace, new aspects of myself to discover. Ireland would always be my home, she was a magical place of beauty and mystery, she had taught me to live in joy and harmony, rather than fear and shame.

The energy of Mary Magdalene who spoke to me from the altar, reconnected with me when we began our journey, compelling me to write my story as we sailed across the seas. I knew my story had importance and I followed my inner call to share it. She believed in me as her messenger and guided me, weaving ancient teachings and wisdom throughout my story.

Once, I did not know who I was without my victim story, yet the more I wrote, the more I realised how far I was removed from the fearful, shamed, bitter and powerless girl of my story. I did not need to write my story to heal me. I had healed long before I set foot on the ship. I wrote from a place of empowerment to inspire other women to rise from their trauma and reclaim their power.

I wrote by day and by night. I wrote under the sun and the moon. I wrote on the deck while watching the brilliant dance of the ocean. I wrote hidden away in the cave of the cabin, allowing me to dive into the discomfort of the darkness. In shining a light on my past trauma and owning my story, I illuminated the dark corners of my soul with the most radiant Divine Light.

I shed the imprint of my ancestral lineage, honouring the ancient women of my bloodline, yet adamant that the shame, lies and patriarchal beliefs about the physical body, sex, sexuality and fertility where eroded and replaced with the truth of the beauty and power of the feminine, her sexual energy and her fertility.

I was determined that my daughters, their daughters, and granddaughters would be empowered to embrace the wholeness of their being, both the feminine and masculine, and my sons, their sons, and grandsons would break the patriarch mindset, and honour all women, just as Ceallach and Dòmhnall had done.

My writing was a solitary experience that was both invigorating and exhausting and saw me distance myself from Ceallach and Marigold, often writing through the night and sleeping during the early morning. Ceallach respected the significance of this journey, and the imminent birth of our child as a rite of passage. He gave me the space I needed, while also being present to hold and rock me during the unease of my transition.

As we drew closer to our destination, excitement and nervousness spread amongst the passengers, in anticipation of the unknown. At first, I confused the flutter in my stomach with my own excitement, yet when I felt an unfamiliar tension grip my rounded belly I realised that our baby was coming much earlier than anticipated. I believed we would be settled in the cottage on the land Dòmhnall had bought before the baby arrived, but the brilliance of the new moon called to her and she told me it was time.

Aunt Maeve and Marigold walked the deck of the ship with me for hours, and I felt an endless wave of love engulf me as I marvelled at the blessing of having these beautiful wise souls by my side. As the surges intensified, Aunt Maeve massaged my back and breathed with me through each contraction, while Marigold sang, creating a sacred birthing circle for me to transition into motherhood and our baby into life.

She summoned the Goddesses of air, fire, water and earth to support me in birthing with ease and grace, and to ground the soul of our baby into her body ready for her new life. She sang to the blessed Mother Mary. To the spirit of Mammy and the mothers of my bloodline seeking guidance and protection as I birthed and moved into motherhood. Finally, she called on the Mother of Mothers, the ancient one who knows all, to teach me the wisdom of birth, to show me the way through the cycles and to connect me with our baby in the physical realm, safely and with love. I moved my body within this sacred space, dancing in harmony with the waves of energy that rose and fell within me. I allowed my body to open and expand. I never doubted her innate knowing. I surrendered myself, while knowing I was held in love. In this space, as the first rays of the sun flickered on the water and shared the sky with the newest of moons, our baby girl graced us with her presence, and neither I, nor the world was ever the same again.

> *Sorcha Aoife Rose,*
> *my bright, radiant light, my warrior rose,*
> *may you shine forever in the beauty of your truth.*
> *Illuminate the path for all women to reclaim the*
> *crown of their sovereignty.*

Epilogue

I am Marigold.

I fell from the stars and landed in a faery garden, or so I have been told. They say that's why I am the way I am. I dance and sing, play the harp and the tin whistle. I pick wildflowers and herbs and make magic potions with Ma Ma. I miss Ma Ma, already. I miss Cynthia, too. I am sad. I feel it deep inside my heart and it aches like it is going to crack open with the pain, and then I dance, and I cry as I dance and all the sadness floats away, across the oceans into the yesteryears, done. My heart weaves herself back together, the healing threads binding pieces of me. I am stronger for my grief, wiser for my pain.

'The most gifted flower faery these parts have

seen in a long auld while,' that's what Ma Ma would say of me. 'Touched with the trinity, for sure.' Cynthia would laugh as they watched me in awe of my ways of seeing, feeling and knowing. They are my gifts, I know this to be true and to be sure there are those times when they feel more a burden than a blessing.

I am just a child, sometimes I do not want to see, nor feel, nor know in the ways that I do. I see and feel people deep within their soul and I know their story, the past and also what lies ahead. I do not like knowing what lies ahead.

When I was very little lying in my beloved Cynthia's arms, I saw what lay ahead for her and I did not want to know. I saw the cemetery and I felt the pain of Ma Ma and Maeve and Dòmhnall and Ceallach and I knew why she was taken so early. I did not know what to do with all this knowing, and I held it close to me, fearing if I spoke of it, it would become real. It was truth, regardless of my speaking of it or not. I learnt to trust and be guided by my gifts, not to fear them.

As Maeve and Clara write through our journeys across the seas, reliving the stories of their past, so others may learn from them, I feel their rawness and vulnerability, the surges of anger and resentment rising and falling away again. I hold them in a container, knowing the remnants of the past often resurface giving us the opportunity to go deeper in our healing.

I feel the calling for forgiveness. Forgiveness of the man by the woman. And I see within me, my own soul needs to forgive. I am shown the violation of my mother, she who bore me, by a cousin and I feel the guilt of her mother who refuses to acknowledge the story she knows to be true. She covers her up and sends her away to the field to birth me alone, in shame. The lines of my ancestors call me to forgive.

The young woman I am to become begs me to forgive, he who will break me. I see me, dancing and free and I see him seething, intent on destroying the purity and beauty that lies within.

Within the container I hold the stories of the feminine, Clara and Maeve's, my mothers and grandmothers and my future self, the past and the future held in the present as I offer forgiveness to the masculine.

And I pray:
Holy Father, Blessed Mother,
Light of the Universe.
Open my eyes, help me to see like you.
Open my ears, help me to hear your guidance.
Open my mind, help me to know the truth.
Open my heart, help me to purify and love.

And I meditate on the oneness of the feminine and masculine and feel the vibration of unity. My consciousness alters and in turn creates a shift in the consciousness of all in remembering the truth, the power of love over fear, the power of forgiveness over resentment.

On one side of my mind I see the masculine, the form taking at times that of Colin Stanley, Vincent, my father, other times a faceless representative of all. I see a light in the centre of his heart, the Divine Light that exists within all. I witness the magnificence as it blossoms from the centre outward, away from the physical form, ever expansive and more golden in its luminance. The physical form of the masculine begins to melt and fades away so that nothing remains but the truth of the Divine Light.

On the other side of my mind I see the feminine, the form taking at times that of Clara, Maeve, Cynthia or myself, other times a faceless representative of all. I see a light in the centre of her heart, the Divine Light that exists within all. I witness the brilliance as it blossoms from the centre outward, away from the physical form, ever expansive and more golden in its luminance. The physical form of the feminine begins to melt and fades away so that nothing remains by the truth of the Divine Light.

I witness the glorious moment when the light of the masculine meets the light of the feminine, merging to become one.

In seeing, feeling and knowing the sacred union of the masculine and feminine, a new truth is created, a Divine Truth where there is no separation between male and female, where oneness and harmony prevails.

Day after day, night after night, as the ship sails, I meditate on this vision that brings together the masculine and feminine as one, knowing that the potentiality of this powerful practice in the creation of this truth.

And I pray that all people remember the power of this vision and work with it, so that all who are to come will know no other truth—the exquisite harmonious dance of *all* that *is*.

Acknowledgements

Clara and Maeve, I am blessed that you chose me to share your story with the world. Thank you for trusting me as you opened in your vulnerability. This powerful writing experience is one I will never forget. It is my honour to bring your story from *beneath the veil*.

Luke, my love. This life we share is certainly an extraordinary ride. And you just keep going with me, riding the wave to who knows where, trusting in me, as I Become more me. I am the lucky one.

My babes, Kokoda, Lucia, Xavier. I know how much you love me as a mother and how proud you are of me as an author, and you will never know how important that is to me. I become more me so that you become more you.

Koko, thank you for bringing me my early morning coffee as I wrote with the rising sun. I love you and your thoughtfulness.

Cici, thank you for connecting with Clara and caring so much about her story. I love you and your kindness.

Xav, yes, you can come to this book launch, I couldn't image not having you by my side, beaming with pride. I love you and your fervour for life.

Mum, you are the strong powerful woman who does life your way, not caring what anyone else thinks. Thank you for instilling this most important lesson in me—to show up in the world in my truth, to do it my way—to be me.
"If everyone else jumped off the Harbour Bridge, would you?"

Dad, Ireland was your home and we grew up knowing it was our home, too. I feel it within the cells of my being every time I return. I truly believe the seed for this book was planted when you took us 'home' to your Ireland when I was seven years old. I wish you were here to share this moment with me.

Natasha Gilmour, you are deeply woven into the golden threads of this story. There was never going to be anyone else to edit *Beneath The Veil*. The 'ladies' knew they could trust you to work your magic on their stories and you gave them everything to ensure she blooms. We know this is a special one, and I am so grateful for sharing her with you, she would not be what she is without your sage touch. Your belief in me and the stories I have been gifted to write, fuels my dreams and illuminates my visions.

To my beautiful friend Karen Seymour. You were so important in the writing of this book. Your intuitive connection to Maeve, is one of those special, hard to explain links between two worlds. I value your love, support and belief in the power of this story and being by my side as she came through. Thank you for being you.

Karen McDermott, I adore making magic with you. Thank you for believing in me as an author and 'knowing' the importance of storytelling in creating change in the world. Ours is such an important connection and I am very grateful that we found our way to one another, both professionally and personally.

Tracy McKelligott, Louise Kipa, Brooke Stevenson, thank you for backing me as we launched *Let's Go Home*. Your belief in me was instrumental in maintaining the energy flow of Halia in the world and cementing my belief in myself as more than a 'one book' author. *Beneath The Veil* was gifted to me, right when I believed in myself enough as an author worthy of taking powerful, inspiring, healing stories to the world.

Maja Otic, my friend and cover designer. I thank you for your belief in me, my books and for somehow converting the visions I have for my book covers into reality. You are a creative genius and I value our very special connection.

To my family, friends, clients and readers who continue to support me as an author, thank you. Every review, message, text or card I have received from those of you who have read *Let's Go Home* speaks to my soul and affirms to me that the words I have been gifted to write are important.

To those who came before me, my ancestral mothers and fathers, the wise women and men who have walked this sacred path, I am deeply honoured to follow you and I am blessed to be guided by the wisdom you bestow upon me in the most beautiful mystical ways.

To those who will come after me, my daughters and son, their daughters and sons, and their granddaughters and grandsons, may you be empowered to embrace the wholeness of your being, both the feminine and masculine.

May you honour and shine in the beauty of your truth and may you illuminate the path for all to return to the Divine Light.

About the Author

Bernadette O'Connor is an internationally acclaimed author, a Kinesiology Practitioner and Advanced Theta Healer.

Bestselling author of *Let's Go Home: Finding There While Staying Here*, Bernadette has guided thousands of people to listen and come home to themselves. She embraces a methodology that acknowledges the unison of mind, body, emotions, vibration, spirit, and teaches others how to create harmony through intuitive guidance, overcoming fear, removing emotional blocks and tuning into their inner wisdom. In her book *Let's Go Home*, Bernadette reveals her long-hidden gift of connecting to past life incarnations and guiding others through soul lessons.

Renowned for devotion and service, Bernadette has featured in publications such as *YMag®, Enrich, Woman Rising* magazines, and on female.com.au.

Words are a powerful connector for her, the golden threads of wisdom she weaves richly and profoundly through her writing connect her to a wide audience: she conveys her messages through a higher vibration that works magically.

Bernadette lives in Newcastle, Australia with her husband, three children and cat Miss Frankie.

Connect with Bernadette on
Facebook: www.facebook.com/bernadetteoconnorauthor
Instagram: www.instagram.com/bernadetteoconnorauthor
Website: www.bernadetteoconnor.com

Lifting the Veil

Thank you for sharing these pages with me.
If you like this book and want to go deeper, receive free teachings by signing up for my newsletter at
www.bernadetteoconnor.com

Let's Go Home

FINDING THERE WHILE STAYING HERE

Available in all good bookstores and at
w w w . b e r n a d e t t e o c o n n o r .